CAROL FINCH

THE LONE RANCHER

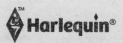
Harlequin®

TORONTO NEW YORK LONDON
AMSTERDAM PARIS SYDNEY HAMBURG
STOCKHOLM ATHENS TOKYO MILAN MADRID
PRAGUE WARSAW BUDAPEST AUCKLAND

This book is dedicated to my husband, Ed, and our children,
Kurt, Shawnna, Jill, Jon, Christie and Durk.

And to our grandchildren
Livia, Harleigh, Blake, Kennedy, Dillon and Brooklynn.
And to Kurt's and Shawnna's children,
whenever they may be. Hugs and kisses!

ISBN-13: 978-0-373-29664-4

THE LONE RANCHER

Copyright © 2011 Connie Feddersen

Recycling programs
for this product may
not exist in your area.

Cahill Cowboys

Texas's Finest

In the heart of America's Wild West, only one family
matters—the legendary Cahills.

Once a dynasty to be reckoned with,
their name has been dragged through the cattle-worn mud,
and their family torn apart.

Now the three Cahill cowboys
and their scandalous sister reunite.

With a past as dark as the Texas night sky, it's
time for the family to heal their hearts and seek justice....

CHRISTMAS AT CAHILL CROSSING
by Carol Finch October 2011

THE LONE RANCHER
by Carol Finch November 2011

THE MARSHAL AND MISS MERRITT
Debra Cowan December 2011

SCANDAL AT THE CAHILL SALOON
Carol Arens January 2012

THE LAST CAHILL COWBOY
Jenna Kernan February 2012

Dear Reader

Welcome back to Cahill Crossing, Texas! Last month you met Lucas and Rosa in the *Snowflakes and Stetsons* anthology. They are on hand to watch fireworks explode between Quin Cahill, eldest son of the town's founding family, and Adrianna McKnight—Rosa's cousin from Boston.

Quin manages the 4C Ranch alone while his estranged siblings chase their own rainbows. He is obsessed with keeping his father's dream of expansion alive, but Adrianna buys the neighboring ranch he has his heart set on. The feisty female won't budge from the spot. How can Quin concentrate on day-to-day ranch duties and round up pesky rustlers when Adrianna distracts and intrigues him as much as she infuriates him?

Adrianna refuses to sell out, because she is here to prove to herself—and her annoying neighbor—that she is more than a pampered heiress. When she tries to outdo Quin at every turn, it fuels a personal feud and the whole town wonders *who* is going to strangle *whom* first.

Grab hold of the saddle horn with both hands, dear reader. This wild ride is teeming with fast-paced adventure, mystery, suspense and romance. I hope *The Lone Rancher* brings you a few smiles and several hours of reading pleasure.

Best wishes,

Carol Finch

Prologue

According to Quin... Two years earlier...

Quin Cahill shrugged out of his best black jacket and tossed it over the back of Pa's favorite leather chair. He watched his two younger brothers and sister, also dressed in black, file into the parlor behind him. If he'd spent a more hellish week in his life, he couldn't recall it. Receiving the awful news that both of his parents had died in a wagon accident during their return trip from Wolf Grove had been a devastating blow. So many raw emotions—grief, frustration and guilt, to name only a few—had hounded him every step of the funeral procession.

Despite the regret and sorrow that weighed so heavily on his heart, he knew it was his obligation to call this family meeting and get on with life, as Ma and Pa would expect him to do.

Quin inhaled a deep, cleansing breath—and stumbled over a myriad of memories that floated through every room of the spacious ranch home. Resigned to fulfilling his duty as head of the Cahill family, Quin stared somberly at his brothers and sister before focusing his full attention on Bowie, who was two years his junior.

"Bowie, you're in charge of raising, breeding, training and selling our extra horses," Quin stated. "You'll give orders to the hired hands who work with our remuda."

"I have a job, in case you've forgotten, brother," Bowie snapped. "I can hardly oversee the horse operation, the livestock and hired hands if I'm already working as the sheriff in Deer County."

Quin tossed Bowie an annoyed glance, then turned his attention to his sister, Leanna. "Annie, you'll be in charge of the meals, our house and its staff, just like Ma."

His sister narrowed her blue eyes and pursed her lips. She looked a lot like Ma when she did that, Quin mused.

"Why do we have to change things right now?" Leanna asked. "We haven't even dried our tears yet. I need to go upstairs and bawl my eyes out. And honestly, I'd rather move out on my own than meekly follow the path you lay out for me."

After she'd given her two cents, as Bowie had, Quin sent her a silencing frown. "This isn't about what you want, Annie. It's about what's best for the 4C. We are family and we stick together."

Quin half turned to face his youngest brother. "Chance, you'll be my second-in-command."

Chance stepped forward, looking every bit as defiant as Bowie and Leanna. "So I'm your hired hand?"

"You'll be in charge during the spring and fall while I'm on cattle drives," Quin tried to placate him.

"Maybe I don't want to stay on the 4C Ranch," Chance spouted off.

Quin's temper tried to slip its leash, but he grabbed on to it with both hands. Unfortunately, Bowie spoke out again, ruining what was left of Quin's good disposition.

"I have my hands full as a lawman and I'm not staying at the ranch. You may have bossed us around as kids, but we're not kids anymore. Ma and Pa are dead. That's the end of an era."

Quin felt as if he'd been sucker punched. Bowie was defying Pa's wishes and he damn well knew it. "How ungrateful can a man get?" He scowled. "You think you're honorable and responsible enough to draw lawman's wages? You can't even own up to family responsibility." He looked Bowie up and down and smirked. "You're hardly a model sheriff. You need to resign and take your rightful place on the ranch, as Pa wanted."

Bowie puffed up with indignation and took a challenging step toward Quin. "I'm good at what I do."

"You should be using your supposed talent to round up the bandits and rustlers that threaten the 4C and your own family," Quin countered. "Do I need to remind you that Pa was none too thrilled when you walked away from here to defend people you didn't even know?" He glared angrily at Bowie. "You *disappointed* Pa. He grumbled to me plenty of times. And who do you think got stuck with the extra chores? It sure wasn't Annie or Chance."

"Is that why you're mad? Because of the extra work?" Bowie snorted.

No, Quin thought, it was because he felt as if his family was ignoring the hopes and dreams of their parents. His past resentments didn't hold a candle to the sense of betrayal roiling through him right now.

"Hell, hire another hand or two," Bowie suggested flippantly. "It's not like we can't afford it."

"How would you know what we can afford?" Quin taunted. "You haven't been around much and I'm fed up of covering for you. I'm surprised you even bothered to attend today's funeral."

The snide remark had the desired effect—insulting Bowie, who growled furiously. Not to be outdone, Quin growled back.

"You hightailed it out of here after Clea North jilted you. Can't blame her for thinking you weren't good enough for her." Quin knew Clea was a sensitive subject, but Bowie was playing hell with his temper and he was past controlling it now. "You thumbed your nose at family obligation, pinned on a badge and refused to compromise for anyone."

"All I've ever done is compromise!" Bowie yelled. "And walk in your shadow for all of my twenty-nine years! Well, I'm sick of it! I'm not quitting my job to become your errand boy!"

In a fit of temper, Bowie shoved Quin against the wall. Quin fell against Ma's treasured porcelain wedding bowl, cutting his right hand in the process. The keepsake crashed to the floor and shattered into pieces—just like the broken dreams of his parents.

Annie cried out behind them, but Quin was too intent on returning the angry shove. He lowered his shoulder and knocked Bowie into Pa's big leather chair, then he shook off the sting of the bloody slice on his hand.

"Accept your responsibility," Quin commanded harshly. "Let someone else get his head blown off defending law and order. I need help with this ranch. It belongs to all of us. Our first obligation is here and here you'll stay."

Bowie bounded to his feet and glowered at Quin. "Go to hell and take your orders with you. Nobody put you in charge."

"Someone has to take charge," Quin defended hotly. "You aren't around often enough to do it."

"You're not Pa," Bowie hurled derisively. "You'll never be able to fill his boots, no matter how hard you try."

The verbal jab prompted Quin to thrust back his shoulders and glare heated pokers at Bowie. "At least *I've* been here to fulfill Pa's dream of expansion."

"Yeah," Bowie jeered. "Until you went to the spring cattle sale in Dodge City and got way*laid* by a couple of whores. 'Scuse my language, Annie."

Quin was furious with his brother for hitting another raw nerve. Bowie was right—damn him—but Quin was too proud and stubborn to admit his shame in front of his defiant family. Already, grief and guilt were gnawing at him. He'd failed his parents by gallivanting an extra day during his return trip. The selfish craving for whiskey and women had prevented Quin from driving his parents to the important meeting. Regret was eating him alive.

"I covered for you more times than I care to count while *you* chased after one skirt or another! You *knew*

I might not be back in time. *You* should've been here to take up the slack. *For once*," he retaliated. "Especially when *you* got word that Pa had injured his wrist. You knew he would need help driving to and from Wolf Grove to meet with the railroad executives to establish a town on our property."

"I was working that day," Bowie gritted out defensively. "There was a dangerous prisoner in my jail."

Chance marched over to stand nose to nose with Bowie and Quin. "I'm not staying to take orders from either of you. If I do, I'll never be anything but your kid brother. Pa's gone and I'm through being a ranch hand."

Hearing Chance defect, just like Bowie, was worse than a hard slap in the face. Quin itched to go for both brothers' throats—simultaneously.

"You're part owner of this ranch," Quin muttered between clenched teeth. "It is your *obligation* to work here."

"Ranching isn't in my blood, Quin," Chance flashed heatedly. "I only stayed this long for Pa."

Quin exploded in frustration. "Ma and Pa are barely in the ground and you two are turning your backs on this ranch? Pa wanted us to be the most influential ranching family in Texas and, by damned, we will be!"

"That's what *you* want, Quin," Bowie lashed out.

Chance nodded. "I'm going."

"Me, too," Annie stated decisively.

Quin stared at his kid sister as if she had betrayed him—which she had. "This is our home, our way of life, our *birthright!* You aren't going anywhere and neither are Bowie and Chance," he decreed, his voice pounding like a gavel.

"You just watch," Bowie had the audacity to smart off.

Fists clenched, Chance got right in Quin's face. "I'm damn sure quitting this place."

"Stop fighting and yelling at one another," Annie demanded, stepping between them. "Don't do something you'll regret."

"That goes for you, too, little sister." Quin tossed her a pointed glance. "You have plenty of regrets already. What a shame that Ma's last thoughts were probably about your childish tantrum over a new dress."

Despite the tears filling her eyes, her spine stiffened and she tilted her chin at Quin. "I'm not playing maid to you and I'm not staying on this isolated ranch!"

His temper boiled over when his little sister—the one he'd vowed to protect and defend—became as insolent and disloyal as his brothers. "You'll do as you're told," he snapped in a tone that brooked no argument whatsoever. Not that it did any good, damn it.

"No one made you ruler over us all," Leanna shouted disrespectfully. "You can try to hold the ranch together, but you won't be able to do it alone. Bowie has his own life. Chance doesn't want yours and neither do I."

"You're going to find a job?" he asked caustically. "There's only one place I know where a woman like you can get by doing nothing more than smiling and looking pretty for pay. I can't picture you as a saloon girl."

"If that's where my dreams lead me, then so be it." She stiffened her spine again and went toe to toe with him. "I think we should sell the ranch and each take our share."

Quin felt as if his little sister had stabbed him right through the heart, then given the knife a painful twist.

"Are you out of your mind? Sell off chucks of the ranch? Over my dead body!" he thundered, appalled by the blasphemous suggestion. "Ranching is our way of life. It's who we *are*. We just *buried* Ma and Pa on this land."

"Making a bigger name for the 4C, for the Cahills, won't bring back Mama and Papa," Leanna reminded him.

"This ranch is our destiny," Quin declared.

"Yours, maybe. Not mine," Chance—the traitor—said.

Quin wanted to hit something—beginning and ending with his selfish, betraying siblings. "Fine! Follow your dreams and see how far you get without your family to back you up. I'll be here to see the 4C grow and prosper, doing what Ma and Pa wanted, *expected*."

He flashed a hard, steely-eyed stare. "All profits go into expanding this ranch. If you leave, you're walking away with no more than the clothes and belongings Ma and Pa *bought* for you."

Chance scoffed. "More than what I expected."

"Take your favorite horse and get the hell out of my sight!" Quin shouted at all of them.

"I hardly think we need to ask your leave for that," Bowie said, and smirked.

Quin made a stabbing gesture toward the front door, as if his brothers and sister were too dense to know where it was. "Go! Defy your legacy if you want. You might as well walk over our parents' grave on your way past, too.

"You think leaving here will help you find out who you are?" Quin looked them up and down—thrice. "I can save you the trip. You're *quitters* and I'm ashamed to call you family."

Chance muttered something foul that Quin didn't ask him to repeat.

Bowie looked as if he wanted to smash his fist into Quin's face. Quin almost welcomed coming to blows to appease his frustration. However, Leanna grabbed Bowie's arm and said, "No, Bowie, don't make this worse."

"Stay out of it, Annie," Bowie snarled, shaking off her hold.

"None of you are worthy to bear the Cahill name," Quin hurled hatefully. "Maybe you should take an alias to hide your shame for defying Ma and Pa. I sure as hell don't want to claim any of you!"

Bowie glared holes in Quin's starched shirt, spun on his boot heels and stalked out.

In tormented fury, Quin watched Chance and Leanna fall into step behind Bowie. He called them every name under the sun as he stormed onto the porch to watch them mount up.

When all three stared at Quin as if *he* were the black sheep of the family, proud defiance took control of his tongue. "Don't think I'll beg you to come back because I won't!" he bellowed before they rode away.

Quin reentered the house and slammed the door so hard dust dribbled from the woodwork. He wondered if he'd ever see his traitorous family again. Overwhelming feelings of grief and anger, not to mention the deep sense of betrayal, left him thinking he didn't give a damn what became of his family.

Quin scanned the empty hallway—and felt his heart

twist in his chest. Deafening silence filled the home that had once brimmed over with lively voices and bustling activity. He'd never felt so alone and abandoned in his thirty-one years of existence.

And he blamed his brothers and sister for every moment of his misery...

Chapter One

Cahill Crossing, Texas springtime, early 1880s

Quin Cahill dismounted from his horse, then stared at the string of saloons and dance halls that lined the north side of the newly completed railroad tracks. He doubted his parents would have approved of the disreputable businesses that had sprung up in the town that bore their family name....

The tormenting memory of losing both parents at once—not to mention the devastating family split that had followed—put a scowl on Quin's face and left an empty ache in his heart. Squaring his shoulders, Quin forced aside the bleak thought and decided to treat himself to a drink at Hell's Corner Saloon before he crossed the tracks to the respectable side of town to pick up supplies.

"Afternoon, Quin," Sidney Meeker, the baldheaded, dark-eyed bartender, said as Quin strode across the planked floor.

Quin nodded a greeting as he leaned against the bar. He glanced around the saloon to note several unfamiliar faces at the poker tables. Cardsharps, he supposed, all waiting to prey on off-duty soldiers from nearby Fort Ridge, the cowboys from neighboring ranches and trail drives and the tracklayers who were constructing iron rails westward.

Sid arched a questioning brow as he dried off a shot glass, then set it aside. "How are things going on the 4C? Still having trouble with rustlers and squatters cutting your fences?"

Quin took a welcomed sip, allowing the liquor to slide down his throat and wash away the bitter memory of his brothers and sister bailing out on him and how hard he'd worked to take up the slack. "Not as much trouble as I had a year ago," he said before he took another drink.

"That's good news for you and the other ranchers in the area." Sid absently wiped the scarred bar with his dish towel. "Especially the new owners of the ranch west of your spread. I saw 'em climb off the train this morning."

Quin jerked up his head and frowned. He had been trying to purchase that run-down ranch for six months. Some highfalutin family had bought out the other investors from Boston and England that had run the spread long-distance—which almost never worked. Quin had written several letters to the headquarters in Boston and made a generous offer to M. G. & L. Investment Group. He had received notice that someone named McKnight had acquired most of the shares.

Sid grinned, exposing his horselike teeth. "It was a sight to behold at the new train depot. Boxcars of fancy furniture, a new breed of cattle and stacks of lumber arrived with 'em." He inclined his bald head toward the door. "Folks scrambled out of here to watch. Most of the ones who showed up at the station were offered jobs of transporting wagonloads of belongings to the ranch."

Quin smiled wryly, then took another drink. This was the perfect chance to meet his new neighbor—who wouldn't last long when he realized the ranch house had fallen into disrepair and part of the livestock had been stolen because only a skeleton crew of hired hands had been retained to watch the place.

"Quite an entourage," Sid continued as he propped both elbows on the bar. "One well-dressed gent with fancy manners and three women. They purchased a two-seated carriage from the livery and headed west a few hours ago."

Quin's lips quirked in wicked amusement. He could imagine the cultural shock those Easterners would encounter. While it was true that Cahill Crossing had increased in population since the coming of the railroad, social events here were infrequent. Sure, there was the occasional school function to raise money for supplies and church socials—that sort of thing—but nothing compared to the gala affairs rumored to take place in New England.

He predicted his uppity neighbors would turn up their aristocratic noses and scurry back to Boston soon. And Quin was going to be first in line to offer to take the property off their hands. The land west of his ranch had an excellent water source, pastures of thick grass and wooded hills to shade the livestock during oppressive summers and to block the brutal blue norther winds during harsh winters.

Yes, indeed, Quin was going to get his hands on that tract of land, just as he had bought up other available property to fulfill his father's dream of expanding the 4C Ranch.

"And Bowie, Leanna and Chance should be here to help me," Quin muttered resentfully.

Sid arched thick black brows and frowned curiously. "Pardon?"

"Nothing." Quin set the empty glass on the bar, then spun on his boot heels. "I need to pick up supplies. Thanks for the drink, Sid."

Quin mounted the bloodred bay gelding, with its sleek black mane and tail. He'd named him Cactus because of his prickly disposition. Quin had overheard some of his hired hands mutter that Quin and Cactus were a helluva lot alike. Though Cactus was a bit hard to handle at times, the horse had amazing stamina and endurance that was invaluable on trail drives. Plus, Cactus had never abandoned Quin the way his two brothers and sister had when the going got tough.

Tugging the packhorse behind him, Quin passed the train depot and Château Royale Hotel—the fancy new establishment constructed to accommodate passengers from the railroad and stage depot. He smiled as he dismounted at the general store on Town Square. How he wished he had been there to see the look on McKnight's face when he arrived at the run-down ranch house. No doubt, the man would be begging Quin to take the mismanaged property off his hands. Very soon, Quin would add another tract of land to the sprawling 4C Ranch.

* * *

Adrianna McKnight gaped at the clapboard ranch house that cried out for a fresh coat of paint and the bare windows that needed bright curtains. There were no gardens to give the place a speck of color. Nothing to welcome her home.

"Good heavens! I traded cooking in a posh Boston mansion for *this?*" Ezmerelda Quickel, the short, round-faced, red-haired cook, chirped as she stared goggle-eyed at her new home.

Adrianna pasted on an optimistic smile as she swiveled around to glance directly at Ezmerelda, who had half collapsed in disappointment on the backseat of the buggy. "I'm sure we'll be in a more positive frame of mind after we recuperate from our exhausting journey. Hopefully, the interior of the house is in better condition than the exterior."

"Let's hope so, Addie dear," Beatrice Fremont, the longtime housekeeper, harrumphed distastefully. "But I have the uneasy feeling I'll face a pile of dust and I'll be sneezing my head off while I try to set this residence to rights."

Hiram Butler, her man of affairs who was like an honorary uncle, glanced this way and that, then said, "I knew Texas claimed to be wide-open range country and wooded hills, but goodness! Our nearest neighbor must be miles away!"

Honestly, she was surprised anyone had volunteered to make this long journey after she had purchased the shares in this Texas ranch. Save those shares belonging to her first and only cousin, Rosalie Greer Burnett. Rosalie had cautioned Adrianna in her last letter that the property had been neglected because the previous manager had embezzled money meant for the upkeep of the home. But *this?*

Adrianna had planned to construct a new addition to enlarge the existing house but she hadn't anticipated remodeling the entire residence! Still, she needed this change of address, this new challenge to prove to herself that she was capable and that she counted for something besides tramping around ballrooms in Boston, fending off adventurers who sought to attach themselves to her vast fortune.

By heavens, Adrianna Kathleen McKnight was going to put this ranch on the map—or die trying! She wasn't the witless debutante her so-called friends in Boston pigeonholed her as. She had disappointed her departed father because she had only made a halfhearted attempt to become the dignified lady he had expected her to become when he introduced her into society. Adrianna *had* tried for her father's sake. Unfortunately, she had been unhappy and she had been untrue to *her* nature, while trying to live up to *his* expectations.

Now, after Reuben McKnight's lengthy illness, Adrianna had taken Cousin Rosa's suggestion to move west and begin a new life for herself. She would make her father proud that she had inherited his knack for business. She was not an empty-headed china doll destined to become the trophy wife for some snobbish social climber.

Mustering her resolve, determined to meet the difficult challenge, Adrianna grabbed hold of her full skirts so she wouldn't swan dive from the carriage, subsequently embarrassing herself in front of all the local workers she'd hired to transport and unload her cargo.

"Please cart the luggage upstairs," she instructed in an authoritative tone that would have done her father proud—or at least she *told* herself that he would approve of her emulating his impressive organizing skills. "Then bring in the furniture. I will direct you where to put it."

"What about all this lumber?" one of the off-duty soldiers she'd hired called out.

Adrianna gestured toward the storage building west of the house. "Stack it over there, if you please." Drawing herself up to full stature, she marched onto the porch that surrounded the house. When she unlocked the front door, her spirits suffered a crushing blow. Whatever furniture had once filled the corrupt manager's home was gone. So were the rugs. Dust covered the floors, staircase and windowsills.

"Oh, my," Elda crowed as she poked her red head around Adrianna's shoulder to inspect the place. "Bea, brace yourself, dear. It's as bad as we thought."

When Bea elbowed her out of the way, Adrianna stepped aside, but she clamped hold of the petite housekeeper's elbow, in case she fainted in distress. Sure enough, Bea staggered sideways, as if knocked off balance.

"Lord have mercy!" Bea bleated as her wide-eyed gaze circled the hall and parlor.

"I appreciate everyone's loyalty in coming with me, but if you want to return to Boston and more familiar surroundings, I will understand," Adrianna insisted. "I will purchase rooms at the new Château Royale Hotel in town and you can be on the first train east, if you wish."

Bea strode forward to run her forefinger over the dusty banister. "And leave you in these abominable conditions?" she said, and sniffed. "I stood by your mama and papa and I am not abandoning you. Even if it takes me a month to remove this pile of dust I will get it done."

"I feel the same as Bea," Elda spoke up. "Or at least I think I do. Let me have a look at the kitchen first."

They trooped off in single file and Adrianna sagged in relief when she entered the kitchen to note the stove, pantry cupboards and worktable were where they were supposed to be. She glanced through the dirty window and noticed the summer kitchen stood behind the house.

"I'm staying, too," Elda announced decisively.

"I insist on a bucket of paint to freshen up these plastered walls," Bea said as she fussed with a coil of coal-black hair that had worked loose from the bun atop her head. "And no telling what varmints—the two-legged, four-legged and eight-legged varieties—have prowled around this house."

Adrianna pivoted to face her stoic accountant, who was scrutinizing their new home as studiously as he pored over financial ledgers. "What about you, Butler? Do you wish to return to town and stay at the hotel?"

Hiram Butler drew himself up to full stature—all five foot ten inches—then brushed a speck of lint from the sleeve of his stylish jacket. "I gave your father my word that I would make sure you got off to a good start without him, my dear. I intend to honor that vow."

Adrianna inwardly winced, wondering if all three

devoted employees had made this trip because her father had wrested promises from them on his deathbed.

Adrianna waved her arms in expansive gestures. "You are hereby released from any vow you made Papa," she decreed. "I intend to make a go of this ranch and to be near Cousin Rosa and her new husband. Boston has nothing for me now."

"We are staying," Butler declared after he received nods from Bea and Elda. "You, dear girl, are all the family we have. Besides, I am not going anywhere until I spend more than the passing moment we had at the train depot to determine if that Lucas Burnett character is good enough for our Rosalie."

Adrianna flung her arms around Butler's neck and practically squeezed the stuffing out of him. Then she hugged Bea and Elda. "I love you all and I am humbled by your loyalty during this *adversity*." She stepped back, blinked the sentimentality from her eyes and added, "And this ranch is definitely an adversity I intend to overcome. The first order of business is to get our bedrooms into a habitable state."

She spun on her heels to breeze through the empty dining room. "We need a place to collapse after a hard day's work."

"That is exactly what we have ahead of us," Bea insisted. "As soon as I change out of my traveling clothes I will roll up my sleeves and get started on this place. At least our bedrooms will be free of dust by tonight."

While the threesome directed traffic to have their belongings carted upstairs, Adrianna strode outside to oversee the stacking of lumber and the corralling of her herd of purebred Herefords into the pens beside the oversize barn.

Although Adrianna had sold the opulent mansion in Boston, she had retained the country estate where she had grown up raising prize cattle and horses. The place held sentimental memories of the freedom and happiness she had enjoyed during the first eighteen years of her life.

Before she had been instructed to behave like the proper, dignified lady her father insisted she become—and never could.

"Never again am I going to try to live up to anyone's expectations," Adrianna vowed fiercely. "This is my independence day. I'm going to make something of myself!"

Quin trotted Cactus through the pasture, taking the shortcut to the neighboring ranch. He leaned out to open the adjoining gate that led into McKnight's pasture and noted the convoy of empty wagons moving in the direction of town. Too bad the McKnights hadn't reversed direction *before* unloading their belongings. It would have saved them time and money.

He had seen this scenario several times before. Investors from England and Ireland had purchased Texas ranches and unknowingly hired incompetent managers. In the past eighteen months Quin had purchased two English-owned properties at rock-bottom prices and added pastures, bunkhouses, line shacks, barns and ranch homes to the sprawling 4C Ranch.

Unfortunately, he couldn't gloat over his hard-earned success to his siblings because he only knew where

Bowic was—and they weren't speaking. He suspected Chance and Leanna had kept in contact with Bowie. But Quin had no clue where the two youngest siblings had begun the new lives they were so hell-bent on leading. Well, he hoped they were happy.

At his expense, of course. They didn't care if he worked himself into an early grave to make the ranch the largest and most influential spread in the whole damn state.

Just as Earl and Ruby Cahill had dreamed of doing.

Ranching wasn't in their blood, his siblings had said. Quin wasn't sure Cahill blood ran through their veins. How could they be so different and still be related? That question continued to confuse him. And damn it, what was wrong with the life they were born to? Wasn't it good enough for the lot of them?

He thrust aside his exasperated thoughts, then urged the muscular bay into a gallop. He smiled in anticipation as he surveyed the home, barn, sheds and bunkhouse that sat on a hill surrounded by a copse of shade trees. One day this property would belong to him, along with the spring-fed fork of Triple Creek.

It was only a matter of time before A. K. McKnight packed up and went home where he should've stayed in the first place, Quin assured himself confidently. Yankees had no place in Texas. They weren't accustomed to the rigorous demands of managing thousands of acres, controlling predators and battling rustlers. What in hell were these people thinking?

Quin rolled his eyes when he saw several cowboys draped over the corral fence, surveying the newly arrived livestock. Those Yankees thought the Hereford breed could withstand harsh weather conditions and compete for grass in pastures with longhorns?

"Those white-faced cows had better be hardy," he said, and smirked. "Otherwise, they'll be dropping like flies and wolf packs will make a feast of them." Sure, he had crossbred livestock, hoping for the best characteristics possible, but he had seen too many English breeds fail miserably in this climate. He hoped the McKnights had plenty of money to cover their losses.

Anxious to meet his short-term neighbors and present his offer, Quin bounded up the steps two at a time, then rapped loudly on the door. After knocking a second time, the door finally opened. He sized up the lanky, hazel-eyed man in a stylish suit. He looked to be in his late forties, judging by the strands of gray mingling with brown hair. The well-dressed gent looked down his hawkish nose, as if Quin didn't measure up. To what Eastern standard Quin didn't know—or care.

"A. K. McKnight?" Quin presumed as he grabbed the man's hand and gave it a firm shake.

The man wriggled his hand loose and stepped aside. Then he said, "And you are…?"

"Quin Cahill, your neighbor to the north and to the east," he replied as he entered the hallway that was cluttered with the fanciest furniture he'd ever laid eyes on. Even his mother's fine taste in furnishings didn't compare to this stuff, he mused.

"Come sit down, Mr. Cahill…if you can find an empty space in the parlor. I'll return in a moment."

Quin nudged a stack of boxes out of his way to make room for himself on the sofa. He waited an impatient moment for McKnight to drag his uppity posterior back to the room that was heaped with displaced furniture. Quin had a ranch to run and he didn't intend to waste unnecessary time before presenting his offer and haggling over a fair price.

"I don't see anyone, Butler," came a woman's voice from the doorway of the parlor.

Butler? Quin frowned, puzzled. He presumed the man he'd met was A. K. McKnight, not the butler. So where was this McKnight character? Was he still back East?

Quin surged to his feet to locate the source of the feminine voice. He blinked in surprise when he spotted a riot of tangled chestnut curls surrounding a bewitching face smudged with dirt. The woman stood five foot five and looked to be in her mid-twenties. Her faded gown was a mass of wrinkles and grime. Cobwebs clung to the mane of shiny hair and stuck to her well-endowed bosom. He couldn't help but notice the fetching creature had the kind of shapely body that could stop traffic on the bustling streets of Cahill Crossing. Her tempting assets certainly had *his* undivided attention.

So this was the housekeeper—and no telling what other services she performed for the master of the house. Quin wondered if she had been sent to offer him a spot of tea before she scuttled back to her daytime duties.

"Nothing to drink for me, honey," he said as he removed his hat and tossed out his best smile. "I have a business proposition for McKnight, then I'll be on my way."

She tilted her head to study him from a pensive angle. "What sort of proposition?" the shapely young housekeeper inquired.

None of your business, sugar, he thought, but he said, "I prefer to discuss the details with Mr. McKnight." He glanced over her mussed head, wondering if the gent had arrived in Texas yet.

"I am A. K. McKnight."

Slack-jawed, he turned his attention back to the woman. *"You?"* he croaked when he finally found his tongue.

Her chin tilted to a challenging angle that reminded him of his sister—wherever the hell she was these days.

"I am Adrianna Kathleen McKnight," she introduced herself with icy formality.

"But who was the man I met?" he asked, baffled.

"Butler."

"You call him *butler?*" This tenderfoot was a snob, he decided.

"His name is Hiram Butler. It amuses him to let people think he is a butler, not an amazingly efficient accountant."

Quin smirked. "I can see he has a killer sense of humor."

She stared down her pert nose at him, the same way the stuffy Butler had done. "You are one of the town founders, I presume. Or are you a shirttail cousin of some sort?"

Her critical tone and her crisp Eastern accent made him bristle, for it sounded suspiciously like she had made a snap judgment and found him sadly lacking. "I'm named after my grandfather, Quinton Cahill." He veered around two stacks of furniture to tower over her. "So, yes, Ca-Cross is named after my family and I manage 4C Ranch."

"I like your abbreviated version of the town name," she remarked. "I shall remember to use it so I can I fit in."

"It won't matter, sugar, you are way out of your element in Texas," Quin said under his breath.

She studied him challengingly. "Come again, Mr. Cahill?"

He flashed the most winsome smile in his repertoire—which, admittedly, wasn't extensive. "I came by to offer you a fair price for this property. I tried to buy it six months ago. But now that you've seen the poor condition in which the former overseer left this spread, I figured you'd have a change of heart."

"Did you now? I had no idea you had the ability to read minds. Another service you helpfully provide, I'm sure."

He ignored her caustic comment. She looked peeved, for reasons he couldn't understand. Since he had very few dealings with Yankees he had no clue what made them tick.

"I wanted you to know I'll take this property off your hands. You won't have to fret about it when you leave town."

She clamped her lush lips shut, stared at him with those vibrant cedar-tree-green eyes and said nothing.

"This place is a mess. Half the longhorn cattle herd has been stolen. Probably by some of the cowhands who worked the place. Also, you'll find very little of the comforts and luxuries you enjoyed in Boston."

"That is true, Mr. Cahill. But I am ready and willing to meet the challenges of my new life."

Her comment reminded him so much of the clash

between him and his brothers and sister that he bris-
tled immediately. This woman represented what he
had come to dislike about Bowie, Chance and Leanna.
Why did folks feel the need to strike off to find a new
life instead of sticking to the ones they were born to?
Lives that were familiar and expected. With birthrights,
family destinies and legacies.

This heiress—and he had no doubt she was wealthy
if she had bought out most of the other investors—had
no business trying to manage a ranch in unfamiliar territory. Obviously, she had been groomed for highbrow
soirees, concerts and such.

"Look, *Boston*," he said, discarding an attempt to be
polite and charming. He had his limit, after all. "You
are a greenhorn in rugged country. This is no place for
a lady. The sooner you accept that, the better off you'll
be."

"Will I?" She crossed her arms over her ample bosom
and glowered at him. "Let me assure you, Mr. Cahill—"

"Quin," he corrected.

"—I did not move to Texas on a whim," she continued, as if she hadn't heard him. Or didn't care what he
had to say. He figured the latter was nearer the mark.
"I outgrew Boston and I became bored with shallow
socialites who count their success and importance by
the number of parties they attend and by how many
wealthy aristocrats they know.

"I overheard my so-called friends poking fun at me.
When I saw myself through their eyes I realized no
one in Boston really knew me at all. They didn't give
a whit what I was on the *inside*. They perceived me as

a pampered, helpless heiress who didn't have to lift a finger to provide for myself.

"Furthermore," she said through gritted teeth. "I have been raising and breeding livestock on our country estate since I was ten years old so I am not unfamiliar with the practices and the duties demanded of running a ranch."

How dare this arrogant cowboy come marching over here to persuade her to sell out before she had a chance to meet and greet the ranch hands and to set up house-keeping! Adrianna silently fumed as she raked the big oaf from the top of his raven head to the toes of his scuffed boots. He was six foot two inches of brawn and muscle—and possessed a pea-size brain. Ruggedly handsome though he was in his Western clothing, spurs and leather chaps that showcased the crotch of his breeches—and demanded entirely too much feminine attention—she wanted to double her fist and smash it into the five-o'clock shadow that lined his jaw.

And how dare he nickname her *Boston,* in an attempt to remind her of where he thought she belonged. He wasn't looking past outward appearances and that infuriated her to no end. He reminded her of the opinionated highbrows she had left behind.

Never mind that she had sailed into her cluttered parlor and felt a jolt of unexpected physical awareness when she met the brawny rancher with silver-gray eyes and wavy raven hair. He was nothing like the sophisticated dandies who sauntered through marble foyers, in hopes of charming her into a marriage that would set them up for life with her inheritance. That was a point in his favor—until he opened his big mouth and declared she couldn't manage this ranch and he wanted to buy her property.

Blast it, he had no way of knowing how competent she was, how adaptable she could be when she tried. Hadn't she portrayed the genteel sophisticate to appease her father? Damn this brawny cowboy. He made her want to revert to her hoyden days on the country estate and show him how disagreeable she could be when she really tried.

"I hear we have our first guest," Bea said as she veered around the corner. "Shall I fetch tea?"

"That won't be necessary." Adrianna gestured toward her annoying guest. "Beatrice Fremont, this is Quin Cahill, one of the town founders. Mr. Cahill is on his way out."

"Good day to you, then, Mr. Cahill." Bea tossed Adrianna a bemused glance, then shrugged a thin-bladed shoulder. "I'll get back to work."

When Bea swept out, Elda swept in. Adrianna swallowed a grin when she noticed the cook had unpacked crumpets and toasted them with cinnamon and sugar for their afternoon treat. It didn't matter what was on hand to whip up for snacks or meals. Elda waved her magic wand and always came up with something tasty.

"Ezmerelda Quickel, this is one of our neighbors, Quin Cahill," she introduced hastily. "I doubt Cahill is hungry."

How could he be? Obviously, he was quite full...of *himself.*

"Of course, I'm hungry," Quin insisted as he plucked up a few treats from the tray. "I skipped lunch in order to welcome my new neighbors."

Adrianna gnashed her teeth when the ruggedly hand-some rascal flashed Elda a wide grin and winked down at her. Elda was at least fifty if she was a day, but she let this Texas devil charm her. Elda blushed like a school-girl when Quin *oohed* and *ahhed* over the tasty snacks. The annoying rancher gave new meaning to the cooking term *buttered up*.

Impatient to have Quin gone, Adrianna clutched his arm and grabbed a few crumpets to lure him out the door like a pesky dog that had barged, unwelcome, in the house. She shoved him onto the porch and thought, *And stay out!*

"Nice of you to drop by, Cahill," she said dismis-sively. "Hope to see you in Ca-Cross sometime soon."

He gobbled down a couple more crumpets, then turned to face her. "Accept my offer to buy you out, Boston. Go home where you belong."

She really wanted to clobber him for being so persis-tent and agitating. Somehow, she managed to restrain herself. She was convinced it was divine intervention at work. Either that or the classes on deportment and refinement at the private finishing school her father forced her to attend.

"I have no intention of selling," she assured him in a tone that could barely be considered civil. "Not now. Not ever. I will make this place prosper and then I will be stopping by the 4C to make *you* a fair offer for *your* spread."

His eyes turned as cold as granite and his dark brows swooped down his forehead. A muscle ticked in his sun-tanned jaw. He looked quite intimidating, but Adrianna refused to back down to him or anyone else in the state of Texas.

"First off, Boston, a woman overseeing a Texas ranch, especially one the size of this one, has disaster written all over it. Secondly, as long as I have a breath left in my body, 4C will never be sold off part or parcel!"

Clearly, she had hit an exposed nerve, though she had no idea how or why. But since *he* had hit a sensitive subject with her, she didn't give a flying fig what had upset him.

She fisted her hands on her hips and met his intense glare. "Then it seems we understand each other perfectly. You are going nowhere and neither am I. You stay on your side of the fence, Cahill, and I will stay on mine."

"Fine, then, you upkeep your half of our shared fence and I'll repair my half. That's how it's done in Texas."

"Then that's how I'll do it," she snapped back.

"You've got yourself a deal, Boston. And don't come crying to me when you can't turn a profit with your Herefords or you discover your foreman is as incompetent as you are."

On that ridiculing comment, he whipped around and stalked off to mount the striking bloodred bay gelding.

"And good riddance!" she called after him when he thundered off. She lurched toward the house, muttering under her breath. Adrianna vowed, there and then, to make this place prosper, if for no other reason than to assure that cocky cowboy that she was made of sturdy stuff.

He represented the opinions of narrow-minded men—and apparently there were as many in Texas as there were in Boston, after all—who didn't think a woman could survive and thrive in a man's world. But someday Quin Cahill would apologize for dismissing her as incompetent, she promised herself fiercely.

On that defiant thought, Adrianna stomped into her run-down house and put her bottled anger to good use by setting her bedroom to rights...before she collapsed in exhaustion that night.

Chapter Two

"Addie K.! I'm so glad to see you!" Rosalie Greer Burnett called out excitedly when Adrianna entered the fashionable boutique on Town Square. "I was afraid you'd be so busy settling in that you wouldn't be in town for a week."

Adrianna gave her beloved cousin an affectionate hug, then surveyed the shop filled with racks of stylish gowns and hats that Rosa had designed herself. She had struck out on her own to follow her dream and she had a successful shop to show for it. Plus, Rosa had married the previous month and she looked so happy she was about to burst her seams.

"Was the house in better condition on the inside than the outside?" Rosa asked anxiously. "Are Butler, Elda and Bea satisfied here?"

"They are undertaking the challenge but the interior needs as much attention as the outside."

"Do you need more help? I could—"

Adrianna flung up her hand, then shook her head.

A curlicued strand of hair tumbled from her hastily assembled coiffure and dangled by her cheek. She shoved it out of the way and said, "We are managing fine. You have your shop to tend and a husband to boot." She frowned disapprovingly at her blond-haired cousin. "And by the way, I am none too happy that you couldn't wait to marry Lucas until the railroad tracks were completed so I could move here. You know I wanted to help with your wedding."

"We, um, decided not to wait that long." Rosa's lovely face turned pink. "I already waited twenty-six years to find the perfect man for me, after all."

"I'm thrilled for you, Cuz, really I am. But I thought we'd made a pact to become spinsters together and let the male population of Eastern society go hang." She wrinkled her nose distastefully. "I have only been here a few days but I'm not sure Western males are better than their counterparts. What was that nonsense you fed me about men in Texas being more tolerant and accepting of women who decide to enter careers usually filled by men?"

"It's true," Rosa declared. "Texas is far more forgiving than New England. Men and women have to work hand in hand to run businesses and build homesteads and ranches. There is more Spanish influence here and women enjoy more rights than we did back East where English influence still reigns supreme."

"Maybe you should tell that to Quin Cahill," she grumbled sourly. "I don't think he knows it."

Rosa blinked thick-lashed amethyst eyes. "Quin came to call? I haven't even told him we are cousins. I wonder how he knew."

"He didn't. He doesn't," she clarified. "The annoying rascal swaggered over to offer to buy the ranch. I would have shot the infuriating man for the insult of nicknaming me *Boston* and insisting a woman rancher was an inevitable disaster, or something to that effect. Lucky for him that I hadn't unpacked my pistol before he showed up."

Rosa's jaw dropped open. "Quin said that?"

"Yes, so don't invite me to any activity you plan to host if his name is on the guest list. We have an understanding that we will take a wide berth."

Adrianna strode over to survey the bolts of expensive fabric piled on the shelves. "I'm hoping you have time to design breeches and blouses to suit my needs. I intend to take an active part in running the ranch and I refuse to do it in a hampering dress."

Rosa groaned. "Please tell me that you aren't reverting to your teenage persona of hellion and hoyden."

Adrianna elevated her chin to a rebellious angle. "Those were the best years of my life. I was allowed to be myself."

"I know, Cuz. I remember the freedom we both enjoyed at your country estate." She smiled ruefully. "Things were much better when your parents, and mine, were indulgent and less concerned about introducing us into Boston society."

Everything had changed when Rosa's father died shortly after Adrianna's mother passed. Rosa's mother married a decorated naval officer, Commander Hawthorne. They had sold their home in Boston, packed up Rosa and moved to Maryland. Adrianna's father had sent her off to boarding school, then bustled her into high society, hoping to make a proper match that bore his stamp of approval.

Reuben McKnight had not been pleased that Adrianna rejected one proposal after another. But Adrianna, who discovered her so-called friends and acquaintances were jealous of her wealth and cared nothing about her, had refused to fit into that pretentious world.

"Luckily, Lucas doesn't complain when I straddle a saddle on his prize horses." Rosa smiled in satisfaction. "For a man who was once known as a hard-bitten part-Comanche and ex–Texas Ranger, he dotes on me. Life doesn't get better, Addie K."

"My life is improving by the day," Adrianna insisted as she scooped up several bolts of sturdy-looking fabric. "I need five sets of breeches and shirts for chores and riding. In addition, I'd like you to make one of your most creative gowns and have it ready as soon as you can design it."

Rosa frowned, befuddled. "I thought you planned to become the independent, free spirit Uncle Reuben stifled, in hopes of making you the most sought-after debutante in Boston. Why do you need a dress?"

"Because I intend to host the largest party Ca-Cross has ever seen, and for one night I need a stylish gown."

"Ca-Cross?" Rosa's lips twitched and her jewel-like eyes twinkled in amusement. "You sound like Quin."

Rosa could have chattered all day without saying that, Adrianna thought, disgruntled. She did not want to be compared to that opinionated rascal.

"Never mind him." She flicked her wrist dismissively. "This town-wide celebration will honor your marriage to Lucas and it will be the talk of the county.

With Beatrice and Ezmerelda's organizing and cooking skills, we will have a grand time. Plus, I can become acquainted with the good citizens of Ca-Cross. After all, I will be doing business in town and I want to meet shop owners. Even the ones on the wrong side of the tracks."

Rosa rolled her eyes, "Addie K., I have no qualms about you making a memorable splash in town, but there is no need to become notorious and outlandish. I, for one, prefer to keep a low profile."

Adrianna noted the simple gold band that was nothing like the expensive jewels Rosa had been expected to wear in years past.

"The McKnight-Greer wealth has caused us both endless headaches," Rosa said, then shrugged. "But I suppose we each have our own way of dealing with our demons."

"Yes, we do," she agreed. "We both know you can't trust a man's motives. Lucas excluded. He, of course, is perfect."

"Indeed, he is. I can tell him anything and he won't betray me," Rosa insisted. "But if you wish to be known as an eccentric heiress who wears breeches and rides astride in public—"

Adrianna flapped her arms to silence her cousin. "You just admitted *you* haven't outgrown your hoyden tendencies entirely," she pointed out. "We sneaked out the two-story windows at the estate repeatedly for midnight rides on horses that our parents considered too spirited for dainty females."

Rosa smiled dryly, but didn't refute the comment. "Be that as it may, do not drag me into this rebellion of yours." She strode off with an armload of fabric and Adrianna followed at her heels. "If Quin set you off with his blundering comments why don't you simply charm the breeches off him? It worked with the men who tried to manipulate you to the altar."

"Cahill is a different breed and requires no finesse," she replied. "I'll make him regret his feeble attempt to persuade me to sell out and return to Boston, where he claims I should have stayed in the first place. In fact, I might become his new neighbor from hell if he continues to aggravate me."

Rosa tossed back her silver-blonde head and burst out laughing. "I'm so glad you're here to liven things up, Addie K. I've missed you terribly. Now I have Lucas, you and my thriving business. Life is good."

Mine is getting better, Adrianna thought to herself. She had spread her independent wings and she wouldn't be stifled, as she had the past seven years. Giving in to her wild, rebellious nature felt wonderful! And she was never going to reside in New England again. It wasn't where she belonged, despite what that infuriating Quin Cahill thought.

"Come meet Melanie Ford, my assistant," Rosa said, dragging Adrianna from her pensive musings. "She has the same kind of magical hands with a sewing machine as Elda Quickel has with cooking. I've already told Mel all about you."

"Thank you…I think."

"It's all good," Rosa insisted. "You can meet Mel and her husband, Cyril, who manages the stage station. He usually drops in to take Mel to lunch. Then you and I can dine together since Lucas is working at the ranch all day."

Adrianna frowned curiously. "You didn't mention where you and Lucas are living. In the apartment upstairs or at the ranch?"

"Both places, depending on our workload," Rosa explained. "If you want to stay the night in our apartment while we are at the ranch, overseeing the construction of our new home, you are always welcome to use it."

"Thank you. And, Rosa?"

"Yes?"

"I'm ever so glad to be here with you."

Rosa grinned over her shoulder. "Me, too, Cuz. Texas is perfect for you. You'll see."

Adrianna followed Rosa into the workroom to make her first official acquaintance in Ca-Cross. Meeting Quin didn't count because she didn't consider that aggravating rascal a potential friend. And just wait until he found out what she had in store for him.

Call her *Boston,* would he? Dismiss her as an ineffective ranch manager? Ha! He would rue the day he belittled her when she was hell-bent on making a fresh new start. She had yet to begin to put Quin Cahill in his place!

Quin was dead tired. He'd spent the past week riding the range, sorting out the calves he planned to take on the spring cattle drive to Dodge City. Although the railroad had finally reached Ca-Cross, the cattle buyers from Chicago meatpacking companies sent their agents to Dodge, so Dodge was where Quin headed each spring and fall.

He breathed a sigh of relief when he glanced down the rolling hill to see his house, bunkhouse, barns and sheds. As soon as he and his cowhands corralled the cattle he'd brought in for branding, he planned to soak in the bathtub for at least an hour. Maybe more. Then he planned to prop up his aching legs and catch a nap. After that, he'd amble down to the bunkhouse to see what the chuckwagon cook had stirred up for supper.

Once his men penned up the special group of calves that represented the 4C's finest beef stock, Quin glanced around the area and frowned. "Where's Rocky Rhodes?" he asked the men that had remained behind to tend daily ranch chores.

The cowboys glanced away and tried to look exceptionally busy. Unease trickled down Quin's spine. "Damnation, is Rock hurt? Or did he receive word that his family in Missouri needed him?"

Quin always counted on Rock, his efficient foreman. Rock had a good rapport with the cowboys and he was an expert on cattle. Quin never worried when he left for a trail drive because Rock was in charge.

"Well? Where is he?" Quin demanded impatiently.

Skeeter Gregory, the leather-faced, wiry cowboy who was Rock's right-hand man, glanced down at the toes of his boots, as if they suddenly demanded his absolute attention. He dragged in a breath, then said, "Rock ain't here no more. He quit four days ago and he left me in charge."

"He quit?" Quin roared in disbelief. "What the hell for?"

A strange silence descended on the group of cowboys. Even the bawling calves that had been weaned from their mamas piped down for a moment.

Skeeter squinted up at him. "He got a better job offer and he told me to tell you no hard feelings."

"A better job?" Hell's jingling bells! No one paid better wages than 4C. That's how Quin had kept the top hands after his family of traitors had ridden off to make new lives for themselves and left him short-handed.

Quin bounded from the saddle and stalked up to Skeeter, who still seemed exceptionally fascinated with the scuffed toes of his high-heel boots. "What the hell is really going on?" Quin demanded sharply.

"You ain't gonna like this, boss," Skeeter mumbled.

"I already don't like it. Where is Rock's new job?"

Finally, Skeeter's hazel-eyed gaze lifted to face Quin's annoyed frown. "That pretty Miz McKnight came over to hire him to run her spread."

"What!" Quin bellowed in outrage. Wasn't it enough that he'd spent the past week seeing that feisty female creep into his dreams each time he bedded down on the hard ground? Damn it, he didn't even like Boston McKnight all that much. Well, sure, she was strikingly attractive with that body built for sin, those thick-lashed green eyes, that shiny chestnut hair and lush mouth that all but begged to be kissed—if only to shut her up. Her defiant attitude rubbed Quin the wrong way. He liked his women soft-spoken and engaging.

That did not begin to describe Boston.

"She'll pay dearly for this prank," Quin muttered as he lurched around, then stormed off. When a thought shot through his mind, he stopped short, then wheeled back to his cowhands. "Anyone else planning to join the McKnight spread?"

"We weren't asked," Skeeter replied. "Just Rock."

Growling under his breath, Quin made a beeline for the house to enjoy the long-awaited bath he'd promised himself. He breezed inside, greeted by the same silence that had met him for the past two years. His housekeeper, who only showed up three days a week, had taken a job in town so she wouldn't have to travel to and from work each day. Quin hadn't been home long enough to replace her. Now he was alone in the gigantic three-story house, thanks to his selfish siblings jumping ship after their parents' tragic deaths.

Although his stomach was growling something fierce, Quin finished his bath, then dressed quickly. He stuffed his feet in his boots and his shirttail into his breeches, then hurried downstairs. He grabbed his best Stetson from the hook beside the door and breezed outside to fetch a horse. Not Cactus, he mused. His favorite mount was as exhausted from the roundup as Quin was.

Ezra Fields, the lanky, bearded cowboy who had signed on more than two years earlier, was waiting with a fresh horse. "Figured you were headed for the McKnight spread," Ezra drawled. "Figured you'd want to give ole Cactus a rest."

"Thanks," Quin murmured as he descended from the porch.

"Don't know what that McKnight gal is trying to pull," Ezra remarked as he handed over the reins. "She came riding astride on her dapple-gray thoroughbred to see Rock."

Riding astride? Now why didn't that surprise him?

"She flashed a big smile and showed off her shapely figure in trim-fitting breeches and shirt."

That sounded like something that hellion would do. Divert a man's attention while she pulled her clever stunts.

"She could've lured more cowboys to join her but she turned all her charm on Rocky Rhodes that day," Ez went on to say. "You think she'll be back to hire away more cowhands while you're out? You think she's trying to undermine the 4C?"

Well, I do now! She is going to catch an earful from me, Quin thought resentfully.

"No telling what that seductive woman promised as fringe benefits to lure Rock away," Ezra commented. "You know how bashful Rock is around women. I'd call him a pushover. Not like you. You don't back down to nobody."

Quin bounded onto the saddle and thundered off. Ezra was probably right. Boston had used her charm on Rock, who rarely worked up the nerve to ask a woman to dance at the occasional town social. Poor Rock, he thought. Boston would chew him up and spit him out if he crossed her.

Well, she won't have the chance, Quin vowed resolutely. He would get his ranch foreman back before that sneaky female sank her claws into Rock and ripped him to shreds.

The moment Quin reached the McKnight Ranch, he headed directly to the house. Aggravated though he was, he noticed the house and veranda boasted a fresh coat of white paint and construction had begun on the new addition. But he wasn't here to admire the changes. He wanted to have it out with Boston.

His hands curled into fists, itching to put a choke-hold on her lovely neck. Muttering, he rapped on the door—hard. Butler showed up two minutes later. Quin suspected the stoic accountant purposely left him waiting on the veranda.

"How nice to see you again, Cahill," Butler said—and didn't sound the slightest bit sincere.

"Same to you." Quin glanced over Butler's dark head. Not a hair was out of place, as usual. "Where is she?"

"Where is who?" Butler blinked and tried out a mock-innocent stare. Quin didn't buy it for even a second. Butler was as annoying as his boss.

"You know perfectly well who I'm talking about," Quin snapped irritably. "Where's Boston and what prank is she planning to play on me next?"

"I don't have the vaguest notion what you mean," said Butler. "However, if you are asking after Addie K., she is sorting her Herefords. I doubt she has time for you right now. Maybe you could call again next week…or the week after."

Quin gnashed his teeth so hard he nearly ground off the enamel. He glared at Butler, who obviously didn't have much use for him. Not that Quin cared what Boston's man of affairs thought. The sooner Boston and her entourage left Texas, the happier he'd be. *Joyous,* in fact.

Lurching around, Quin strode toward the barn and the surrounding corrals. To his amazement, Rock and the skeleton crew of cowhands had their arms draped over the top rail of the fence, watching Boston wander around the white-faced cows that she had shipped from New England. To his amazement—and the fascination of every cowboy—she was wearing the formfitting breeches Ezra mentioned. The tan-colored garment accentuated her small waist, the enticing curve of her hips and the well-defined shape of her legs. The breeches were tucked into her boots and her long chestnut hair lay against her spine in a thick braid.

And that blouse! Damn, thought Quin. The top two buttons had come undone. Or more likely, she had unbuttoned them to hold the cowboys spellbound and leave them wondering when another button would work loose to expose more cleavage. For certain, the garment was custom-made to display Boston's full bosom to its best advantage.

One of Rosa's designs, Quin suspected. No telling how much Boston had paid Rosa to create garments that diverted male attention away from the fact that she was an annoying little hellion.

Despite the resentful thoughts chasing one another around Quin's head, he watched her intently. She carried a stick as she wandered through the herd of Herefords, speaking softly to them. She tapped one and then another on the rump to single them out, then directed them into a separate pen. She seemed to be selecting heifers that carried the characteristics she wanted to breed into her next crop of calves. Quin was unwillingly impressed, though he'd cut out his tongue before he complimented the little vixen for her ability to spot quality beef on the hoof.

"These heifers will be penned up until my boxcar of shorthorn bulls and cows arrive next week," she called over her shoulder. "These heifers are old enough to breed and they are familiar enough with the place to be released into a pasture with the incoming registered bulls."

When she fastened the gate, she pivoted around—and halted abruptly. Quin's narrowed gaze zeroed in on her, revealing none of the masculine appreciation that had bombarded him a few moments earlier. All the resentment that had spurred him during his ride hit him full force.

He watched her gaze dart to Rocky Rhodes—the six-foot, blond-haired, blue-eyed cowboy about Quin's age—who stood at a distance. Quin focused his hard glare on his former foreman who suddenly became fascinated with the toes of his boots, just as Skeeter had earlier.

"Please see that all the Herefords have plenty of feed and water," Boston requested as she passed around a dazzling smile to the crowd of cowboys.

Then she squared her shoulders and walked toward Quin. Her chin tilted and her deep green eyes drifted from the top of his hat to his chest and hips. He caught himself wondering if she found him the slightest bit attractive. Not that he cared what she thought of him, of course. He was just curious, was all.

"How nice to see you again," she commented as she closed the gate.

"That's what Butler said. I didn't believe him, either." Quin clutched her elbow and propelled her around to the back of the barn to ensure privacy. If he decided to strangle the smarmy little minx, he didn't want her bewitched cowhands rushing to her rescue.

She jerked her arm from his grasp and stared him down. "The last man who tried to scuttle me off, in an attempt to seduce me into accepting his marriage proposal, received a kick in the crotch," she informed him tartly.

"No need to fear for your virtue, only your life," he growled as he rounded on her. "How dare you sneak over to my ranch while I was away to steal Rocky Rhodes!"

Her chin jutted out and he mentally kicked himself when his gaze dropped to the lush curve of her mouth. Anger and desire battled inside him and he hated that he found her so wildly attractive when he wanted to strangle her.

"I'm sure he's delighted, considering the intimate perks you're probably offering him and the other cowboys who work here."

Her gaze narrowed to glittering green slits. "What is that supposed to imply, Cahill?"

He gestured toward her clothing. "I'm surprised your cowboys can concentrate on what you tell them when you wear garments that fit like a coat of paint."

Her back went ramrod stiff, which drew his rapt attention to her out-thrust breasts. Quin's gaze focused on the gap between the buttons of her blouse and the cleavage beneath—and hated himself for his fierce attraction to this firebrand.

"You expect me to trounce around in a cow pen in a cumbersome dress?" she hissed like a disturbed cat. "That's impractical. Furthermore, I don't need your approval. In fact, I couldn't care less what you think of my wardrobe and of me!"

Quin loomed over her, pressing her against the barn wall, trying to intimidate her. He outweighed her by a hundred pounds and was at least ten inches taller. However, it didn't seem to matter that he could crush her like a bug. She refused to cower, even when he snarled, bared his teeth and tried to frighten her into submission.

"You listen to me, hellcat. I want my foreman back and I don't want you to set foot on my property to lure my men to your spread again."

"Business is business, Cahill," she sassed him. "I will hire whomever I want in order to turn this ranch into a prosperous endeavor. I intend to integrate my Herefords into my present herd of longhorns and breed the finest group of them with the shorthorns due in next week." She stabbed him in the chest with her forefinger. "*You* stay out of my way and off my ranch."

He grabbed her finger before she poked a hole in his breastbone. "And you stay out of mine, Boston."

She jerked sideways and he reflexively snaked his arm around her waist to hold her in place. This little snip wasn't leaving until he dismissed her. Unfortunately, Quin forgot what he intended to say when her body slammed into his and she grabbed hold of the collar of his shirt to give him a shake.

Quin wasn't even sure how it happened, but he blinked in surprise when he realized he was kissing the breath out of Boston and she was kissing him right back. It made no sense whatsoever. He wanted to choke her…didn't he? And she wanted to rip him to shreds… didn't she?

Before he could form reasonable answers to those befuddling questions, his brain broke down. He devoured her dewy lips. Damn, she tasted good and she felt like the devil's own temptation in his arms. He could feel the imprint of her hips against his groin, feel her breasts meshed against his heaving chest. He went on kissing her as if his very life depended on it...until he was forced to come up for air.

They stared at each other wide-eyed, gasping to draw air into their starved lungs. Quin took a step back and was surprised that his knees buckled slightly. He was not surprised, however, to realize that the ache south of his belt buckle was pulsing in rhythm with his pounding heartbeat.

"That was uncalled for!" she spouted off, breasts heaving, face flushed.

"You started it," he countered—and realized he sounded ridiculously childish. But damn it, this woman made him loco.

"Me?" She glared pitchforks at him. "I'd rather kiss my horse. Do not ever do that again or I will have the city marshal bring assault charges against you."

"Not before I file charges against you for trying to entice me into letting you keep my foreman."

She reared back a doubled fist but Quin grabbed hold of it before she socked him in the jaw. "Do us both a favor and go home, Boston. Clear out of Texas. I'll pay you exactly what you paid for this floundering ranch."

"You can rot in Hades, Cahill," she spewed furiously. "Furthermore, I cannot believe my cousin calls you friend. You are an infuriating beast of a man!"

"Your *cousin?*" He stared stupidly at her.

"Rosalie Greer Burnett," she said in a huff. Then she wrested her fist from his grasp. "Her mother and my father were brother and sister. I thought Rosa had better taste."

"That's why you moved here?" he asked, dumbfounded.

"Partly." She rearranged the blouse that had somehow become twisted when she kissed him half to death. "I told you, I'm making a new life for myself in a place that is *supposed* to be more accepting of women who want more than to become a wife to a man who thinks he's entitled to boss her around. As if she doesn't have a brain in her head and needs a man's permission to do the slightest thing. You, I suspect, are nothing like Lucas. He treats Rosa as his equal partner, not his chattel."

"You don't know me well enough to know how I'd treat my wife," he pointed out. "*If* I decide I want one. Which I *don't*."

"Nor do I care to know you any better than I do now." She made another stabbing gesture with the same forefinger she had poked into his chest earlier. "Now get off my property. And do not come back unless you send advanced notice so I can gird up for battle before you arrive."

He smirked sarcastically. "Boston, you don't need advanced warning. You're pricklier than my horse Cactus."

"I can see why your horse might be contrary," she shot back. "Having *you* ride him is barely tolerable, I suspect."

He smiled devilishly when she clamped those kissable lips shut and looked as if she wished she could retract that reckless remark. "Cactus has no complaints. It might be more enjoyable than you think, Boston."

She puffed up like an offended cobra. "I have work to do and I have no time to listen to your rude, suggestive comments," she all but shouted at him, her bosom heaving in outrage. "Good day, Cahill, and good riddance!"

Quin swooped down to pluck up the Stetson she had knocked off his head while she practically climbed all over him to get closer so she could kiss him senseless. Moreover, she was *not* pinning that hot, breathless embrace on him. He hadn't started it…had he? It was all *her* fault.

On that righteous thought, he crammed the hat on his head and veered around the corner of the barn to see the cowboys watching him warily. He sent them a clipped nod, then glared at Rocky Rhodes, the turncoat. Scowling, Quin headed to the hitching post in front of the house to fetch his horse.

Halfway there, an inspiring thought assailed him. He smiled mischievously as he untethered his horse and led the animal around to the back door of Boston's freshly painted house.

Chapter Three

After her encounter with Cahill, Adrianna inhaled several restorative breaths to regain her composure. Then she tamped down the unwelcome and unexpected sensations still undulating through her body. Good heavens, if she didn't know better, she'd swear her physical attraction to that infuriating cowboy overshadowed her fierce dislike of his character and personality.

Why she had allowed Cahill to kiss her blind and stupid defied reasonable explanation. And despite what he'd said, *he* had started it...hadn't he?

She did not go around kissing men on a reckless whim. Not ever. She didn't trust the male gender. They were a devious, manipulative lot. Well, except for Rosa's beloved Lucas, she amended. The two of them had stopped by the previous afternoon to see what changes she had made in the house. It was sweet, really, the way the newlywed lovebirds held hands and whispered to each other.

Adrianna was happy for her cousin, but she felt a bit

left out, too. Her expectations of moving to Texas and re-creating the days of her youth when she and Rosa had been inseparable hadn't panned out. There had been a time when Rosa was as cautious of the agenda of men as Adrianna was. But Rosa's obvious love for Lucas changed her perspective.

Adrianna discarded her wandering thoughts and strode off. She wanted to check her remuda of horses to ensure the long train ride hadn't distressed them. And tomorrow, she would ride into town for the second fitting for her new gown and pick up two more pairs of breeches that Mel was working on. Adrianna planned to take Elda and Bea with her to arrange the grand party. Celebrating Rosa and Lucas's marriage was going to be a gala affair.

According to Rosa, hosting parties on Town Square worked perfectly. But in case of a spring storm, Adrianna supposed she would have to reschedule....

Her thoughts trailed off when one of her employees, Chester Purvis, nearly plowed into her as she rounded the corner of the horse barn. The stocky, shaggy-haired cowhand who was a few years older and had pale brown eyes reached out to steady her before she collapsed on the ground.

"Sorry about that. You okay, Miz McKnight?"

She flashed a nonchalant smile. "I'm fine."

"I was afraid Cahill planned to rough you up a bit after you hired away Rocky Rhodes." Ches leaned closer than Adrianna preferred so she shifted away. "Cahill is a man to be reckoned with, ya know. His brothers and sister shoved off the first chance they got. Plus, that Cahill Curse makes him mean-spirited."

She frowned, bemused. "What curse?"

"Well, some folks in these parts claim the Cahills bribed the railroad agents to get the town placed on their property so they could sell lots and rent buildings to shopkeepers. Then, of course, there was the wagon accident that killed Ruby and Earl Cahill. Not to mention how rustling and fence cutting increased as a result of the curse."

Adrianna frowned pensively. She would have to remember to question Cousin Rosa about the supposed Cahill Curse. Maybe that's what made that brawny, gray-eyed cowboy irascible and hard-nosed. Not that Adrianna intended to excuse his behavior. Still, she was curious about the loss of his parents and the rift that sent his brothers and sister away from the ranch.

"Thank you for the information, Ches," she said before she strode off.

Ches was a step behind her. "Cahill didn't threaten you or anything, did he, Miz McKnight?"

She stopped short, causing Ches to bump into her. She backed up a step and tried not to wrinkle her nose when she got a whiff of the cowboy, who was overdue for a bath. She made a mental note to purchase a bathtub for the bunkhouse.

"Don't concern yourself with me, Ches. I can take care of myself when it comes to dealing with Cahill."

He inclined his shaggy head, then touched his hand to the rim of his grimy hat. "Yes, ma'am. Just wanted you to know that me and some of the other boys are here to back you up if Cahill tries to pressure you."

Adrianna watched the bowlegged cowboy stroll off to tend his chores. It sounded as if Ches Purvis and the other hired hands envied Cahill's wealth and influence in the area. She wondered how many of her employees shared his opinion that Cahill deserved all the bad luck that came his way. Then she wondered if Cahill's hired hands resented *her* for hiring away Rocky Rhodes and not them.

Well, in some ways she supposed she was like Cahill. She didn't give a whit about public opinion. She was following her father's policy of surrounding herself with exceptional employees. That, according to Reuben McKnight, was the secret to financial success.

An hour later, Adrianna entered the house, anxious to devour one of Elda's delicious meals, then sink into a relaxing bath. She ambled into the kitchen, surprised to see Bea and Butler slicing bread, cheese and some sort of meat she couldn't identify.

"Where's Elda? She isn't feeling ill, is she?" Adrianna asked in concern.

"No, she's fine," Bea replied as she grabbed the whistling teapot off the stove. "She took a new job."

"What?" Adrianna crowed in astonishment. "After all her years of loyalty to us? Why would she do that?"

Butler pivoted to face her. "Cahill showed up at the back door and lavished Elda with so many sticky-sweet compliments I developed an instant toothache just listening to them."

"She joined the enemy's camp?" Adrianna howled in dismay.

Bea calmly took the supper tray and whizzed into the dining room that now boasted a china cabinet, table and chairs that had once graced the lavish mansion in Boston. "Now, now, dear, don't fret. There is method to Elda's defection. Although Cahill promised to pay her exceptionally well to cook and clean for him, she intends to remain there only temporarily to see what goes on at 4C. She plans to report her findings to you."

Adrianna scoffed. "Since when does Elda engage in clandestine espionage?"

Butler snickered as he toted cups of steaming tea into the dining room. "You're aware the household staff at the Boston estates provide a network of information. How do you think rumors about who was cheating on whom and who was going bankrupt on an ill-advised investment began circulating? For a fee, you can find out the dirt on the highest echelon of aristocrats and politicians. Elda is using that tactic."

"But still…" Adrianna mumbled. "Elda is family and family is supposed to stick together."

Bea arched a brow. "You hired away Cahill's foreman to whip this ranch into shape, but mostly you did it to annoy your neighbor, didn't you?"

"Well, yes," she admitted begrudgingly.

"Then there you go," said Butler as he plunked into his chair. "Now sit down and eat. Bea and I will be better prepared for tomorrow's meals."

"No need," Adrianna replied. "Tomorrow we will purchase supplies in Ca-Cross and arrange Rosa's wedding celebration. There are several restaurants in town. We'll try their fare."

"I'm ready for a day away from painting, dusting and cleaning," Bea said enthusiastically.

The threesome ate in companionable silence but Adrianna inwardly fumed over Cahill's audacity of charming Elda out of the kitchen and escorting her to his house. Blast that dark-haired demon! First, he had kissed her senseless, then he had swiped Elda, who was an honorary aunt, same as Beatrice.

Later, while Adrianna was lounging in her fragrant bath in her private quarters—that she had painted herself and spiffed up to feel like home—she wondered if loneliness was part of the reason Cahill had lured away Elda.

According to Chester Purvis, Cahill's siblings had left him to manage the ranch alone. Maybe he'd grown tired of rattling around in that big three-story stone-and-timber home by himself. The conflict between her and Cahill might have been the perfect excuse for him to have someone else in his house.

Adrianna was cautious not to sympathize with Cahill's problems because she did not intend to soften toward him. He had insulted her, after all. He deserved to find himself living next door to a neighbor from hell. And just because that impossible man had kissed her—and she had liked it—didn't mean she had the slightest respect or affection for him. He was a man cursed, if Ches Purvis was to be believed. Adrianna had enough challenges ahead of her without tripping over a big, swarthy stumbling block with mercury-colored eyes and sensuous lips that tasted—

Adrianna jerked upright in the bathtub so quickly that she accidentally slopped water on the floor. "Forget about that," she lectured herself sternly. "Forget about *him*."

She settled back into the tub and smiled wickedly. "I wonder how much it would cost to hire Elda to poison Cahill? That would put the ornery rascal out of his misery for good."

* * *

Adrianna had to admit it was a relief to leave behind the *rat-tat-tat* of hammers all the livelong day. Although she was anxious to complete the new addition that would become her spacious private parlor, bedroom and office, she was eager to get away and visit Rosa.

"There aren't many options for purchasing supplies and personal items," Bea remarked as they halted the wagon in front of Rosa's shop, which faced Town Square.

"We'll manage," Butler insisted as he helped the housekeeper down.

Adrianna frowned curiously when she noticed Butler held on to Bea—and she to him—a moment longer than necessary. If Adrianna didn't know better...

She studied the twosome from a different perspective. "How long has this been going on without my knowledge?"

Butler stepped protectively in front of Bea. He met Adrianna's speculative gaze and stood his ground. "For a dozen years. We were careful in Boston, because gossip mills can grind you up, you know. If you object to our, er, friendship—"

Adrianna waved him to silence, then hopped agilely to the ground to brush dust from her breeches and shirt. "If you recall, I moved to Texas to enjoy my independence. I'm pleased you and Bea are exceptionally fond of each other. I merely meant that no one bothered to enlighten me. I'm ashamed that I've been so wrapped up in my own misery the past few years I failed to notice."

Butler and Bea looked relieved that Adrianna hadn't scorned their liaison.

She grinned impishly at them. "Now, if the day comes that you decide to make it legal I will be honored to host a party for you." She strode ahead of them. "Come see Rosa's shop. She has done very well for herself and, like you, she has become good at keeping secrets." She paused to stare somberly at her employees. "Rosa doesn't want anyone to know that she's an heiress so mum's the word."

The twosome nodded agreeably before they followed Adrianna into the dress shop.

Quin trotted Cactus into town to pick up the payroll so he would have it on hand to pay his cowboys. He also wanted to ensure the rent that the banker, Willem Van Slyck, collected monthly for him had been deposited in the ranch account. Although Quin had told Bowie, Chance and Leanna that he was pouring all the profits from town rentals and cattle sales into ranch improvements and expansion, he had paid his siblings dividends—in case they needed a financial boost. Of course, they would have to *contact* him—which they hadn't. Quin wasn't worried about Bowie's finances since he'd had a job before leaving 4C. Not the kind of job their parents had approved of but Bowie was drawing sheriff's wages. Quin had no idea what Leanna and Chance were doing to make ends meet. Nevertheless, the money awaited them when they finally came to their senses and returned home where they belonged.

Like Boston—who never should have ventured west to disrupt his life and take the starring role in his dreams. Damn the woman. He kept playing that tantalizing kiss over and over in his mind and wondered if perhaps he had been the one who had initiated it. For certain, she fit against his body as if she had been made for him....

Now there was a thought that rattled him to the extreme.

Yet, maybe he had been going about dealing with Boston all wrong, he mused as he halted in front of Hell's Corner Saloon. Perhaps he should have charmed Boston as he had charmed Elda Quickel into cooking and cleaning for him. She was a gourmet cook of the highest order. His taste buds nearly went into riot remembering the delicious fare she had served him. Besides, it was nice to have someone join him at the dinner table—and he had insisted on that. No need for Elda to eat alone in the kitchen, after all.

His thoughts flitted off when he saw Lucas Burnett and his black-eyed wolf dog—named Dog—moving along the respectable side of the railroad tracks. Lucas was riding his favorite horse called Drizzle and leading four Appaloosa-and-mustang crosses that he had culled from his prize herd.

"Where are you headed, Burnett?" Quin called out.

Lucas inclined his raven head toward Town Square. "I'm meeting Rosa for lunch. Then I'm taking the horses to Fort Ridge to sell. Care to join us for lunch, Cahill?"

Quin veered away from the saloon to join Lucas. "So...how is married life treating you? Haven't seen much of you since Rosalie put a ring through your nose."

"Torment me all you want, Cahill," Lucas replied, unruffled. "I'm happy. Thanks to Rosa's influence, I don't feel quite so much like an outcast in town. Since everyone adores her, they tolerate me."

"Why didn't you tell me that McKnight hellion is Rosalie's cousin?" Quin accused abruptly.

Lucas shrugged his broad shoulders, then cut Quin an amused glance. "First off, I haven't seen you lately because we have been on our honeymoon. Secondly, you didn't ask."

"Well, I'm asking now. How can your sweet wife be related to that snippy heiress who thinks she can manage a sprawling Texas ranch without going broke like her Eastern- and London-based predecessors?"

"Addie K., as Rosa calls her, inherited a staggering fortune from both sides of her family," Lucas explained without bothering to elaborate on Rosa's financial connection—or lack thereof. "Addie K. could likely buy and sell you a few times over if she had a mind to, Cahill."

The teasing comment and the mischievous grin with which it was delivered made Quin squirm in the saddle. "No doubt that's what set off that firebrand when I offered to buy her ranch the first day she arrived."

Lucas barked a laugh and his shoulders shook with amusement. "You tangled with the wrong female, friend. According to Rosa, Addie K. doesn't have much use for men. Too many adventurers and gold diggers were after her fortune. I think that's one of the reasons she came west."

Quin recalled Boston making a similar comment about her lack of faith in the motives of men in general. Lucas, of course, received a free pass because Boston apparently approved of her cousin's marriage. As for Quin, he hadn't been welcoming or friendly. He'd wanted something from her, just like every other man of her acquaintance, he suspected.

Until the previous evening, Quin hadn't added getting his hands on Boston's curvaceous body to his list of *wants*. He wasn't proud of it, but the truth was he desired the chestnut-haired hellcat whose sassy mouth amused him, annoyed him and aroused him all at once.

"So what do you say, Cahill?"

Quin snapped to attention, then scrambled to find his place in the conversation. Damn it, fantasizing about Boston had thoroughly distracted him. Finally, he gave up and glanced guiltily at Burnett. "Sorry, what did you say? I was woolgathering."

Lucas grinned knowingly. "I can see why. Addie K. is exceptionally attractive."

"Who said I was thinking about that mouthy shrew?"

Lucas's thick black brows arched a notch higher and he grinned broadly. "I'm not as stupid as I look, Cahill."

"Don't put money on it," Quin muttered as he followed Lucas, who tethered his string of horses outside Rosa's shop. "After all, you married into the family so that makes you Boston's cousin-in-law. You have my sympathy."

Several women filed from the shop, carrying packages and smiling in satisfaction. Lucas, Dog and Quin waited until the women had vacated the boardwalk before they ambled inside. Quin stopped dead in his tracks when he heard bright ringing laughter and witnessed the sparkling smile that lit up Boston's face. He hadn't expected her to be here. He certainly wasn't prepared to see her laughing. Usually she only glared poison arrows at him.

Obviously, Quin brought out the worst in her, for as soon as she spotted him her smile disappeared. Then she focused on Lucas and walked over to hug the stuffing out of him.

"I'm so glad you're here to join us," she enthused, ignoring Quin as if he was one of the many bolts of fabric crammed on a shelf. "We can discuss my plans for your wedding celebration over lunch."

"Now hold on a minute—" Lucas tried to object as he stared pleadingly at Rosa.

Boston waved him off as if he were a pesky mosquito. "I wasn't here to attend my cousin's wedding but you won't deprive me of hosting a grand party so the whole town can congratulate you on your marriage and I can meet my new neighbors."

Lucas stared helplessly at his lovely, lavender-eyed wife and Quin almost felt sorry for the ex–Texas Ranger. Especially when Boston snapped her fingers in front of his nose, demanding his undivided attention.

"Rosa broke her solemn promise to me," she told Lucas. "We were going to become spinsters together and denounce all men everywhere. Then you came along to steal her heart. My only consolation is this party to celebrate her happiness." She gave him the evil eye. "Do not fight me on this, Lucas, or I will make your life miserable."

"And she can, too," Quin interjected before he could bite back the taunt. "Take my word for it, Burnett."

When she turned her glittering green-eyed glare on him, silence descended on the boutique. Quin hated to admit that, glare or not, he'd wanted Boston's notice. It beat the hell out of being ignored as if he were invisible. He suddenly remembered that he had considered changing tact. Maybe he could treat the shrew with kindness rather than taunts and see how that worked. It probably wouldn't matter, given her cynical opinion of men and her dislike of him in particular.

Quin removed his hat, then bowed slightly from the waist. "I apologize, Miz McKnight. That was uncalled for. You are here with family and I am intruding." He nodded a polite greeting to Rosa, Bea and Butler. "If you will excuse me, I have an errand to run."

He noticed Boston was watching him intently with those lustrous eyes that could mesmerize a man if he stared into them for a prolonged period of time. That must have been what had happened the previous day, he decided. He had gotten lost in those beguiling eyes and found his lips feasting on her as if he were starving for the taste of her.

Quin turned to leave and Boston said from behind him, "How is Elda? I miss her, you know."

"And I enjoy having her and her amazing meals," he replied, glancing over his shoulder at her. "My family went their separate ways to *find themselves*—whatever that means—and my house has been empty until Elda arrived." He lifted a questioning brow. "How is Rock settling in? My men miss him. I miss him. He is a valuable employee."

"He fits in perfectly," she assured him, not smiling, which was too bad because Quin wished he could be the reason for the joyous expression he'd witnessed earlier. But he was an unwanted outsider and Boston wanted him gone. *To hell,* he suspected.

"Addie K.," Rosa scolded her cousin. "Where are your manners?"

Quin pivoted to see Boston struggle to paste on a

polite smile but it didn't come close to reaching her eyes. "By all means, Cahill, join us at the Porter Hotel across the square after you conduct your business. We would love to have you join us for lunch."

That was the most insincere invitation he'd ever received. "Thanks, but no. I don't wish to intrude."

"Well, maybe some other time, then," she said dismissively. "I'm sure you're anxious to be on your way."

"Addie K.!" Rosa sent her a withering glance. "What has gotten into you?"

Boston flashed her blond-haired cousin an exasperated frown, then strode directly up to Quin. "My apologies, Cahill. Of course, we'd be delighted if you joined us for lunch."

He decided to accept, if only to annoy her. Indeed, she had aggravated him—so they were even. Since misery loved company, they could make each other miserable over lunch.

"I'll be there," Quin said before he turned on his heel and walked out.

The jingling bell over the door announced Quin's departure. Adrianna inhaled a relieved breath. Then she pivoted to face her meddling cousin—God love her because Adrianna didn't at the moment. Rosa had forced Cahill on her.

"I would appreciate it dearly, Cuz, if you wouldn't shove Cahill at me. We bring out the absolute worse in each other."

"Really?" Lucas said, and snorted. "We hadn't noticed."

Adrianna glanced at her new cousin-in-law. His coal-black eyes twinkled with devilry. She could see why Rosa had become enamored with Lucas. He was big and rugged and he looked nothing like the prissy aristocrats who sauntered down the streets and ballrooms of Boston. Sort of like Cahill's unpretentious, straightforward manner—

She chopped off the thought. She was not giving Cahill credit for anything. However, there had been a moment earlier when his sincere apology had almost got to her. She wondered what it would be like to call him friend rather than exasperating antagonist.

"I have a few errands to run myself before lunch." Adrianna strode toward the door. "I'll meet you at Porter's in thirty minutes."

The instant she stepped outside her gaze landed on Cahill and she watched him stride across the square to the bank. He walked with a hypnotic economy of movement. He was graceful in an utterly masculine sort of way. Too bad she disliked him so much, she mused as she headed in the opposite direction to contact the owners of another restaurant on the northwest corner of Town Square.

Rosa suggested including all of the shopkeepers in providing food, drinks, tables and chairs for the grand affair. According to Rosa, she practiced the same policy when she held her annual Christmas celebration. All the businesses in town chipped in for food, entertainment and fireworks for a Fourth of July festival, she was told, so she wouldn't have problems gaining cooperation.

Twenty minutes later Adrianna scurried across the square to the meat market and came face-to-face with Cahill when he exited the bank. She blew out her breath and blurted out, "I'm sorry for sounding so rude earlier. It was most impolite."

"I won't be joining your family and friends for lunch," Quin said stiffly. "You can make up an excuse for me."

She clutched his arm when he started off. "You are coming to lunch," she said in no uncertain terms. "But first I want to know what this supposed Cahill Curse is all about."

Quin scoffed. "It's pure nonsense, manufactured by locals who believe my family deserved bad fortune because we have enjoyed wealth and success. It doesn't seem to count that we worked long and hard for what we have accumulated."

She nodded in understanding. "I've overheard similar comments in Boston because of my family's influential position and fortune. The devil is out to get us, or at least he should be because our family cannot possibly have amassed so much wealth without swindling someone."

"Precisely," Quin said, then smiled faintly. "It's easier to cut someone else down to your size instead of blaming your misfortune and shortcomings on yourself." He stepped back a pace, then doubled at the waist. "So let's start over, Boston, er, Adrianna," he suggested. "I made several remarks at our first meeting that I regret."

She eyed him consideringly, trying to decide if he was giving lip service or if he was sincere. This time, however, she was careful not to stare overly long into those silver-gray eyes. She had made that crucial mistake yesterday and she had blacked out, only to regain her senses and realize she was kissing Quin as if there were no tomorrow. It had been the most unsettling moment in recent memory. *Correction. Ever.*

"Apology accepted, Cahill, er, Quin. I probably overreacted. I'm intent on making something of myself in Texas. It is important that I become as successful and business-minded as my father because I could never become the docile, soft-spoken lady he expected me to be when I entered Boston society."

"What happened to your mother?" he asked gently, showing another side of himself that she rarely glimpsed.

"She died when I was sixteen. It was a devastating loss and it changed my father drastically. He became obsessed with transforming me into the genteel, gracious sophisticate my mother was. But I couldn't be the extension of all that she was."

She expelled a heavyhearted sigh, amazed that she was sharing a long-kept confidence with her antagonist. What the devil had come over her? They were standing right smack-dab in the middle of Town Square. Of all the places for a confidential conversation, this was *not* it.

"And who are you really, Adrianna?" he asked, studying her intently.

"The independent woman you see before you who doesn't want to conform to the standards men in society have established for women. I want to confront challenges, to test myself and achieve my own goals."

He smiled wryly. "Then let me say you are well on your way, Adrianna."

A compliment? She glanced at him cautiously. Her knee-jerk reaction was to question a man's compliment and determine his hidden agenda. "Are you trying to charm me, Quin?"

His sensuous lips twitched in amusement. "Is it even possible?"

She grinned back. "Considering your lack of charm? No."

"Touché. I'm not known for my devastating charm."

She bubbled in laughter—and realized that she had been so intent in conversation with Quin that she hadn't realized the other four dinner companions had ambled up behind her.

She glanced back to see them staring curiously at her, making her self-conscious. "About time you showed up," she said as she turned on her heel. "Cahill and I were just saying that we'd likely starve to death before you got here."

Adrianna sashayed up between Bea and Butler to hook each one by the elbow, leaving Cahill to fall into step with Lucas and Rosa. The unexpected intimacy of her conversation with Cahill disturbed her. It seemed they had passed a milestone of some sort. It was more dangerous somehow. Indeed, it was safer to be at odds with him. If she lost that edge, she would be fighting a battle with herself, because he presented the kind of alluring temptation that was unfamiliar to her.

Desiring a man was unchartered territory for Adrianna. Didn't she have enough going on in her new life without stumbling into perilous pitfalls like that? She didn't need further complications.

Quin Cahill was about as complicated as it got!

Chapter Four

 $\sim\!\!\infty\!\!\sim$

Two days later, after savoring Elda's tasty breakfast, Quin stepped onto the front porch. He frowned warily when Ezra Fields strode toward him. "Something wrong, Ez?"

The lanky cowboy nodded grimly. "Thought you'd wanna know there's some cattle missing from the west pasture. Most of 'em we branded recently. They're some of the calves you planned to drive to Dodge City in a few weeks."

Quin whirled around to grab his hat. Ezra was still standing on the lawn when he exited the house. "Something else?" Quin asked as he jogged off to saddle Cactus.

"Yeah, I stepped out of the bunkhouse after dark last night and I thought I saw some torches to the west," he reported as he tried to keep Quin's quick pace. "I didn't think much about it then. Just figured McKnight's cowhands were riding fences. After some of our cowboys checked this morning and found your calves missing, I got to wondering if rustling was what I saw last night."

Quin gnashed his teeth. If this was round two of Boston's mischievous pranks, he didn't find it amusing. Repairing fences and gathering scattered cattle cost time and money.

Hell's jingling bells! He should have suspected something like this, he mused angrily. At lunch earlier in the week, that green-eyed hellcat had been sociable and she had even flashed him several smiles after they had shared confidences in the middle of Town Square. Like a fool, Quin thought they had reached a truce. Apparently, she was still peeved at him for making the blundering mistake of insisting she should return to New England where she belonged. Which she should, of course, but try to tell *her* that and see where it got you!

"Want me to help search for your cattle, boss?"

Quin glanced behind him, so wrapped up in his bitter thoughts that he'd forgotten the cowboy was a few steps behind him. "No, Ez. I can handle this."

"You don't think that spiteful chit did this, do you? Just like she hired away Rock?"

Quin didn't reply, just stalked into the barn to toss a saddle on Cactus's back. "Go back to your chores. I'll see what I can find out."

With practiced ease, Quin prepared Cactus for riding, then thundered west. Well, so much for the amiable thoughts and erotic fantasies about Boston that had been spinning in his head. She'd tried to lure him under her spell by dropping her hostility, plying him with smiles and treating him like a friend rather than her worst enemy.

Damnation, what a skilled actress she was. But then, he suspected she'd had plenty of practice in the crowded ballrooms and theaters of New England. And to think he'd even felt sorry for her when she confided her father had pushed her to be something she hadn't wanted to be. She had freely admitted to being a sassy hoyden, he reminded himself. But her striking beauty and the unruly desire that prowled through him when he came within five feet of her had made him vulnerable.

Well, no more of that, Quin fumed as he spurred Cactus into his swiftest gait. He and that hellion were going to have an honest-to-goodness showdown. Maybe not with pistols at twenty paces, but he was going to chew her up and spit her out if *his* cattle were locked in *her* pasture!

Adrianna smiled secretively as she lounged in bed, choosing to be lazy this morning rather than hitting the ground running as she had been doing lately. Last night, Quin Cahill had invaded her dreams and she kept seeing him smiling down at her before he drew her against his masculine body and kissed her, caressed her, bedeviled her.

The man could be amazingly charming and amusing when it was his wont, she recalled. He'd told delightful stories about life on the range and cattle drives during their luncheon in town. Then he'd walked her to Rosa's Boutique, gently guiding her with his hand to the small of her back. His incidental touch had sent pleasure and desire swirling through her.

Perhaps Quin had softened now that they had shared confidences. Maybe he had begun to respect her and accept her for what she was. They might become friends… And perhaps in time they might become something more….

Her speculative thoughts shattered when someone rapped on the door. "Addie K. dear, one of the cowhands wants a word with you. Are you decent?" Bea called from the hallway.

"Tell him I'll be down in two shakes." Adrianna bounded from bed, ran a brush through her wild, curly hair, then donned the new pair of breeches and shirt Rosa had made for her.

She frowned in concern when she saw Ches Purvis lounging against the post on the porch, his arms crossed over his chest. She noticed immediately that he had made use of the new bathtub she had placed in the bunkhouse two days earlier. He wasn't as ripe as he usually was, she noted gratefully.

"Is there a problem?" Adrianna questioned.

"Yes, ma'am," Ches said soberly. "Rocky came back from sorting off your longhorn cattle for the spring trail drive and he noticed some of your purebred Herefords are missing from the east pasture where he put 'em yesterday afternoon."

"What about the ones I separated and left in the pen for breeding to the shorthorn bulls?" she asked anxiously.

"They're still there, ma'am," the shaggy-haired cowboy confirmed. "I checked 'em myself before I came to the house." He started toward the barn, opened his mouth, then clamped it shut.

"Obviously there's something else on your mind, Ches," she said impatiently. "What is it?"

"Well, Rocky was speculating about whether this was one of Cahill's pranks to retaliate because you hired him away from the 4C. We didn't want to check 4C pastures in search of your prize heifers without your permission. Don't need to start a range war if there is a reasonable explanation."

Blast it, Adrianna silently muttered. That sounded exactly like something Cahill would do, the ornery rascal. First, he had insulted her, then he'd stolen Elda. Then he'd changed tactics and become the attentive companion at lunch in town. She had let her guard down to the point that her instinctive attraction to him had invaded her dreams and left her aching for his touch. She'd even felt sorry for him because his brothers and sister had lit out and he didn't know what had become of the younger two.

Damn him! He had purposely set her up to humiliate her. The short-lived truce was over and the private feud was on again. Just when she had accepted the inarguable fact that she found him attractive and enjoyed his companionship he had betrayed her feelings for him.

"You want that I should saddle up and check around to find your missing Herefords?" Ches asked.

"No. I'll tend to that task myself," she managed to say without biting off the cowboy's head. She shouldn't kill the messenger, just because she felt like blowing the deceptive Quin Cahill to smithereens. "Please saddle my dapple-gray gelding. I'll be down at the barn in a few minutes."

Cursing Cahill with every step, Adrianna whirled

around, then bounded upstairs to fetch her boots and pistol.

"Where are you going with that?" Butler asked when he saw the weapon she had clutched in her fist. "This isn't Boston, but I doubt you can blast someone to kingdom come without serious repercussions, even in Nowhere, Texas."

"We'll find out," she growled as she barreled downstairs.

Butler blocked her path at the bottom of the staircase. "You better not be planning to shoot someone, Addie K.... If you are, is it anyone I know?"

"Yes, that rattlesnake named Quin Cahill," she muttered.

Butler's brows shot up his forehead. "I thought we liked him now."

"No, he was pretending to be nice, but that snake shed his skin. Damn men everywhere. Easterners or Westerners, they are all the same!"

Butler clamped his hand around her forearm when she tried to veer around him. "I hope you are excluding me, my dear girl. If you can count on nothing else, never doubt that Bea and Elda and I are loyal to you—"

His breath came out in a whoosh when Adrianna impulsively hugged him zealously. "I know. It has comforted me greatly for over a decade, Hiram. I'd be lost without you."

She stepped back, tucked the pistol into the band of her breeches, then strode toward the door.

Behind her, Butler called out, "If you decide to shoot him for whatever it is he's done this time, don't kill him.

You would not look good behind bars, m'girl. Please try to restrain yourself *this once*."

Adrianna nodded without looking back. She headed to the barn, serenaded by the *rat-tat-tat* of the carpenters nailing down the rafters for her new addition. She should borrow one of their hammers and pound some sense into that devilish cowboy, she thought spitefully. She had allowed Cahill to make a fool of her because she had fallen for his suave charade. Heavens, she had seen through the practiced charm and silver-tongued flattery of enough adventurers and charlatans in Boston. How humiliating to be fooled by that rugged cowboy!

"You sure you'll be all right riding off by yourself?" Ches asked worriedly when she bounded onto Buck-shot's back, then reined east. "There's bears and lobos lurking around this area, even during daylight hours."

"I'll be fine." She gouged the dapple-gray gelding in the flanks to race toward the fence separating her ranch from the 4C. "My cattle had better not be in Cahill's pasture," she growled as she raced off.

Quin glanced up and glared at Boston, her hair billowing around her as she flew across the pasture like a witch on her broom. The long-legged gray thoroughbred ate up the ground in graceful strides, he noted. Quin would have admired Boston's horse and her riding skills if he weren't so furious with her latest prank. As it was, he stared at her through a red haze and waited for her to approach so he could bite her head off.

"Get off my property, you thief!" she yelled at him as she brought Buckshot to a skidding halt.

"Me?" he roared, then made a stabbing gesture toward a dozen longhorns grazing in her pasture. "How many of your men did you pay a bonus to burn *your* brand over *my* fresh brand?"

"Don't be an ass, Cahill," she snapped back, her green eyes throwing hot sparks. "And don't pretend to be the injured party here. A half-dozen of my pedigree heifers are missing. I have no doubt you stole them from this pasture to breed to those mongrel longhorns you call a prize herd!"

Quin snorted in disgust. "I wouldn't want your white-faced cattle rubbing hides with my hardy breed."

Her chin lifted and she glowered at him. "Herefords are prized for their adaptability to rugged terrain and harsh climates. At least *my* cattle have genetics and they are known for their good dispositions," she flashed. "Unlike you and your wild-eyed herds that stampede with little provocation."

Quin thrust out his arm to call her attention to the fresh brand on his cattle. "Explain that, Boston. Is this your idea of turning a profit? Stealing the neighbors' cattle and selling them as your own? Was that your father's policy, too?"

She reined her dapple-gray thoroughbred up beside him, her breasts heaving with each angry breath. Ordinarily, Quin would have been distracted by her arresting feminine assets, but not today. He was too angry. As angry as he'd been since his brothers and sister betrayed his parents' dreams and left him to do all the work. Now he was being betrayed by the attraction he felt for a woman who didn't even belong in his world. A woman who had struck off to be something besides who she was. Just like Bowie, Chance and Leanna. Damn it, Boston was just like them! Maybe that's what aggravated him so much.

"What the blazes?"

Adrianna's surprised tone of voice jerked him from his frustrated musings. He studied her closely, then reminded himself that she was an accomplished actress who had made him believe their feud had ended and they were on amicable terms. Ha! She had buried her hatchet, all right. In his *back!*

"Amazing that you can feign surprise when you've been caught red-handed," he said scathingly. "I can *smell* burned hide on my cattle."

She jerked up her head in defiance. "I am not responsible for this."

"You mean you weren't on hand when the deed was done?" He smirked. "Don't toss out misleading comments to make yourself look innocent, Boston. One of my men saw torchlights here last night." He waited for her to follow him a short distance, then he pointed to the ashes of a small campfire. "And here is where you and your thieving cowboys heated your iron in an attempt to cover up the 4C brand."

"You did this to make me look guilty, didn't you?" she accused harshly. "You are trying to ruin my good name and reputation, in hopes of sending me back to Boston. Well, it won't work, Cahill. I did not order my men to rustle your cattle and I certainly didn't do it myself. You pulled this prank to cover your own thievery when you stole my Herefords!"

He stared at her as if she were insane. Or he was. He wasn't sure which because the woman made him crazy. Whatever the case, this feisty, intelligent female had him listing like a ship on a storm-tossed sea. He hated her. He liked her. He desired her. He wanted to be nowhere near her… Because, even as furious as he was with her, he couldn't trust himself not to grab hold of her and kiss the living daylights out of her for making him lose control of his self-restraint.

"Where are you going?" he called when she whipped Buckshot around and headed east.

"To find my Herefords," she threw over her shoulder. "If they are on your property, I'm going to shoot you a couple of times for lying to me, even if I did promise Butler that I wouldn't kill you. But you make me so mad I don't care!"

When she leaned out to open the gate, Quin circled his stolen cattle, herding them through the opening. After he'd shut the gate behind him, he chased Boston across his pasture to a wooded hillside. A moment later, he realized she was following tracks as expertly as he did. Damn, he hadn't given Boston full credit for her skills and abilities. She was knowledgeable about her cattle and she could ride expertly—even in the darkness, no doubt. Which proved she was perfectly capable of stealing his cattle, maybe even branding them herself, so she wouldn't have to involve her hired hands in her mischief. Then they wouldn't have to lie when he accused them of rustling.

"A-ha!" She growled in outrage, then pointed into the underbrush between the trees. "And what have we here, Cahill? Are you going to lie through your teeth and tell me that my heifers opened the adjoining gate and came over to your property for a change of scenery?"

Quin did a double take when he saw the red heifers in the underbrush. "I did not order the theft of your Herefords!"

Boston scoffed caustically. "No? So you did it by yourself so you didn't have to involve your cowboys?"

He muttered under his breath when she threw his accusation back at him.

"Very clever, Cahill. You have surpassed my expectations of your shrewd and devious tactics to bankrupt me and send me packing to Boston. How dare you try to lay the blame on me!"

She glared at him, angry with him, angry with herself for thinking he was a cut above the rest of the males on the planet. But she was wrong. Cahill was the absolute worst because he had the power to hurt her with his deception and his lies. She was fiercely attracted to him and that made her vulnerable. She had given him the benefit of the doubt about his change in attitude toward her in the past few days and he had betrayed the smidgeon of trust she had placed in him.

Blast it, she had countered every devious ploy from aristocrats in their quest to control her fortune, but she had tripped over this swarthy, gray-eyed rancher who wanted her land and wished her back to Boston.

Worse, he had humiliated her by pretending to befriend her and then double-crossed her. She really wanted to shoot him but she had promised Butler she wouldn't.

Quin rode his bloodred bay gelding up beside her, then stared her squarely in the eye. "I did not remove your heifers from your pasture, Boston," he said gruffly.

"You can despise me for a hundred good reasons but not for this because I am not responsible."

She elevated her chin so she could look down her nose at him. "Then I suppose you're going to tell me it's the Cahill Curse casting shadows of doubt on your honor and integrity."

His gaze narrowed and his thick brows flattened on his forehead. "Only the spiteful and ignorant believe there is such a curse to punish my family for its wealth and prosperity. We've had this discussion already and I expected better from you."

She blew out her breath. "All right, I concede that was a low blow. But you have to admit this incident makes *you* look bad, Cahill."

"You, too, Boston," he countered. "In fact, I wonder if this was a premeditated prank to put us at odds again."

"We've been at odds since I set foot on Texas soil," she reminded him.

He eased Cactus closer, his muscled leg brushing her knee. "Not always," he murmured in a husky drawl that sent unwanted heat coiling deep inside her.

Then he leaned out to curl his gloved hand around the back of her neck, drawing her face steadily toward his. His eyes, which could sometimes look as cold and hard as a tombstone, now gleamed like mercury. They hypnotized Adrianna in one second flat. She didn't protest when he brushed his mouth over her parted lips. Desire burned through her when his hand glided over her shoulder to follow the curve of her breast. She caught her breath when he rubbed his thumb over her beaded nipple.

She felt helplessly drawn to him, helpless to protest

when he hooked his arm around her waist and lifted her off Buckshot to settle her on his saddle facing him.

"Tell me that first kiss we shared was no good, that there was no heat between us," he whispered as he arched upward, brushing his arousal against her inner thighs, now draped intimately over his legs. "Tell me it was just my imagination, Adrianna. Then tell me that when we were laughing and talking over lunch it was nothing more than two people being polite in front of friends and family."

She looped her arms around his neck and squirmed closer, surprised by her own brazenness. Then she reminded herself that this was who she was—a woman who dared to meet challenges and enjoy adventures of all kinds. Cahill, she decided, was the most erotic and tempting adventure of all.

He groaned when she rubbed provocatively against him. "God, woman, you're going to be the death of me, one way or another, I swear."

"Then before your demise, tell me that you kissed me first, just as you did today," she teased, her voice crackling with erotic pleasure as she pressed her lips lightly to his and caressed the wide expanse of his chest. "Tell me you want me for who I am, Cahill."

"I want you like crazy," he growled huskily. "And I hate that I have no willpower when it comes to you. Hell, I'm not sure I can trust you."

"And I can't trust you," she replied as she unbuttoned his shirt, itching to explore his hair-roughened chest.

When she dragged her mouth from one exposed male nipple to the other, fire shot through Quin's overly sensitized body like a sizzling lightning bolt. He surged instinctively against the V between her legs, resenting the layers of clothing separating them, resenting the reckless need she provoked so easily from him.

If there was a hell, then he was most surely in it, Quin decided as her warm lips skimmed over his chest, stirring so much pleasurable torment he swore he was one of the newly damned. Then her hand drifted over the band of his breeches to the low-riding double holster that draped his hips. He knew she was aware of how much she had thoroughly aroused him. When her hand flitted over his throbbing length beneath the placket of his breeches Quin struggled to catch his breath.

"Careful, Boston," he choked out. "You keep that up and you'll find yourself flat on your back beneath me and there will be far more than accusations going on between us."

"Empty threats, Cahill." Her vivid green eyes danced with mischief. "Nothing will happen that I don't approve of—"

Adrianna's voice fizzled out when he ran the back of his hand over her breasts, sending pleasure sizzling through her. He flashed a devilish grin as he used his teeth to pull off his glove so he could unfasten her blouse. Then his hand splayed over the rise of her breasts and dipped beneath the flimsy chemise to caress her. Adrianna forgot to breathe when he took one nipple, then the other, between this thumb and forefinger and plucked gently. She almost passed out when he dipped his head and drew the beaded peak of her breast into his mouth and suckled her.

The burning ache between her legs became so pronounced that she moaned and impulsively arched against his hard length. Cactus shifted beneath them, rocking them together and apart provocatively.

Adrianna was trapped in a haze of hungry desire when Quin pushed off the stirrups, dragging her to the ground and onto the grass. He half covered her with his powerful body, then leaned down to kiss her as she'd never been kissed before. He stole the breath right out of her lungs, then gave it back so tenderly that she nearly wept.

She wasn't aware that she'd clamped her fingers in his tousled hair to hold his head to hers so she could kiss him until she tired of it—and wondered if she ever would feel that way. The sensation of his mouth moving expertly over hers, his tongue stabbing provocatively between her teeth, while his hand cupped her breast, had her chanting his name as if she were entranced.

Then he eased his hips between her legs, his hard arousal settling over the place that burned so fiercely and wantonly for him that she arched upward, wondering what it would be like to be flesh-to-flesh with him, easing this maddening ache that burned her self-restraint into charred ashes.

Her breath clogged in her throat when his wandering hand dipped beneath her waistband, easing the loaded pistol aside to stroke her belly. His hand moved lower as he held himself suggestively above her. He kissed her until she begged for whatever he was depriving her of. Then his fingertips glided over the moist heat between her thighs and indescribable pleasure flooded over her in tidal waves.

When he dipped his fingertip inside her, stroking her gently, arousing her to the extreme, she gasped. Then the most incredible sensation imaginable reverberated inside her. Heat and pleasure spread through every part of her body and shimmered with one breathtaking sensation after another. She blinked up at him, astonished by the intense pleasure that expanded with each erotic stroke of his fingertip.

"Quin?" she rasped, unsure what she was asking, wanting.

He smiled down at her, then kissed her again. "Do you want me, hellcat?"

"You know I do," she said raggedly. "I want—"

Her voice dried up when Quin suddenly jerked away, then hastily pulled her blouse back together and stuffed her discarded pistol into her hand. Then she heard the thunder of hooves and the whinny of their horses greeting the new arrivals.

"Damn it," Quin muttered as he jumped to his feet. "Of all the rotten timing!"

Three of his cowhands were galloping toward them and Boston had yet to button her blouse and rearrange her gaping breeches after he had touched her intimately. And what's more, his body was throbbing with the want of her and his men would know exactly what had happened if he didn't get himself under control—and quickly.

Swearing under his breath, he swooped down to haul Boston to her feet. Then he guided her deeper into the underbrush so they could make themselves presentable and pretend all they had been doing was herding her Herefords from the grove of trees.

"I did *not* order my men to show up here to embarrass you and put you in a compromising position, Boston," he felt compelled to tell her before she got the wrong idea. "Just so you know, I'm aching for you like crazy. This is pure torment. An interruption is the very last thing I wanted."

She smiled shakily as she rearranged her clothing and plucked leaves and grass from her hair.

Turning his attention to the Herefords, Quin picked up a fallen branch to tap one heifer on the rump, as he'd seen Boston do in her corral. The others fell into step behind the lead heifer to exit the trees and underbrush.

By the time Skeeter, Ezra and another hired hand named Otha Hadley arrived, the Herefords were walking west toward the gate, while Boston spoke softly to them.

"Everything okay, boss?" Ezra asked, then nodded a polite greeting to Boston.

"No, there are suspicious goings-on," Quin replied as he mounted Cactus. "A dozen of my cattle are carrying Boston's brand and a half-dozen of her Herefords are on the wrong side of the fence." He stared hard at his men. "Any of you know anything about how that might have happened?"

Skeeter thrust back his shoulders, offended. "No, boss. You know I ride for your brand. Always have. I'm not the one who ran out on you. Maybe you should ask Rocky about that."

Boston took exception. "I can assure you that Rocky Rhodes had nothing whatsoever to do with this." She pulled herself onto the dapple-gray thoroughbred. "I hired him because his reputation is impeccable."

"Was. Not so sure about that now," Ezra mumbled,

then sent her an accusing glance. "A man's head can be turned by a pretty face and come-hither smiles."

"That's enough." Quin glared at the lanky cowboy. "Apologize to the lady, Ez."

"Sorry," he grumbled without looking up. "Don't know what came over me."

"Boston and I will put her cattle where they belong. I'll see you back at the barn later," Quin said dismissively.

After the men rode off, Quin berated himself for risking Boston's reputation for what might have been a tumble in the grass—with an audience of cowboys. Apparently, the self-control he'd spent thirty-three years perfecting wasn't as ironclad as he thought. Either that or he had a chink in his armor that went by the name of Adrianna McKnight.

"I'm sorry for accusing you of rustling," she murmured as she herded her cattle toward the gate.

"Same goes for me…and I'm sorry about—"

"Don't apologize for something that was as much my fault as it was yours," she interrupted. "I hope to see you at Rosa and Lucas's wedding celebration, Cahill."

When she rode off, leaving him to drive his rebranded cattle to the corral, Quin expelled an audible sigh. He decided he needed to swing by Triple Creek for a cold soaking before he headed home. Otherwise, he was going to reduce himself to a pile of frustrated coals. Even now the memory of lying with that green-eyed temptress burned him up—inside and out. Quin wondered if there was a cure for this insane craving for Boston.

"Yeah," he muttered bleakly. "Being dead for a week should cure it."

Chapter Five

Quin spent another long four days riding through various pastures, sorting off calves he planned to drive to Dodge City. More often than not, his thoughts strayed to the tantalizing tryst he'd *almost* had with Boston. The woman was getting to him, though he had told himself repeatedly that she represented the same attitude as his siblings who had ventured off to find a new life that didn't include him.

Well, maybe it wasn't so bad, he mused as he and his cowboys herded the calves to the corral for branding. Maybe he'd become too entrenched in ranch life to realize his siblings didn't share their father's dream or the same passion for the land. Maybe Quin had pushed them too hard, too fast.

For certain, he'd made several cutting remarks that he'd like to retract. In addition, he shouldn't have tried to delegate ranch duties so soon after his parents' funeral. Between the heart-wrenching tragedy and the natural friction between siblings, the situation had spiraled out of control and tempers had flared—to the extreme....

"Hey, boss, you need to have a look at this."

Quin jerked to attention and twisted in the saddle to see Otha Hadley waving his hat in the air. Frowning warily, Quin reversed direction to see a skinned carcass concealed by tall grass. The hide was gone, along with meaty flesh.

"Someone butchered your calf, right here on the spot." Otha pointed to the gunshot wound between the eyes. Then he glanced at Quin. "Surely that lady rancher wouldn't do this."

Quin was through blaming Boston for swiping and rebranding his cattle. "I think something else is going on here," he murmured pensively. But damned if he could figure out what and who might be responsible.

Otha cut Quin a quick glance. "Rumors circling the bunkhouse say that lady rancher is trying to undermine your ranch 'cause you offered to buy her out and it made her mad."

Quin gnashed his teeth. "Cowboys can be worse than old hens when it comes to spreading gossip."

Otha removed his hat to rake his blunt-tipped fingers through the tuft of wiry red hair. "I reckon you're right, boss. Half the boys blame the lady rancher and the others think the curse is at work again."

Quin shot the bowlegged cowboy—who was five years his junior—a withering glance.

"Well, boss, you gotta admit that the thieving, butchering and fence cutting has picked up again. It was pretty bad before and after your folks died, God rest their souls. Then it tapered off awhile. Now it's cranking up."

Yes, it was, thought Quin. It had begun with Boston's arrival. However, it wasn't as if other ranchers in the area hadn't suffered similar problems. Just not to the extent the 4C had. Then again, 4C covered more territory and pastured considerably more cattle and horses than the other spreads.

"Uh, boss, I was wondering about taking some time off this weekend for that city-wide celebration those foreigners are planning for Rosa and her ex–Ranger husband."

Quin frowned pensively when Otha referred to Boston and her entourage as *foreigners*.

Otha shifted awkwardly in the saddle, then crammed his stained hat back on his red head. "Ya see, I met this real nice girl and—"

"Sure, you deserve a break after riding with me each time I've sorted calves," Quin cut in, and then watched the cowboy's freckled face turn a deeper shade of red. "Is this real nice girl anyone I know?"

His blush deepened. "Her daddy's a tracklayer and she works at Monty's Dance Hall. Don't think she rightly belongs in that place but she says money is hard to come by so she smiles and dances with cowboys and soldiers for a fee."

Quin hoped the woman in question wasn't feeding Otha the same line she fed other customers. The cowboy didn't need his heart broken. Of course, Quin wasn't sure what that felt like because the 4C had consumed his life for as long as he could remember. His liaisons were infrequent and impersonal. The occasional scratching of an itch, so to speak.

He knew his brother Bowie had had his heart broken once by Clea North. Quin grimaced, remembering his snide comment about Bowie's rejection. Salt to a wound, he mused regretfully. Quin had struck out when Bowie had landed on a sensitive nerve about his delay in arriving home to help his parents tend to the business of signing contracts with the railroad.

"I'm thinking about asking Zoe Daniels to marry me," Otha commented as he reined toward 4C headquarters. "There's that cabin up north that once belonged to the previous English owners of the property you bought last year." Otha stared hopefully at Quin. "I wondered if we might rent the place. I could keep a watchful eye on your northern pastures since I'd be riding home in that direction every night."

Quin nodded. "It might be nice to have a full-time hand keeping up with those far-removed pastures. But the place needs some repair, Otha."

The cowboy beamed excitedly. "I know 'cause I looked it over pretty good the last time we rode through there. But I can make the repairs myself."

Quin leaned out to shake Otha's hand. "Then we have a deal. I'll pay for the materials for repair if you do the work in your spare time. I hope things work out for you and Zoe."

Otha smiled so widely he nearly split a lip as Quin turned his attention back to the butchered calf. Someone was preying on 4C and other spreads in the area and Quin would dearly like to know who was behind the rustling, butchering and rebranding of his cattle.

Exhausted from long days of hard work and extensive hours in the saddle, Quin glanced south. He was anxious for a soaking bath and one of Elda Quickel's gourmet meals. Not that the chuckwagon cook didn't do his best, but the older man's fare couldn't compare to Elda's. Quin could almost taste the cook's delicious baked bread from here.

Adrianna waved to Elda, who was making her second visit since she had moved into the 4C ranch house.

"I brought cookies," Elda announced as she bustled up the steps, with the handle of her basket draped over her elbow. She halted to admire the gleaming woodwork and recently polished floors. "My, Bea has this place shining, doesn't she? Knew she would."

"How are things at 4C?" Adrianna asked as she grabbed a couple of melt-in-your-mouth cookies.

"Quiet." Elda held out the basket for Bea and Butler, who showed up the moment they heard her voice. "It's sad, really." She plopped down on the parlor sofa. "That man left everything as it was before his parents died. Why, he didn't even move into the master suite, and you can tell that not one stick of furniture has changed position in the office or parlor. It's like a monument to the past."

Adrianna frowned thoughtfully. Why hadn't Quin moved on with his life and made the ranch house a reflection of his own tastes? She, on the other hand, had sold the mansion in Boston and only kept the country estate that held fond childhood memories of a life similar to what she experienced now. She had chased new dreams and adventure while Quin Cahill remained entrenched in the past. Maybe being intolerant of change was who he was. Why else would he live in his parents' shadow and allow their dreams to become his?

It dawned on her that they were alike but in different ways—if that made sense. Cahill kept his father's dream *alive,* as if he were the extension of his will. Adrianna wanted to *prove* she was as capable as her father was.

"You should see the other four bedroom suites." Elda paused to munch on a cookie. "They must look exactly like they did when his brothers and sister moved out two years ago." She leaned close and said, "But Quin didn't confide what caused the rift. He did say he planned to leave things as they are. Maybe forever. Who knows?"

"He told me that his siblings had no intention of running the ranch and they wanted to make their own lives, make their own choices after their parents were gone," Adrianna said.

Butler smirked. "So that's why he didn't approve of you pulling up stakes and moving to Texas. You did exactly what his family did and he didn't like it."

Adrianna nodded, then grabbed another tasty cookie while the older threesome chitchatted companionably. Leaving them to their reunion, she wandered outside to consult Rocky. After Elda left, she went upstairs to put away the laundry Bea had washed. She gasped in alarm when she noticed a plume of smoke rising in the distance. It looked as if it was coming from the 4C, perhaps near the grove of trees and underbrush where she had located her missing Herefords—and found herself about to succumb to her secret desires for Quin.

Lurching around, Adrianna bounded down the staircase to alert Bea and Butler. Then she dashed outside to round up her hired hands to help her smother the fire. And blast it, she hoped Quin didn't believe she was responsible for this latest mischief. Especially not after that steamy incident in the grove of trees. He'd likely think she had tried to lure him in, soften him up, then strike out in another spiteful retaliation.

"Fire!" she yelled at the top of her lungs.

Men darted from the corrals, barn and bunkhouse to see her pointing northeast. Adrianna grabbed the nearest saddle horse and a gunnysack that Rocky tossed to her. She raced across the pasture at breakneck speed. By the time she and her men opened the adjoining gate and headed north, six 4C ranch hands galloped over the rolling hill toward them.

She became the recipient of six accusatory glares. No doubt, gossip in the bunkhouse blamed her for the woes on 4C. Conversely, her employees thought Quin and his men were responsible for stealing her Herefords the previous week.

"You sure we should be helping Cahill?" Chester Purvis asked as he trotted his horse beside her. "He probably thinks you started this fire to get even for swiping your heifers."

She frowned in annoyance when several other cowboys nodded in agreement with Ches. "We are not starting some silly range war over incidents likely instigated by outlaws and rustlers," she declared sharply. "Is that clear?"

"Okay, but if you ask me, it's the Cahill Curse at work again."

Adrianna jerked up her head and glared at the scruffy, slow-talking cowboy—Pokey O'Reilly was his name—

who had spouted the comment. "I am not the superstitious sort and I don't expect any of my employees to be, either. If you want to believe in voodoo nonsense, then collect your wages and leave."

That shut them up in a hurry, thank goodness. Adrianna doubted she had changed anyone's opinion but she didn't have to listen to such foolishness. She suspected someone was preying on the 4C because it was so large and it was impossible to oversee so many thousands of acres. Plus, someone wanted to lay the blame on her, the newcomer. Why her reputation and respectability was being sabotaged, she didn't know. She wasn't sure how to find out, either.

She discarded the troubling thought and hightailed it across the pasture to reach the site of the grass fire. Thankfully, there wasn't enough wind to engulf all the trees. In addition, the area was nearby Triple Creek so they could soak their gunnysacks with water, then pound out the flames.

Adrianna was hard at work smothering the fire when she glanced sideways to see Quin racing beside a hundred head of longhorn calves that he'd herded from his northern pastures. His narrowed gaze landed on her and she thrust out her chin, daring him to point an accusing finger.

She noticed that every cowboy on hand glanced between her and Quin, waiting to see if a shouting match broke out. She decided to turn rumor of their supposed feud on its ear. When Quin dismounted, she walked up to him, pushed up on tiptoe and placed a kiss right smack-dab on his lips.

There, thought she. That should quell any rumors of

a hostile feud between them. "We came as soon as we saw the fire, Quin," she said loudly.

She met those silver-gray eyes that were fringed with thick black lashes and she saw a faint smile crease his lips. Despite the heavy five-o'clock shadow that rimmed his jaw, he looked irresistibly attractive. Of course, she'd realized how vulnerable she'd become to the man several days ago—which is why they had ended up tumbling around in the grass and she'd been unable to keep her hands off him.

"Thanks, Boston. We appreciate your help."

He dropped a quick kiss to her lips, grabbed the gunnysack from her hand, then jogged off to beat down the flames. She fell into step behind him to toss aside the potential kindling of fallen branches. They worked tirelessly side by side for an hour to ensure the embers had cooled so flames wouldn't erupt later to destroy the shadowy grove the cattle favored to beat the blistering summer heat.

"I'm grateful for the extra help!" Quin called to Adrianna's cowboys. "If you have an emergency, my men and I will gladly return the favor." He glanced around the area. "I just hope this grass fire isn't a diversion for other destructive activities, like the butchered calf we found on my north pasture."

Adrianna blinked in surprise while the cowboys mumbled in speculation about who'd done the deed.

"I also noticed the adjoining fence had been cut a mile north of here. No doubt, a gang of rustlers is preying on our area, so everyone on both sides of the fence will have to remain on guard. I don't want to lose men or cattle to bloodthirsty thieves."

He cupped Adrianna's elbow to usher her toward her saddle horse. "Come on, Boston, let's check another stretch of fence to make sure no one has been up to more mischief."

While Rocky Rhodes led Boston's employees back to her ranch, Quin asked his fire volunteers to drive the cattle he'd collected to the corrals for branding.

When they were alone, Quin scooped her up in his arms, set her on her mount, then asked, "What was that unexpected kiss about, Boston?"

"You're an intelligent man, figure it out, Cahill."

He nodded his shaggy head, then reminded himself he was in need of a haircut. He wondered if Elda was as handy with scissors as she was with spoons and spatulas. Otherwise, he'd have to ride into town to seek out the barber.

"I suppose you thought you were quelling gossip about your involvement in my suspicious fire," he said as he stuffed his foot in the stirrup and swung onto Cactus's back.

She scraped a recalcitrant strand of chestnut hair away from her sooty face and Quin battled the urge to lean over and kiss her again. But he was reluctant to become as sappy as Otha Hadley—who had visions of happily-ever-after with Zoe Daniels dancing in his head. Boston made it clear on several occasions that she didn't trust the motives of men.

Not that he blamed her for being a cynical heiress, mind you. He'd had his share of manipulative fathers and mothers shoving their eligible daughters under his nose because the Cahills had money, influence and property. You never knew who was sincere and who had dollar signs in his eyes when money was involved. As for Boston, she was on a crusade to establish her independence and prove her ability to run a ranch. She resented a man telling her what to do.

Quin already knew firsthand how well that went over.

"What are you grinning about, Cahill?" she questioned. "Someone tried to burn down your pasture and barbecue a few calves. Nothing amusing about that."

He studied her sooty face and the dark braid that tumbled over her shoulder to lie temptingly against her breast. He groaned inwardly, remembering how it felt to skim his hands and lips over her lush flesh and feel her arch toward him.

She snapped her fingers in his face to grab his attention. "What is wrong with you, Cahill? Sleep deprived?"

Something else deprived, he thought, then said, "No, just distracted by thoughts of our last encounter on the very site someone set this fire."

His comment caused her face to go up in flames. "You should know that was out of character for me," she mumbled, avoiding his direct stare.

"Momentary lapse of sanity?" he supplied helpfully, then smiled because being with her and playfully teasing her made him happy. Not as happy as touching her intimately...

Careful, Cahill, you don't want to end up like brother Bowie, who got his heart trampled. And damn! I'm suddenly sympathizing with him.

"Yes, let's blame it on a momentary lapse of sanity," she replied aloofly. "That's what it was."

He noticed the proud tilt of her chin and decided Boston was as cautious as he was. Emotional vulnerability could lead to humiliation and disaster. Quin wanted no part of it.

"Whatever the reason, I should warn you that kissing me with an audience of cowboys is an invitation to more gossip."

She expelled a frustrated breath. "I was trying to dispel the notion that we are feuding, because my cowboys were quick to assume you would blame me for the fire. I wanted them to think we are on friendly terms."

"It might backfire," he cautioned as they trotted toward the treed hill where the grand ranch house his parents had built stood like a fortress overlooking the barns, sheds and corrals at 4C headquarters. "I suspect the next round of gossip will suggest that I'm trying to *romance* your ranch out of you because driving you out of Texas hasn't worked worth a damn."

She snapped to attention and scowled. "Blast it, I should have thought of that. From feud to affair. Well, I suppose we'll have to keep our distance to quell that rumor."

Quin smiled wryly. "Or I could insist that I've decided I don't want your ranch and that I'm after your luscious body."

Although he'd meant to tease her, she stared at him very seriously, surprising him. "No more and no less?" she asked.

"Would you be offended if I answered yes?"

His appreciative gaze drifted from the rise of her ample bosom to the trim indentation of her waist. Suddenly, he wished she was straddling *him* and no one was around to catch them doing wildly erotic things to each other. The tantalizing thought sent unappeased desire rippling through him and he gritted his teeth to prevent groaning aloud.

Her deep-green eyes locked with his and he nearly fell off Cactus when she said, "It would be only for your pleasure and mine. We won't expect favors of any sort. Agreed?"

Hungry need pounded him like a sledgehammer. He had been too long without the sexual favors a woman could provide. Not to mention that wanting Boston in the worst way had been eating him alive since he'd met her.

"If it's your intent to torment me, Boston, it's working. But the answer is yes. I want you. Badly. No strings. No expectations. That is, if you want me, too.... Do you?"

She smiled impishly as they approached his house. Instead of answering his provocative question, she asked one of her own. "Mind if I come in? I haven't toured your place yet. I'm curious what a real Texas ranch house looks like."

"I'd like to show you my bedroom," he said under his breath. Unfortunately, that wasn't going to happen because there were too many cowboys lurking around. It would have to be a quick tour.

"Elda!" she called out when the stout cook appeared at the door. "How nice to see you. Cahill is giving me a tour of his home. I hope he's treating you well. Otherwise, he will answer to me."

Quin noticed the exchange of glances between the two women. He knew Boston had spoken loudly to ensure the curious cowboys knew Elda was their chaperone, but whatever had passed between her and Elda excluded him.

Disappointed that yet another erotic fantasy had gone up in smoke, Quin watched the seductive sway of Boston's hips as he followed her into the house. He didn't want to turn to one of the soiled doves who lived in the red-light district on the wrong side of the tracks, but he needed some relief. Perhaps the ten-mile trek to Wolf Grove for supplies was in order. Still, he doubted another woman would satisfy him when this spirited hoyden was the only one he wanted.

It didn't take long for Adrianna to realize Elda's assessment of Quin's home was right on the mark. All of his sister's clothing hung in her wardrobe and the room must have been left exactly as she had decorated it. The same went for Bowie's and Chance's quarters. Quin's bedroom was neat and tidy but the master suite didn't have that lived-in look.

Adrianna shivered uneasily. It was clear that Quin hadn't moved on. She wondered if he had taken time to mourn the loss of his parents or simply harbored resentment against Leanna, Bowie and Chance.

She glanced discreetly at Quin as he led the way to the third-floor rooms that looked to be a play area for children and extra space for guests. She was sure Quin thought it was his duty and obligation to live his father's dream. The man didn't have a life of his own, she mused. He was the extension of his father's desire to own half of Texas.

When they returned downstairs, Adrianna cast aside her insightful musings to stare appreciatively at the stone fireplace and mantel in the cozy den. "This is a very impressive room, Cahill." She inclined her head toward the stuffed longhorn head hanging above the mantel. "A Hereford would look better, considering it is the breed of the future."

Quin smirked. "You decorate your fireplace as you want and I'll do mine as I want, Boston. I like it the way it is."

"I'm sure you do," she murmured as she wheeled toward the front door. "Thank you for the grand tour. I'd better be going. Tomorrow will be a long day. The shorthorn cattle I bought were delayed but they are due in tomorrow."

She heard him mumble something about sticking to longhorns if she knew what was good for her, but she didn't ask him to repeat it. With a wave to Elda, Adrianna stepped onto the porch to admire the view. She felt Cahill's presence behind her, inhaled his scent and felt the stirring of undeniable desire. She wondered if she would be bold enough to carry through with her suggestion of a noncommittal tryst—to experiment with the brief moment of passion Quin had introduced her to that day in the grove of trees.

"Sure you don't want to sneak back here after dark?" he whispered from so close behind her that his warm breath caressed her neck and made her weak in the knees.

Adrianna relied on the flippant responses she had used when aristocrats tossed propositions at her. "Not tonight, Cahill. I'll let you know…."

He frowned down at her and she suspected he realized he had received a practiced response leftover from her days in Boston's high society.

"I should go," she murmured as she descended the steps.

"I'll be here if you need me…for one reason or another," he said softly, invitingly.

She halted to glance up at the brawny cowboy that sported a bristly beard and shaggy hair. He looked rough-edged and rugged…and those leather chaps always drew her attention to the crotch of his breeches. Adrianna inhaled a steadying breath and walked toward her horse. She wondered how much longer she would be able to control the unruly desire Cahill always managed to stir inside her.

No strings, she mused as she rode home. A simple experiment with passion. It was a man's way so it was going to be her way, she reminded herself. After all, she had come to Texas to live without the infuriating restraints applied to women in the East. She just hadn't expected her new philosophy to include sexual pleasure. But Quin Cahill was a hard man to resist.

She wondered if Cousin Rosa had had the same problem when it came to the brawny ex–Ranger.

Adrianna smiled to herself, wondering if that's what Rosa had been talking about when she said that she and Lucas didn't want to wait that long. She suspected she was beginning to understand what Rosa meant.

Chapter Six

"I hope everything will run smoothly at the wedding party tonight," Bea fretted as she fluffed the sleeves of the new gown Rosa had created, then smoothed a wrinkle from Adrianna's dress after fastening the back of the garment.

"With you and Elda at the helm, I'm sure this festivity will go off splendidly," Adrianna reassured her housekeeper. "And you look lovely, I might add. That yellow gown accentuates your complexion and your dark hair."

Bea pinched Adrianna's cheek playfully. "You are good for me, sweetie. Make me feel half my age."

Adrianna studied her own reflection in the cheval glass that stood in the corner of her room. She wondered if Quin would perceive her as the debutante her friends in Boston saw. Expensively dressed, privileged, blue-blooded. He claimed he wasn't after her money, but she knew he would snatch up her ranch at the drop of a hat. And her body, if she decided to accept his offer...

The erotic thought roiled through her, triggering the same wicked pleasure she had experienced when she had been in his arms—twice—in the past two weeks. She wasn't accustomed to being wanted for her body, only for her social connections and her fortune. She supposed she should have been insulted by Quin's comments and horrified with her own responses concerning no-strings-attached trysts. However, the truth was she had been tempted to follow Quin to his room a few days earlier to find out what all the fuss was about.

Rosa could clue her in but Adrianna was too embarrassed to ask for specifics.

Somehow, Adrianna had managed to resist the reckless urge that had been hounding her, but that didn't mean the temptation to find out what other sensations lust provoked was lost on her....

"Do you agree?" Bea prompted, staring curiously at her.

"Oh, sorry, I was mentally listing the duties I want to tend to when we arrive in town for the party," Adrianna lied.

Bea's lips pursed in wry amusement. "Of course you were, dearie. You've done a lot of woolgathering of late. Somehow I don't think it has anything to do with managing this ranch or overseeing arrangements for tonight's party."

"I have no idea what you are suggesting," Adrianna said aloofly, then flicked an imaginary speck of lint off her gown.

Bea sniffed in contradiction. "Of course you do and we both know it. And for the record, I'm beginning to like Cahill. Hiram still has some reservations, but he is like a protective father where you're concerned. A woman of your rank and wealth must always be cautious of men's ulterior motives." She glanced meaningfully at Adrianna. "It doesn't matter if the man in question is an Easterner or a Westerner."

Adrianna tucked a curly strand of hair into the coiffure pinned atop her head, then spun toward the bedroom door. "I suppose the recent rumors suggest Cahill is courting my ranch because he made it clear he wants to buy it."

"I'm afraid so," Bea murmured unhappily. "I hope I haven't got too-high hopes in Cahill. One must always be on guard. I don't want you to be disappointed or heartbroken."

"I plan to avoid both," Adrianna murmured as she led the way down the steps to where Butler waited.

He smiled at Beatrice as if she were the most breathtaking creature to walk the face of the earth. Now that Adrianna had figured out what was going on between her man of affairs and housekeeper they were open in their affection for each other. Adrianna had noticed the same tender expression on Lucas Burnett's face when he stared at Rosa.

What would it be like to become a confidante, devoted friend and lover to a man? she wondered. She doubted she'd ever find out. She'd rejected dozens of proposals in the past seven years. Yet, the man who had drawn her interest and her provocative speculations was devoted completely to 4C Ranch.

His obsessive passion for preserving the family legacy had caused a rift with his siblings. Did Quin ever regret the absence of family in his life? Had he invited them back and they had turned him down?

Adrianna cherished her freedom and independence, but she had Beatrice, Butler and Elda—the cook who now saw herself as some sort of espionage agent who had infiltrated the 4C. Adrianna smiled at the thought. If her cook craved adventure and intrigue, then so be it. Still, Adrianna missed Elda and her delicious meals. She wondered how long Elda would camp out at Quin's house.

"Are we ready?" Butler questioned as he stepped between Adrianna and Beatrice to escort them to the door. "I hope the weather cooperates for this outdoor affair. I noticed a bank of dark clouds piling on the southwestern horizon. I have no idea what that implies in this part of the country, but I do not want it to rain on Rosa's grand parade."

Neither did Adrianna. Much planning and expense had gone into the festivities that included tables heaped with food and gallons of punch. Rosa had cautioned Adrianna that ruffians from the Wrong Side had disrupted her Christmas party on the square. Lucas and Quin had put a stop to it, but it was difficult to exclude rapscallions—who arrived inebriated—when you invited the whole town to a social affair.

What she didn't need was a brawl to add fuel to all the gossip winging around town. Rumors of a curse were still flying. Add to that rumors of the McKnight-Cahill Feud. Now, thanks to her attempt to quell talk of a feud, folks were thinking Quin was trying to charm her into selling the ranch because she had kissed him in front of the cowboys.

Blast it, the solution to one problem had led to another. "You should be used to that," Adrianna mumbled under her breath as she headed for the waiting buggy.

Flying gossip had surrounded her for years in Boston. Men tried to link themselves to her name, in hopes of discouraging competition for her affection. What a pity those gold-digging dandies didn't realize she had no affection to give. At least, not to the likes of pretentious jackasses!

Her thoughts trailed off when she arrived in town and stared across Town Square. She immediately spotted Rosa and Lucas walking toward her, hand in hand. Dog was beside them. Rosa, with her perfect creamy complexion, curvaceous figure and silver-blond hair, looked like an angel. Especially in her blue gown encrusted with rhinestones. Lord, she was like a shining star in a midnight sky.

And Lucas... Adrianna looked him up and down, admiring his masculine build, his high cheekbones and coal-black hair that denoted his Comanche heritage. He looked quite dashing in formal black attire.

Adrianna burst out laughing when she noticed Dog was wearing a rhinestone-studded bow tie. "That burly wolf dog has stolen my heart, Lucas," she insisted. "Name your price. I want him for my own."

Lucas grinned and Adrianna knew immediately why Cousin Rosa had lost her heart to him. Granted, Lucas could look fierce, intimidating and somber...until his expression softened in a smile. He reminded her of Quin in size, stature and commanding appearance. Quin had a softer side, too, though he didn't expose it very often.

Adrianna had discovered it beneath the shady trees on a wooded hillside when they had explored each other intimately....

"You look positively enchanting," Rosa complimented.

Adrianna spun in a circle to display her elegant gown from every angle. "Of course, I only wear the finest formal attire, designed by my genius cousin," she replied. "I was always the envy of Boston's social circle because of my one-of-a-kind wardrobe."

While Rosa praised Bea's and Butler's appearances, Adrianna strode off to check with the waitresses she had hired from local establishments to ensure plenty of food and drink filled the tables. Then she hiked across the square to speak with the band Rosa had recommended to her. There were no flutes or violins, as in Boston's orchestras. But rather banjos, fiddles, harmonicas and a piano transported from one of the saloons across the tracks.

When she glanced around, she noticed people were showing up all at once. They flocked in from every direction to fill Town Square to overflowing. Adrianna hurried off to set up a reception line for Rosa and Lucas. *Greet first, eat second,* she mused as she herded several rough-looking partygoers into a line to congratulate the newlyweds.

Adrianna pasted on a smile and bowed slightly when the string of guests offered their names and greeted her after they paid their respects to Rosa and Lucas. *So far so good,* she decided. Thirty minutes had elapsed and no fights had broken out.

"Adrianna McKnight," Rosa said formally, as she

inclined her blond head toward a petite woman who looked to be about a year or two older than Adrianna. "This is Merritt Dixon. Like us, she is a businesswoman in Cahill Crossing. Merritt owns the Morning Glory Boardinghouse near the opera house."

Adrianna clasped the lovely brunette's hand and smiled delightedly. "It is a pleasure to meet you, Merritt. We businesswomen need to stick together and encourage others to open their own businesses."

"I agree," Merritt replied. "The more, the better."

Adrianna would have liked to chitchat with Merritt but the next man in line grabbed her hand and pumped it enthusiastically. "Glad to make your acquaintance, Miz McKnight. I'm Ned Womack. I'm your neighbor to the west."

Adrianna smiled politely as she surveyed the man's bushy brown hair, caterpillar-like eyebrows and bulbous nose. He looked to be in his early forties and he was by no means attractive. But his small mouth split into a smile and she decided he was more genuine than most men she knew in Boston.

"Lost my wife last winter to influenza and I've been shopping around for another one to help raise my two boys," he continued as she wriggled her hand from his tight grasp. "You interested?"

Beside her, Rosa and Lucas sputtered and coughed to camouflage their laughter. Amazingly, Adrianna managed to keep a straight face. "Thank you for your kind offer," she said with practiced ease. "But I'm focusing my efforts on organizing my ranch so that it runs effectively."

Ned leaned in close to say confidentially, "Then watch out for Cahill. He tried to buy me out last year."

Apparently, Adrianna wasn't the only one offended by Quin's offer.

"I hear he's planning to charm you out of your property since he couldn't force you to sell outright."

Adrianna inwardly grimaced but manufactured a smile as Ned walked off. Quin had predicted this would happen, and it was her fault. Now what was she supposed to do to quell the new rumor of being romanced out of her property?

Speaking of Quin… Adrianna glanced down the receiving line, wondering what had detained him. He was supposed to escort Elda to town. Where the blazes were they?

Before she could scan the area thoroughly, a bald-headed, dark-eyed man with thin black brows stepped up in front of her. "Sid Meeker is the name," he introduced himself. "I'm the bartender at Hell's Corner Saloon. Not that I expect you to visit the place, ma'am, but it's nice to meet you all the same." He waited a beat, then said, "You looking to get married anytime soon?"

Adrianna shook her head. Given the men in Ca-Cross outnumbered women, she wondered if every eligible bachelor planned to propose. Apparently, getting to know each other wasn't a prerequisite. Wedlock seemed to be a convenient alliance. At least the Western approach was straightforward, unlike the devious manipulation she had faced in Boston.

Adrianna cast aside her wandering thoughts to greet a well-dressed gentleman who bowed over her hand. He was over six foot tall, lanky and there was a smattering of gray hair mixed with black strands that were slicked away from his gaunt face. He had brown eyes, a long nose and looked to be approaching fifty.

"Donald Fitzgerald, I'm your neighbor to the south," he said as he drew himself up to full stature, then flashed a cordial smile. "I hope you are settling into our community."

"Yes, and I'm delighted to be here," she replied.

She felt someone tug at her sleeve, then she glanced over her shoulder to see the blonde waitress hired to cater food.

"Miz McKnight, I think one of those ornery miscreants from Wrong Side spiked our punch," she muttered.

Adrianna tossed Fitzgerald an apologetic smile. "Please excuse me, sir. I have an errand to tend."

She followed the tall, long-legged waitress to the tables, then sipped the punch. "Definitely spiked," she wheezed. "Do you suppose it's lethal?"

The waitress shook her frizzy head. "I tasted it, too. I'm still standing. Probably the work of those rowdy tracklayers that scoff at the idea of a highfalutin party like this. I suspect they're trying to bring the rest of us down to their ill-mannered level."

"Dilute the punch as best you can and test it periodically," Adrianna advised.

"Yes, ma'am. I'll tell the other girls to be on guard."

When Adrianna strolled away from the refreshment area to rejoin the receiving line, she noticed several women standing aside. They appeared young and unattached. Adrianna suspected they plied their wares on the north side of the tracks and had been shunned by the so-called decent folks. But Adrianna wasn't here to judge as she had been judged. She refused to conform to accepted standards. In fact, this was the first time she'd worn a dress since she stepped down from the train.

"Have any of you met Rosa?" Adrianna asked as she halted in front of the five young women. "She's my cousin and she is one of the nicest people you will ever meet."

"We've seen her at a distance and all of us would dearly love to buy one of her marvelous dresses," Margie, the brunette-turned-spokesperson said, then pointed at Adrianna's gown. "You're wearing one of her creations, aren't you?"

Adrianna nodded, grinned, then added, "She also designed my breeches and shirts. I am convinced that somewhere back in history some spiteful little man decided women should be restrained and hampered by cumbersome dresses. That's why it is taking us longer to assume control of the world."

The women giggled, but Adrianna wasn't kidding. In her opinion, women had been held back, held down and pigeonholed entirely too long. She wanted to be remembered as one of the new breed of females who did not need a man to resolve her problems or to cut a wide swath to protect her from whatever adversity she countered. Women needed a change in attitude, she decided, and she would promote independent thinking every chance she got.

"Come along, ladies. If you admire Rosa's talents with fabrics and her independent spirit, then you should meet her."

Despite several puzzled glances to her left and right, Adrianna led the procession of women to the receiving line that had dwindled to a few dozen. Rosa greeted the women graciously, as anticipated, and then watched them amble toward the refreshment tables.

"Are you trying to prove a point?" Lucas asked, his obsidian eyes bearing down on her.

Adrianna elevated her chin. "Of course I am. Do you think I'm an empty-headed moth fluttering from one flame to the next? Those women might not have the advantages I've had in life, but they greatly admire Rosa's sense of style and her willingness to set up a business. Moreover, I do not intend to draw lines that indicate different social classes. The West is supposed to be the place where hard work and ingenuity are more important than pedigrees. Am I right?"

"Oh, good, this is a rally for women's rights," came an amused voice from behind her. "I was afraid it might be just a dull wedding reception to honor my friends."

Quin's wry amusement transformed into stunned amazement when Boston spun around to greet him. Her stylish emerald-green silk gown swirled around her. The décolleté of the formfitting dress dragged his attention to her full cleavage. Then he yanked up his gaze to notice the sophisticated coiffure that accentuated the sleek column of her neck—where he wanted to place about a half-dozen kisses. For starters.

Gracious! He'd never seen Adrianna in anything except breeches—which was tantalizing enough. Well, there was that faded old gown she'd worn while giving her new home a good scrubbing, he amended. But this! She looked like a regal princess, not the sassy, spirited hellion who had clashed with him repeatedly and heatedly in the past.

Quin wanted to grab her hand, drag her off to a dark corner and devour her with hungry kisses. He suspected he wasn't the only one, either, for he noticed several men staring admiringly at her. They were all but licking their lips in anticipation of having her to themselves for a few steamy moments.

"Cahill, so glad you could finally make it," she greeted.

When she smiled, it set off an explosion of lust that he'd been battling for days. His silent pep talks to discard erotic thoughts of Boston hadn't worked worth a damn. Nothing smothered his tantalizing memories of her.

She glanced this way and that. "Where's Elda? You're late and she is likely upset because it's her mission in life to oversee events involving food."

Thunder rumbled and lightning flashed in the approaching cloud bank. Boston frowned at the sky, as if daring the storm to disrupt her party. Quin bit back a grin and thought Mother Nature had best not tangle with the strong-willed firebrand in emerald green. Mother Nature might lose.

"I don't know where Elda is now but I can tell you where she's been." Rosa gestured toward the table where several cakes and pastries had appeared.

It had taken Quin an extra half hour to load the desserts Elda had been cooking for the past two days. And believe it, the red-haired cook was fussy about transporting her desserts properly so they wouldn't be damaged!

Adrianna's laughter filled the empty spaces in the region of Quin's heart as she turned dancing green eyes back to him. "Let me guess, Elda turned your kitchen into a bakery and you were not allowed within five feet of the door for fear you might cause her cakes and pastries to collapse."

He nodded, smiled stupidly—and didn't care that he had. "I've lived on hardtack and johnnycakes for two days," he reported. "I'm thinking of sending her back to you."

When the band struck up a tune, Rosa grabbed Lucas's hand and towed him away. Dog, decked out in his sparkling bow tie, trailed after them.

"Burnett has been dreading this dance since you scheduled your party," Quin confided. "He doesn't like limelight."

"He will just have to get over it because the first dance is always reserved for newlyweds," Adrianna remarked, then grinned impishly. "Small consolation for the grand prize of Rosa's everlasting affection, if you ask me. She and I lost faith in men until Lucas came along. Which goes to prove, I suppose, there is no logical explanation for affairs of the heart. Now, I'm forced to share her companionship with that brawny ex–Ranger and his wolf dog."

There it was again, Quin mused, that staunch declaration that Boston needed no man to make her life complete. He certainly hadn't needed a woman, not with his rigorous schedule and endless duties to keep 4C running efficiently.

But still…sometimes at night, when the silence consumed the house and seeped into his soul, he wondered if he should select a wife and fill the family home with a child to carry on the Cahill ranching tradition that his brothers and sister discounted as insignificant. What if Quin's future children did what Bowie, Chance and Leanna had done? The next generation might scatter in the wind to seek their fortunes and stumble into disaster.

Thunder rumbled in the night and Boston glared at the sky in defiance. "Don't you dare ruin the party."

"Miss McKnight? Quin?"

Quin gave himself a mental slap, then glanced sideways. The sixty-year-old banker sported a neatly clipped mustache and beard. He was in charge of collecting town rent and monthly installments for the loans Quin carried for residents who purchased Cahill land in town. The older man approached, then bowed politely.

"We haven't met yet," the banker said, clearly dazzled by the enchanting beauty in green silk. "I'm Willem Van Slyck. My son, Preston, is around here somewhere. He'll want an introduction, too."

Boston curtsied gracefully. "A pleasure to meet you, sir. Thank you for coming this evening."

"It is nice to have an Eastern heiress among us," Willem remarked. "Western society must seem lacking in sophistication, compared to what you are accustomed to."

Quin could feel Boston tense beside him. Of course, Van Slyck had no idea that the heiress had no use whatsoever for exclusive social circles and name-dropping.

"On the contrary, sir," she replied through a smile that Quin noticed did not reach her eyes. "I'm fascinated with life in Texas and I'm relieved to have left that other world behind. In fact, I'm considering the idea of joining the trail drive to Dodge City when I sell my cattle next month. It should be a memorable adventure."

Quin choked on his breath and the banker's blue eyes nearly bugged from their sockets. Boston slid Quin a challenging glance, daring him to object to her plans.

"Well, um, if I can be of financial service to you in the future, Miss McKnight, do not hesitate to stop by the bank," he said before he went on his way.

"You dashed Willem's hopes of forming an elite social circle in Ca-Cross," Quin commented.

"He can form one without me. I left that pretentious lifestyle behind for a dozen good reasons."

"Do your *good reasons* have a name?" Quin questioned, staring interestedly at her. "Someone specific who destroyed your faith in high society men?"

She turned away, disregarded his question, then frowned thoughtfully at Willem's departing back. "Is there a Mrs. Van Slyck?"

"No. I don't know what became of Willem's wife," Quin said. "As for Preston, he works at the bank with his father...when it suits his whim. I think Willem is disappointed that his son doesn't live up to expectations."

Boston hooked her arm in his and urged him forward. "I need to check the refreshments. Are you hungry?"

"Of course. I told you, I've been on a steady diet of hardtack for two days," he reminded her.

She arched an amused brow when Quin drew the attention of a flock of women beside the dance area. "It seems several females would eagerly line up on your doorstep to dance. Or better yet, become part of the Cahill family. Maybe they are interested in helping Willem form an elite social circle."

"They should look elsewhere. I'm not good marriage material," Quin assured her.

"Nor I."

"Too independent-minded and contrary?" he said helpfully.

She smiled good-naturedly and returned his taunt. "What sensible woman would want to play second fiddle to the 4C? Even if it meant marrying a high-and-mighty Cahill?"

"There might be a few interested takers," Quin contended, then nodded a greeting to Oscar and Minnie Jenkins. "Here's a perfect example. The owners of the Château Royale Hotel have a daughter named Ellen. They have shoved her at me on several occasions and don't appreciate my lack of interest."

"Are they disgruntled enough to grind you up in the gossip mill and besmirch your reputation every chance they get?" she asked as she studied the older couple astutely.

Quin frowned in thought. "I don't know, but that's a possibility, I suppose. I doubt Ellen would be a party to it. She seems timid around me and not particularly disappointed I didn't pursue her."

"Maybe she doesn't prefer domineering ranchers like you," Boston teased, then glared skyward when lightning flickered ominously. "You might crush Ellen's spirit in nothing flat."

"Unlike you, who'd bite my ankle before I could stomp on your spirit." He chuckled, delighting in their playful banter.

"A matched set," she declared. "We will save the poor souls of Ca-Cross from misery if we remain unattached."

"It's settled, then," Quin proclaimed. "We'll do the world a favor. No marriages for the likes of us."

"Agreed…"

Her voice trailed off when Preston Van Slyck swaggered toward them with a full glass of spiked punch in each hand.

"Who is that dandy?" Boston asked distastefully.

"Preston Van Slyck. He's a few years older than you," Quin murmured. "I don't care for the banker's son. He lacks ambition and takes advantage of his father's position in the community. He is a ladies' man of the worst sort, which is why Bowie, Chance and I escorted him off the ranch when he tried to pay Leanna a visit. He disliked being rejected."

Boston nodded in understanding. "He reminds me of the dime-a-dozen dandies in Boston who live on the laurels of their parents and hope to seduce heiresses who can afford to pay their gambling debts and provide residences for their mistresses. Handsome to look at but brimming with false charm as insincere as the day is long."

"You've just described Preston to a *T*."

"Ah, so here you are, my dear," Preston purred as he halted in front of Boston. His devouring gaze swept over her alluring figure not once but twice. "I'm here to say that you are as bewitching and lovely as I've heard tell."

Boston inclined her head in a regal manner that was as standoffish as it could get. Quin could envision her in a ballroom, surrounded by panting fortune hunters like Preston. No doubt, she could spot pretentious scoundrels at a glance.

"Adrianna McKnight, this is Preston Van Slyck," Quin introduced reluctantly.

"I hope you are enjoying our party," she said with stiff politeness.

Preston struck a haughty pose. "I'd enjoy it more if there was more *spike* in the punch, but I can overlook that if you dance with me."

Possessive jealousy stabbed at Quin—at least, that's what he thought it was. He'd never experienced the feeling before and he told himself he shouldn't be feeling it now because he had no hold on Boston. She made it clear she was her own woman and would do as she pleased in this new life she had created for herself and for her family of devoted employees. She didn't need a keeper and didn't want a man's protection.

"No, thank you, Preston," she declined. "Mr. Cahill and I have business to discuss."

Preston smirked as he turned his attention from Boston to Quin. "What business is that? Charming you out of your ranch and anything else he can get away with? Perhaps you should know the Cahills aren't the pillars of society they want everyone to think they are. In fact, I recently returned from Deadwood, South Dakota, where I renewed a former acquaintance. Someone you know well, I believe, Cahill."

Quin frowned warily when Preston smiled like a hungry shark, then swirled his drinks in his glasses.

"In case you didn't know, your sister works at a saloon in Deadwood. I'm sure, as one man to another, we can guess how she makes extra money. She *claims* she pays room and board dealing cards, but with her lovely face and enticing body, we both know how she moonlights, don't we?"

Fury consumed Quin so quickly that he didn't realize he'd doubled his fist, anxious to cram Preston's teeth down his throat. If Adrianna hadn't jerked on his arm, he would have clocked that annoying bastard.

"Are you unusually drunk, Van Slyck?" Boston asked, keeping a stranglehold on Quin's arm. "Or are you always such an ass?"

The clean-shaven, dark-haired rake shrugged off the insult. His blue eyes gleamed with wicked delight. "Oh, did I forget to mention Leanna's illegitimate child? Thought you'd want to know you have a nephew, Cahill."

When Quin tried to go for Preston's throat, Boston clamped him in a bear hug. "Don't spoil Rosa's party because of this pathetic excuse of a man," she gritted out while she glared at Preston with contempt. "He isn't worth the trouble, no matter what lies spew out of him."

Preston took another sip of punch, then looked down his nose at Boston. "I was hoping we could be friends, but if you prefer to consort with the brother of a card-dealing prostitute, then so be it, my dear Adrianna."

He turned an about-face, then swayed slightly to regain his balance. He downed both drinks, then wobbled off to refill his glasses.

"Are you all right, Cahill?" Adrianna asked as she peered into his murderous expression. Clearly, he'd had no idea where his sister had settled. The news, especially delivered from a cad of the highest caliber, came as a devastating blow.

"Whether that arrogant blowhard is telling the truth

Play the Lucky Hearts Game

and get...
2 FREE BOOKS and
2 FREE MYSTERY GIFTS...
YOURS TO KEEP!

yes! I have scratched off the gold card.
Please send me my *2 FREE BOOKS* and
2 FREE MYSTERY GIFTS (gifts are worth about $10).
I understand that I am under no obligation to purchase
any books as explained on the back of this card.

Scratch Here!
Then look below to see what your
cards get you...*2 Free Books*
& *2 Free Mystery Gifts!*

246/349 HDL FJCQ

FIRST NAME

LAST NAME

ADDRESS

APT.#

CITY

STATE/PROV.

ZIP/POSTAL CODE

Visit us online at
www.ReaderService.com

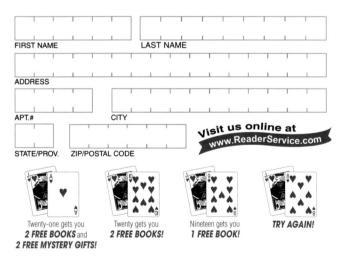

Twenty-one gets you
2 FREE BOOKS and
2 FREE MYSTERY GIFTS!

Twenty gets you
2 FREE BOOKS!

Nineteen gets you
1 FREE BOOK!

TRY AGAIN!

or not, he'll spread the vicious scandal about Leanna and the possibility of a child all over town. It's my fault that she's out in the world, struggling to survive."

He scowled sourly. "The thought of Leanna falling into ruin eats me up inside. I wonder if Bowie knows. And Chance? Is he in some kind of trouble, too? Damn it! It's my job to protect the younger ones and I sent them away in anger."

"You are not responsible for Leanna or Chance," Boston assured him firmly.

He looked down at her and snorted. "I'm not? Then why do I feel as if I cast my sister to the wolves?"

"Because you're her big brother and you believe it's your born duty, just like you believe it's your obligation to carry on your father's dreams to expand the 4C."

Although he glowered at her, his silver-gray eyes flaring with anger, she stepped forward, not away. "I know how your sister feels. At least I think I do," she insisted. "She wants to be her own person, not the extension of a family legacy.

"I wanted my father to appreciate me for who I am inside, but he wanted me to live a fairy-tale life and become the image of my mother. I was to be pampered by some wealthy man who could manage my fortune so I wouldn't have to fret over business. But *you* know perfectly well that's not who I am, Cahill, even if my father couldn't see it. Furthermore, whatever Leanna is doing with her life, I bet she prefers to make her own choices and face the consequences."

Quin blew out an agitated breath, then nodded reluctantly. "You independent females drive men crazy."

"Why? Because we envy what men have? *Choices?*"

she challenged. "Because we want to control our destiny? To vote and to have a say in laws that affect us as much as men?"

"This is no time for one of your barnstorming speeches," he muttered darkly.

"I'm trying to tell you how your sister likely feels," she insisted. "You need to see the world from her point of view, from *my* point of view. Try trading places with me for a week. See how you react to being stifled and treated like a second-class citizen. See how you react to being bossed around by men who think it is their God-given right to do so."

Quin wheeled around, intent on looking up Preston and pounding him into the ground. But Adrianna would have none of that. She grabbed his arm and blocked his path.

"I've met his type before. He delights in tormenting others for his own amusement. It would take a dozen Prestons to make one of you, Cahill. Don't lower yourself to his despicable level. Especially not here. Not tonight."

"Fine, but I need a drink. The punch isn't strong enough to numb the feeling that I've failed my sister, just as my two brothers have failed her. Damn them! They should've told me where she was. She should've sent word to me!" he brooded.

Adrianna suspected Quin's sister had rejected Preston when she realized what a rascal he was. This was, no doubt, Preston's way of retaliating. Unfortunately, *Quin* had to deal with the scandalous gossip about his sister and the rumor about how *he* was attempting to charm Adrianna into selling out to him. Not to mention that malarkey about the supposed Cahill Curse being deserved punishment for his family's prosperity.

She blew out an exasperated sigh while she watched Quin stalk off, looking like a fire-breathing dragon in elegant formal attire. She'd like to shoot that Preston character full of buckshot for blurting out those comments that cut Quin to the core. Wherever Leanna Cahill was, her reputation was being dragged through the mud tonight, compliments of Preston Van Slyck. The offensive, drunken bastard.

"Do not let that scoundrel ruin Rosa's party. Don't *you* ruin this celebration," Adrianna chanted repeatedly as she strode across Town Square. She was itching to blow that man to smithereens for spreading gossip and upsetting Quin to the extreme. "Blast it all, *who* is going to stop *me* from giving that spiteful bastard the shooting he so richly deserves?"

Chapter Seven

Quin stalked across the tracks to chug a few stiff drinks and cool off at Hell's Corner Saloon. Unfortunately, the place had been locked up tight. He glanced south to see Sid Meeker ambling toward him.

"Surprised to see you here so quickly. I wasn't expecting the crowd to leave the party for another hour," Sid commented as he opened the door for Quin.

"I need a drink…or ten," Quin muttered.

He doubted it was possible to drown his troubles and frustrations in a bottle but, at the very least, he wanted to numb his senses to the torment eating him alive. His little sister had a child and no husband? She was a saloon girl or card dealer—or both? Worse, Preston Van Slyck's implication that she had turned to prostitution to support herself was killing Quin bit by agonizing bit.

Muffling a salty oath, Quin threw back his head and gulped the whiskey. He gestured for Sid to pour another drink…and then another.

Thunder rumbled overhead, all too symbolic of the

storm of torment raging inside him. He told himself that his family had abandoned him and the ranch, not the other way around. But the niggling voice inside him whispered that he had forced his siblings into desperate situations. He should head to Deadwood and see for himself whether what Preston said was true. And maybe he would do that after the spring trail drive to Dodge City. By then, he'd have this upheaval of emotion under control. Of course, that didn't mean he wouldn't be tempted to gun down the irresponsible father of Leanna's child who had left her to manage all alone. Damn him to hell and back!

"A fine way for a boy to grow up," he grumbled sourly. "But he's a *Cahill*. The first of his generation. God forbid he faces the same problems with *his* siblings and cousins."

The grim thought prompted Quin to guzzle another drink.

"I think you've had enough, Quin." Sid removed the bottle and shot glass from his reach.

Quin nodded in agreement, then pushed away from the bar. "I suppose you heard the vicious gossip tonight."

Sid bobbed his bald head and smiled sympathetically. "I heard. Maybe there's more to that Cahill Curse—"

Quin exploded in a growl and puffed up like a spitting cobra. "I expected better from you, Sid. We go back a long ways and I call you friend."

Sid heaved a sigh. "Yeah, you're right. You financed this place so I could get a new start. I've been listening to too much saloon gossip instead of putting a stop to it. Count on me to quell some of the rumors, my friend."

Quin nodded, then wheeled toward the door. He

stalked onto the boardwalk and noted that a few torches and lamplights were still blazing on the square. Most of the rowdy crowd was walking toward the tracks to play billiards, monte or poker and to visit the harlots on the Wrong Side.

As for Quin, he was headed to 4C to down a few more drinks. Boston could give Elda a ride home tonight because he was the worst of all possible companions now.

Cursing Preston Van Slyck for spreading vicious rumors, Quin pulled himself into the buggy he'd driven to town to accommodate Elda's desserts. He left the lights of town behind, then burst out with a string of obscenities when he stared northwest. Flames danced in the wind that had picked up in the approaching thunderstorm.

With a sense of urgency, he popped the reins over the horses' rumps and sped off. If lightning had struck a tree on his property, he could expect another prairie fire to destroy the tall grass and endanger his cattle. He'd have to stop a stampede and beat out the fire with the skeleton crew of cowpunchers that was at the 4C. Most everyone who hadn't drawn the short straw had ridden to town for the festivities.

The wind picked up another notch as Quin raced toward home in the darkness. He was reminded of the wagon accident that had killed his parents two years earlier so he tried to use caution, but time was of the essence. He still couldn't precisely tell where the fire was. Distances were deceiving when it came to pin-pointing smoke and flames.

"Of all the…!" Quin roared when he reached the 4C

headquarters and realized the fire was raging at Boston's house. Dear God! Had lightning set the fire that was spreading in the wind?

Quin raced the buggy to the bunkhouse to alert the ranch hands, but no one answered his call of alarm. Swearing foully, he guided the buggy toward the gate between his spread and Boston's ranch. His heart twisted in his chest as lightning flickered above the dancing flames that lit up the night.

"What else can go wrong tonight?" Quin muttered as he glanced skyward. Hell, he wasn't sure he wanted to know. He still hadn't dealt with the frustration Preston had tossed at him and now he expected to face Boston's angry accusations that *he* was responsible for the fire.

Adrianna was busy gathering leftover food when someone tapped her on the shoulder. She half turned to see Butler staring bleakly at her.

"We need to go. Now," he said urgently.

"Why? I have to clean up the area."

Butler clamped his hands on her shoulders, then turned her around to face northwest. She gasped in dismay when she saw the golden flames that sharply contrasted with the black clouds that had swallowed up the moon and stars.

"I don't know whose place it is. Maybe ours or Fitzgerald's just south, or the 4C to the east. But I'll feel better when I know for sure," Butler insisted.

Adrianna set aside the boxes, crates of food and supplies she had collected, then lifted her full skirts out of her way so she could dash off to summon Bea and Elda.

Like Butler, she wasn't as familiar with the area

and it was difficult to tell whose ranch was on fire. She didn't know if the flames engulfed timberland, grassland or structures. Whatever the case, the sense of urgency streaked through her as she raced ahead of her employees to reach the carriage.

"What's wrong?" Rosa called out behind her.

"Fire!" Adrianna threw over her shoulder as she grabbed the reins.

"Sweet mercy! In this fierce gale? That could be disastrous. Do you know where it is for sure?"

"That's what we plan to find out!"

"Lucas and I will be right behind you," Rosa promised as she lurched around to locate Lucas and Dog.

Heart pounding against her ribs, Adrianna pulled herself into the carriage, then helped Butler, Elda and Bea clamber to their seats. All three were gasping for breath when Adrianna slapped the horses on the rumps with the reins, demanding their fastest gaits.

"Slow down before you kill us all!" Elda yelped as she clamped one plump hand on her new hat and put a stranglehold on the metal armrest with the other.

"Want me to drive?" Butler asked as he grabbed hold of the seat to prevent being catapulted onto the street when Adrianna practically took the corner on two wheels.

"Just hold on for dear life," she advised. "We need to find out whose place is on fire and what we can do to help."

"I will be of no assistance whatsoever if I'm dead—" Bea's voice dried up when Adrianna swerved to dodge a drunken cowboy who staggered from the boardwalk to the street.

Thunder rolled and everyone except Adrianna instinctively ducked. She was too intent on trying to follow the road in the darkness. She hadn't lived in the area long enough to race off on a shortcut without plunging the carriage into a ravine or overturning it on a sharp curve.

"Lord! I think the fire is on our place!" Bea howled in dismay as they flew down the road with the wind and dust billowing around them.

Adrianna's thudding heart plunged to her stomach as they passed the turnoff that led to 4C headquarters. She hadn't wanted to wish ill on Cahill or her neighbors, Fitzgerald and Womack, but she couldn't wish a fire on herself. Yet, there was no question now. Her home or barn— she couldn't tell which—was in flames and her prize cattle might be in danger!

Blast it! She had hired workers to carefully pack her family heirloom furniture and transport it all the way from Boston to Texas. The pieces had only suffered a few scratches. Now they could be kindling in a fire. Not to mention the specially designed gowns that Rosa had labored over. And the financial ledgers could be ashes, she thought frantically. Good heavens, there could be nothing left to salvage!

"Will you look at that!" Butler yelped when he realized it was the house, not the barns or sheds, that was burning.

Adrianna raced over the hill to see flames leaping across the rafters of the new addition to her home. Silhouettes dashed hither and yon, splattering water to douse the fire. Without a care for her elegant gown, she drew the back hem between her legs to fashion makeshift breeches. Then she ripped a strip of fabric from her petticoats to serve as a belt. She had the dispirited feeling her improvised garment might be all she had left of her new wardrobe and her new life in Texas. Her world was going up in smoke!

Adrianna leaped to the ground, then raced off to fetch a bucket. Men were dashing about, splashing water on the existing wall of the house, trying to prevent the entire structure from catching fire.

"Boston!" Quin's voice rose in the air, followed by another formidable rumble of thunder.

She spun around to see him, still in his formal attire, tossing a lasso over a smoldering rafter. He yanked—hard—before the rope caught flame. The charred lumber collapsed into a pile—away from the walls of the house. Adrianna rushed toward him, then skidded to a halt when glowing embers settled over both of them. For a moment, she thought her hair had caught on fire. That's all she needed, a bonfire in the windblown coiffure atop her head.

"Hold on to this rope while I toss up another one," Quin barked as he handed her the trailing end of the first lasso. He glanced at her quickly, his silver eyes reflecting the devastating flames. "I swear to you that I had nothing to do with this, Boston. I didn't undermine your ranch. It's likely a stroke of bad luck caused by lightning."

As if to emphasize his point, lightning crackled nearby and thunder exploded overhead once again.

Adrianna flinched but then she gritted her teeth and dragged the smoldering lumber farther from the north wall of the house before the rope burned completely in two.

"Do you believe me, Boston?" Quin asked before he hurled the loop of the rope, snagging another piece of burning lumber. "I wouldn't do this to you. I'd sooner burn down my own house. And why not? *My* family has no use for it. But *you* and your family made this house a home."

Adrianna heard the torment in Quin's deep baritone voice. The cruel tale Preston Van Slyck had spread around town had come as a bitter blow to Quin. He was holding himself personally responsible for his sister's woes and he was angry with his two brothers for allowing it to happen. They should have contacted him so he could have helped...or at least been prepared for ugly gossip.

In addition, he believed Adrianna suspected him of starting this devastating fire that had destroyed the new addition that would become her private living quarters.

"I know you aren't to blame," she assured him as she grabbed hold of his rope to help him tow the peak of the smoldering rafters away from the existing house.

His broad shoulders slumped. "Thanks, Boston. Whatever it takes, my men and I will help make this right."

"Confound it, what awful luck!"

Adrianna lurched around to see Rosa, Lucas and Dog racing toward them. Lucas was out of the carriage in a single bound to lend assistance to Quin. Rosa hopped to the ground while Dog remained on the seat, still wearing his sparkly bow tie, staring at the dwindling flames.

"I'm so sorry," Rosa commiserated as she hugged

Adrianna close. "You can stay in my apartment. It will be a mite cramped with you, Bea, Butler and Elda, but we can set you up at Morning Glory Boardinghouse or at Château Royale Hotel tomorrow night. And don't fret if your clothing is damaged. You can have anything of mine and whatever will fit that's hanging on the store racks. Same goes for your employees."

Adrianna's breath hitched. "Thanks, Rosa."

She cursed herself when tears filled her eyes. Most everything could be replaced, she reminded herself. Her adopted family was safe. Her dream might have gone up in smoke but she could rebuild....

Her thoughts scattered when rain poured down in torrents, soaking everyone in a matter of minutes. Adrianna stared heavenward and sent up a silent prayer for the divine assistance that doused the remaining flames.

When Quin and Lucas signaled that it was safe to enter the house, Adrianna hurried inside to light a lantern. The smell of smoke penetrated the area, but the furniture and drapes appeared to be intact.

Butler scuttled in behind her, then veered toward the safe in the office. "Addie K., fetch one of your hat-boxes," he commanded hurriedly.

Frowning at the odd request, she bounded upstairs to grab a few essential garments and the hatbox. When she returned, Butler waited with a stack of papers and banknotes.

"It isn't a safe, of course, but no one will know the money and financial ledgers are tucked in this box."

Adrianna managed a smile. "Brilliant, Butler. If vandals show up, they won't find anything important, thanks to you."

Butler crammed the important documents and money in the box "Take this and your belongings outside, then send in Bea to fetch her things," he suggested. "Thankfully, Elda's belongings are safe at 4C."

Adrianna scampered outside to see Quin and Lucas frowning at the hatbox. "I haven't had a chance to wear my new hat yet," she said to the men and the cowboys who stared at her as if she was crazy for saving frivolous headgear.

While Elda helped Bea grab a few items, Adrianna set her carpetbag and hatbox under the seat of the buggy. She raked the mop of wet hair from her face, then turned to see Quin towering over her.

"You're staying with me," he said in no uncertain terms.

She smirked in contradiction. "No, I'm not. There are so many rumors and speculations swirling around us right now that the gossip mill will be grinding for a week. Rosa offered the use of her apartment above the shop for the night. We can stay at Merritt Dixon's nice boardinghouse on the south side of the square or Jenkinses' Château Royale near the train depot."

"No, I want you close by so I can make certain you're all right," he insisted sternly.

She tilted her grimy face to survey his rock-hard expression. "What does that mean?"

"It means that I'm not completely convinced that lightning started this fire, Boston. But I sure as hell was not going to voice that speculation in front of your cowboys and mine because that would incite more gossip."

Her mouth dropped open. When she recovered from

shock she clamped her jaw shut. "You think this was deliberate?"

"Four of your men and five of my men were here during the party. All of them were attempting to douse the fire when I arrived. But one of them might have set it, then appeared innocent of wrongdoing by sloshing water on the flames."

"Or someone could have lit the fire and left the scene without being noticed," Adrianna speculated. "Indeed, someone might have hightailed it to town to attend the party. It is impossible to know who is guilty when so many people are milling about."

Quin muttered under his breath. "We can't tell for certain what happened, or where the fire originated, until daylight. Maybe not even then. The rain ruined the chance of finding tracks and following them."

Adrianna nodded glumly. "Why would someone target me? Have I made that many enemies around Ca-Cross already?"

"There are several possibilities," he speculated. "Your former disgruntled foreman might have acted on his resentment."

"Oh, damn, I didn't consider that. George Spradlin didn't like being demoted so he collected his wages and stormed off. I haven't seen him since."

"Then again, someone might be trying to throw suspicion on me," Quin suggested. "Torching your home might be a tactic to keep our personal feud alive. The fire might make you want to retract that kiss you planted on me in front of our men. Contrasting speculations will be flying now."

"So someone wants *me* to blame *you*," she mused aloud. "If I don't fall for your charm, who gains from it?"

"Someone who wants to court you and sees me as an unwanted rival," Quin speculated, then studied her quizzically. "How many marriage proposals did you receive tonight?"

"Several. But compared to the number at a Boston soiree it was an off night. Surely no one would be spiteful enough to break up our potential courtship… or would they?" She expelled a frustrated breath, then raked her mop of hair from her face. "I'm not sure what is going on or why but it is evident someone wants to undermine you, me or both of us."

"You're coming home with me and that's that." Quin scooped her up and plunked her down on the carriage seat before she could object again. "Take your family of employees to my place. I'll be home soon."

While the threesome carted belongings to the carriage, Quin walked up to speak to Lucas, who glanced up sharply, stared in Adrianna's direction, then nodded his raven head.

"Blast it," Adrianna grumbled. "Lucas and Rosa don't need to be involved in this. They are newlyweds." But clearly, Quin considered the former Texas Ranger a confidant and he'd shared his suspicions about the fire being deliberately set.

"So much for needing a bath this evening." Butler plucked at his soggy clothes after he had assisted Bea and Elda into the buggy. "Things could have been much worse, I suppose."

They are worse than we thought, Adrianna mused as she turned the carriage toward the 4C. Someone was intent on fueling speculations and gossip about her and Cahill. Someone also wanted to keep Adrianna and Quin's suspicions about each other alive.

Why? Adrianna wasn't sure but she intended to find out.

"You think someone orchestrated that fire to make you look bad?" Lucas focused his dark-eyed gaze on the plumes of smoke drifting in the wind. "Any idea what someone might gain from this?"

Quin scowled, then glanced sideways to watch Boston and her entourage head toward his house. "Don't know, Burnett. Maybe it's a warning for Boston to distance herself from me because I have this so-called curse hanging over my head and now it's rubbing off on her."

Lucas snorted. "Every rancher in the area has been plagued with rustled cattle, stolen horses and fires of some sort. I lost a couple of horses that I had planned to sell at Fort Ridge last week. They were in the pasture one night and gone the next morning."

"Maybe you're right. Maybe I'm overly suspicious," Quin replied. "But it's been a bad week, not just a bad night."

Lucas waited a beat, then said, "I'm sorry about your little sister. Even if the rumors aren't true, it adds fuel to the turmoil surrounding your family name."

Quin scowled. He didn't want to discuss his sister and brothers while frustration boiled inside him. "Thanks for the help, Burnett. Sorry to cut your special evening short."

Lucas peered directly at Quin. "You would have been there if I had needed you, right, Cahill?"

"Of course."

"Then there you go. I have three friends around here. You, Rosa and Dog. Everyone else is a nodding acquaintance. Well, except for Addie K. and her employees," he added with a grin. "Rosa says they are my family now, like it or not."

Quin managed a faint smile as he strode alongside Lucas. "I can count my true friends on one hand. Everyone else thinks I'm jinxed because my name is Cahill."

Lucas chuckled. "Maybe you should change your name, then."

Quin contemplated it all the way home. The knot of tension that tightened his chest eased slightly when he arrived at his house. Lights were blazing in the windows of all three stories. It reminded him of the days when his parents were alive and his brothers and sister were around. He welcomed the company and the distractions tonight, especially after the shocking news about Leanna and the suspicious fire that had destroyed Boston's new addition.

Soaked to the bone, Quin ascended the steps to his room. He stopped short when he realized Boston had made use of the space to change into her customary tan breeches and blue blouse. Even with wet hair dangling around her face she still appealed fiercely to him.

"Sorry," she said as she gathered up her soggy emerald-green gown she had draped over a chair. "I'll get out of your way so you can change clothes."

"No, you can have my room. I'll stay in Ma and Pa's suite." Odd, he'd never given a thought to taking over the spacious two-room living quarters. He had left everything the way it had been two years earlier. But as his brothers and sister had said, Ma and Pa weren't coming back. No matter how hard Quin tried to cling to the past, nothing was going to be the same again.

She eyed him intently. "Are you sure that's what you want to do, Quin? Elda told me that you prefer to leave everything in its place. I can camp out on the third floor, you know."

Quin smiled in wry amusement. "So that's why Elda agreed to come to work for me. She was your spy. Clever, Boston, did you put her up to it?"

She grinned impishly. "No, I didn't have to. Elda thought of it all by herself. Oh, and I recently discovered that Hiram Butler and Beatrice Fremont have been carrying on an affair without my knowledge for a decade. So if you hear someone tiptoeing down the hall after lights out, do not investigate. It might prove embarrassing."

Quin chuckled. "I'll ignore footsteps. Wouldn't want to stand in the way of true love, if that's what it is."

When he spun on his heel, Boston fell into step behind him. "I want you to know that I never, not even for a moment, thought you were involved in tonight's fire."

"Thanks, Boston. I doubt you're in the majority. Too many folks envy the fact that I make money as a member of the town's founding family because I sell commercial and residential lots, carry the loans and collect rent on business buildings. Not to mention that I run an expansive ranch operation. Yet, it's easier to criticize than praise the acquisition of wealth, good fortune and hard work. Not that I've enjoyed much good luck in the past two years."

She followed him to the master suite and halted at the threshold while he lit a lantern in the sitting room. "Do you want to talk about it?" she asked softly.

The prompt set him off. "No, I don't want to talk about my sister, who might have reduced herself to prostitution to eke out a living for herself and her illegitimate child!" he erupted like a volcano.

Adrianna closed the door and watched him pace from wall to wall in the sitting room. Rain pounded against the windows and thunder rumbled outside—and deep inside Quin, as well.

"And I don't want to discuss Chance, who is closer to Annie's age and enjoyed a bond with her that Bowie and I didn't because we were a few years older. *We* were her *protectors* and I failed my baby sister miserably!" he spewed in frustration.

"Damn it, if she's dealing cards in some low-life saloon it's because we taught her to play cards as a kid. What a mistake that turned out to be!" He lurched around, his stomach churning with guilt and regret. "Plus, right before she rode away, I jokingly suggested she become a saloon girl since she had no marketable job skills."

"Maybe Chance is keeping a watchful eye on her," Boston supplied helpfully as she followed him into the bedroom while he lit the second lantern.

"And maybe he isn't." Muttering, he wheeled away from the massive walnut bed to pace toward the marble-top dresser on the far wall. "All Chance ever cared about was being lightning-quick on the draw and deadly accurate with a pistol. Hell, he had better not be someone's hired gun with notches on the handle of his pistol. Ma and Pa would be rolling in their graves, for sure."

"It's easy to think the worst—" she tried to interject, but Quin wasn't through venting his frustration.

"And Bowie, damn him!" Quin reversed direction to wear another path on the carpet. "He should be checking on the younger ones since none of them want anything to do with me. How could he have allowed this to happen?"

"There is a strong possibility Preston was tormenting you for the sport of it." She sank into a chair near the dresser. "You claimed he once pursued Leanna and you ran him off when she tired of him. I can name countless suitors who circulated hurtful stories about me to hide their embarrassment of rejection. The same goes for envious locals starting rumors to make sure everyone believes your success comes at the price of that ridiculous curse—"

"Because I'm supposedly in league with the devil," Quin cut in sourly, and raked his hands through his disheveled hair. "Let's not forget that, Boston."

"The same rumors spread about the McKnights," she informed him, sounding oddly distracted. "Supposedly, prosperous families sell their souls to Satan for power and wealth. The population of Ca-Cross will be ecstatic, I presume, when we are both frying in hell...."

Quin arched a quizzical brow when her voice evaporated. "Boston? Are you all right? Why are you looking at me like that?"

To his stunned amazement, she walked over to unfasten his wet cravat, then tossed it aside. She pulled off his coat and sent it flying in the same direction as the cravat.

He stared bemusedly at her, his eyes glistening like mercury in the lamplight. "What are you doing, Boston?"

"Helping you out of your damp clothing."

"You sure that's a good idea? Remember what happened last time you and I started undressing each other in that grove of trees in the pasture?"

She smiled wryly. "You offered room and board for the night, didn't you?"

"Yes, but I don't expect intimate favors in return. I'm indirectly to blame for that fire, I expect," he reminded her.

She unbuttoned his shirt, anxious to get her hands on his muscular chest…and other parts yet exposed to her curious eyes. Adrianna wasn't sure what had come over her while she watched Quin pace in frustration. She had become utterly fascinated by the way he moved with such masculine grace. The fierce, impulsive need for him overwhelmed her. She remembered all too well how it felt to touch him, to be touched by him. And suddenly, like a bolt from the blue, she *wanted* him—badly.

It was as simple and as complicated as that.

"I have another theory," she murmured as she skimmed her lips over his hair-roughened chest and encircled his male nipples with her forefinger—loving the feel of his muscled flesh flex and relax beneath her hand.

"What theory is that?" His voice crackled and a muffled groan clogged his throat.

"The fire was a warning for *me,* sent from one of

your secret admirers. One of your jealous lovers might have tried to burn down my house for spite."

"I don't have any lovers, jealous or otherwise," he said as he stepped back a pace. "Look, Boston, I know your emotions are in as much turmoil tonight as mine, but this isn't a good idea. Not that I'm not interested, because you know I am. But we've both had a rough evening. If we become each other's consolation tonight, you'll regret it in the morning."

Adrianna thought it over carefully and realized she was not looking for compassion, distraction or consolation. Her desire for Quin—who could be maddening one minute and irresistibly charming the next—had plagued her since she'd met him.

"Of all the men I could have had, Cahill, you're the one I want," she admitted honestly. "You have assured me that you don't need my money and I have no need of your wealth. There are no strings attached, right?"

He cupped her face in both hands and lowered his dark head. "No strings, maybe, but there might be consequences," he warned. "Just ask Leanna, who maybe went to a man for comfort and consolation and bore him a child he won't claim."

She looped her arms around his neck and leaned closer, aware that he was aroused. That did wonders for her self-confidence. For once, she was desired for herself, not for her name, her social status and her fortune. "Are you going to kiss me, or keep trying to talk me out of this? I'm all talked out after hosting the party. I'd much rather kiss you, Cahill."

And so she did. She wanted Quin to forget about the frustrations they'd both experienced tonight. She wanted to feel his masculine body pressed familiarly to hers and to appease the erotic dreams that continually hounded her sleep.

"Are you absolutely sure about this, Boston?" He devoured her lips, scooped her into his arms, then grinned. "This is your last chance at sanity. Don't come whining to me later."

She returned his teasing smile and traced his sensuous lips with her index finger. "I almost never whine, Cahill."

He tumbled with her onto the bed, then braced himself on his arms to loom over her. He chuckled wickedly and said, "Perhaps not, but I wouldn't mind hearing you *beg*."

"I don't do that, either," she insisted loftily.

One thick, black brow elevated and he flashed a devilish grin. He was so playful and endearing that she nearly melted on the spot.

"No? We'll see about that," he purred.

Then he kissed her so tenderly, so seductively, that she considered *begging* for a dozen more tantalizing kisses. But she couldn't speak or think or breathe when his warm lips skimmed her throat. She gasped in anticipation when he unbuttoned her blouse, then cupped her breast.

Desperate need coiled inside her when he flicked her nipples with his tongue. She arched instinctively toward him to align her aching body with his, but he bent his leg over her knees to hold her in place.

"Patience," he murmured, then suckled her breasts. "This might take all night. In fact, I'm counting on it, Adrianna...."

She loved the way her name rolled off his tongue with that husky Texas drawl.

"Then I need someone who moves a lot faster than you because I won't last the night. You're burning me up already," she rasped.

When Quin raised his head, something fierce and unfamiliar blazed through her chest and lodged in the vicinity of her heart. *Oh, for heaven's sake,* she thought. *I'd better not be falling in love with him.* Adrianna had come to Texas for limitless freedom and independence. She had wanted to take complete charge of her life and prove she was as business-minded as her father. She wanted to avoid restricting ties. And look where that had got her!

"I'm not giving you up to anyone else who moves fast, slow or anywhere in between," Quin said hoarsely, jolting her back to her previous remark. "I want you all to myself, Adrianna. I won't be satisfied with anyone but you tonight...."

Chapter Eight

Quin meant exactly what he said. He wanted to be flesh to flesh and heart to heart with Adrianna so badly that he ached from his eyebrows to the soles of his feet. Nothing was going to make that ache go away except being as close as he could get to this green-eyed beauty.

Quin peeled off her blouse, kissing every inch of satiny flesh he exposed. Each time she whimpered his name—first Cahill, then Quin—he smiled in satisfaction. He watched her blush in the lantern light as he cast aside her blouse, then her breeches. He couldn't recall a time in his life when he'd found himself in bed with a woman that he wanted to spend so much time admiring. Her luscious curves and swells intrigued him to the extreme. She was erotic perfection and he wanted to know her soft body better than she knew it herself, wanted to discover what made her moan in pleasure and what made her writhe with urgent need.

"Give me your clothes, *now*," she demanded as she grabbed hold of his open shirt.

"They're too big for you," he teased, then splayed his hand over her belly and slid his fingertips lower, making her groan in torment.

"I want you out of them, *damn it*," she rasped shakily.

"Tsk, tsk," he chastised in a playful tone. "That's no language for a blue-blooded lady to use."

Then he lowered his hand to trace the hot folds between her legs and she nearly came off the bed.

"Quin…" she panted breathlessly. *"Please…"*

"Now, was begging so hard?" he murmured, then dipped his head to trace her moist flesh with his tongue.

He heard Adrianna struggle to draw breath as he eased her legs farther apart to glide his fingertip inside her. He felt her burning around him and he kissed her intimately again. She dug her nails into his shoulders— and ripped the seam of his shirt in her impatience to undress him.

Quin made a feast of her supple body, amazed at how much pleasure he derived in pleasing her. But he became sidetracked when she stroked him through his breeches, then unfastened the placket to curl her hand around his throbbing length.

He wasn't even sure how and when she eased him to his back to remove his trousers but he looked up to see her cedar-tree-green eyes twinkling with triumph at having him stark naked. She nearly finished him with erotic pleasure when she lowered her head and let her long hair caress his heaving chest while she took him into her mouth and suckled him.

Quin squeezed his eyes shut and concentrated on *not* passing out from the indescribable sensations assailing him. His entire body pulsated as she glided her thumb and forefinger up and down his shaft, then followed the titillating motion of her fingertips with her moist lips.

"Mercy!" he croaked, surprised at the odd sound of his own voice.

"My name is Adrianna, not Mercy," she whispered against his throbbing erection.

"Adrianna…" he repeated on a wobbly breath. "Come here."

She didn't stop caressing him and he swore he would explode. He clamped his hands on her hips and turned her sideways. Then he braced himself on his forearms above her. Breathing hard, he stared down into that enchanting face and sparkling eyes that had invaded his dreams more times than he could count.

Quin angled his head to kiss her at the same moment that he pressed intimately against her. She was so hot and tight that he had to battle to prevent plunging recklessly into her. He moved slowly, gently, though it nearly killed him. She tensed slightly when he came into her, then she relaxed as he penetrated deeper. He savored the feel of her moist flesh closing around him until they were one pulsating essence.

When Quin lifted his head to make sure she was all right, she stared intently at him. Then she arched upward, moved restlessly against him, and he nearly lost his tentative grasp on his self-control.

"Adrianna…"

He didn't know what he'd intended to say, but having her name roll off his tongue as he buried himself to the hilt said enough. He felt the fragile barrier give way, assuring him that he was her first experiment with passion. He liked knowing that, though he suspected this feisty, independent beauty would scoff at that possessive sentiment. She resented men's restrictive expectations for women, he knew. She refused to be restrained in any manner and he wasn't foolish enough to blunder into saying something like, *Now you're mine.*

But he *thought* it as he moved rhythmically against her, feeling the scintillating sensations building one atop the other until the heated pleasure became so intense he swore he had burst into flame.

Her body quivered beneath his, around his. He heard her draw in a frantic breath as she clasped him tightly in her arms. Spasms of her climax echoed from her body into his, unleashing the passion he'd tried to hold in check.

Quin groaned as he shuddered helplessly against her. He buried his head in the silken strands of her chestnut hair that splayed across the bedspread, then he collapsed above her, holding her as tightly as she held on to him.

The frustration and tension that had clamored through him over the past few hours melted away with the rain pattering against the window. The storm had broken—the one outside and the one inside—he realized with a contented sigh. He was at peace for the first time in two years, though the world around him was still in exasperating turmoil. But here in Adrianna's encircling arms, they were one body, one soul. Nothing could conquer him…except his obsessive fascination for her.

Honestly, Quin couldn't understand why he'd settled for occasional, meaningless trysts with other women, because being with this spirited, alluring female was so much more satisfying in every way imaginable. Sure as hell, she was going to ruin him, for he couldn't be satisfied merely scratching the proverbial itch again.

When she shifted beneath him, Quin eased away to give her space. When she tried to inch off the bed, he draped his arm over her hip.

"Stay with me, Adrianna…*please*… ."

He could feel her smile against his lips when she kissed him and said, "Now was that so hard, Cahill?"

Then she settled down to sleep beside him all through the night and Quin couldn't recall being so utterly content. The room he'd left untouched for two years became *his* room, and having Boston here with him felt right.

He wondered what she'd say if he told her that? Quin grinned drowsily. She'd probably call him a sentimental sap…and—God forbid!—he'd have to *agree* with her.

When Adrianna awoke the next morning, she was alone in bed, as she had been all twenty-five years of her life. She stretched leisurely, remembering the amazing sensations she had experienced with Quin. A blush crept up her neck to stain her cheeks when she recalled how wild and reckless she'd been with Quin. Something had changed last night, she mused. *She* had changed. Drastically.

Furthermore, she didn't care what rumors were chasing each other around Ca-Cross now that she had taken up residence at 4C until her home aired out. She was close enough to her ranch to oversee the rebuilding of the new addition and the breeding operation of her prize cattle. If she moved to town, she'd waste time traveling back and forth.

Besides that, she'd miss sleeping with Quin.

Rolling from bed, Adrianna freshened up, then dressed in her breeches. She was grateful the hall was empty when she strode toward the stairs. Although her entourage had taken up the rooms once used by Quin's two brothers and sister, Adrianna didn't hear any movement behind the closed doors. However, she did hear furniture scraping against the wood floor as she descended the staircase.

Puzzled, she poked her head around the corner of the parlor to see Quin scooting his father's leather chair to a new position, allowing space for the sofa and chair he had transported from *her* house. The styles of furniture clashed but that didn't seem to bother Quin.

"What are you doing?" she asked as she entered the room.

His silvery gaze ran the length of her body, reminding her that they had been as close as two people could get the previous night. She would have described his look as possessive, but she knew Quin didn't think in terms of possession just because he'd slept with a woman.

No strings, she reminded herself. Last night was about desire and erotic pleasure. She was not the kind of woman who needed commitment from a man. She was a free-spirited adventuress, after all, and Quin Cahill was devoted to the success and expansion of the family ranch. *Married* to it, you might say.

"This furniture wasn't too smoke damaged so I'm including it in the room…to make you feel at home," he added belatedly.

She observed him for a long, contemplative moment. This man, who strenuously objected to change, was making marked changes in here? Just as he had taken up residence in the master suite last night? Good heavens, who knew what this hidebound traditionalist might decide to do next!

"Yoo-hoo! Breakfast is ready," Elda called from the kitchen door.

Adrianna scurried to the dining room. "I've missed Elda's delicious meals," she told Quin, then added confidentially, "Her attempt to spy on you wasn't very informative, anyway. I'm ready to have her back."

He grinned and another chunk of her heart crumbled down her rib cage. Honest to goodness, Quin Cahill could become a ladies' man if he really tried, she decided. His boyish smile could warm the coldest of hearts—and Adrianna had packed hers in ice the past few years so she wouldn't become susceptible to the ploys of gold diggers and greedy adventurers. But now she was in danger of losing her heart to Quin.

Be sensible, Boston, she lectured herself sternly, unaware she had referred to herself by the same name Quin used. She wasn't playing for keeps, she mused as she took her seat at the table. She'd had her fun with Quin and he'd had his with her. This was her temporary residence. She would enjoy him, then walk away. It's what Quin expected—and she had better not let herself forget that.

Later that afternoon, Adrianna and Quin investigated the site of the fire. Unfortunately, they couldn't tell if it had been set deliberately or if it was the result of a lightning strike. True, the peak of the new addition was the highest point on the hill and had yet to be equipped with a lightning rod. The storm could have ignited the fire, she supposed. However, instinct warned her that something else was going on that had nothing to do with Mother Nature hurling random lightning bolts at the earth.

"Should we contact Marshal Hobbs?" she wondered aloud.

"No, not yet," Quin murmured pensively.

"Then the next order of business is to question my ranch hands," she declared as she spun around to head to the barn.

"I questioned my men already," Quin reported. "They said they saw the fire from the bunkhouse and came to lend a hand."

Adrianna received the same information from her cowboys when she interrogated them. Everyone on hand had grabbed buckets to douse the fire, they claimed. No one had spotted her former foreman or other suspicious characters skulking around the house.

"That doesn't mean someone wasn't sneaking around here." Quin fell into step beside her while she checked her Herefords and the black shorthorn bulls that had arrived recently.

"The timing was too convenient. With the party in town, and only a few cowboys on hand, it would have been easy to start the fire and duck out of sight during the gathering storm and darkness." Adrianna frowned speculatively as she veered toward Buckshot's stall in the barn. "I want to check my longhorns and my other herd of Herefords. Maybe the fire was a diversion for more rustling."

"I need to check my livestock, too." Quin grabbed

her saddle and tossed it on the dapple-gray gelding's back for her. "Take Rocky with you, in case you have trouble. I'll meet you at 4C after I check my pastures."

He dropped a hasty kiss to her lips, turned away and then wheeled around to kiss her again. Then he walked off.

Adrianna brushed her fingertips over her mouth, surprised by Quin's impulsive display of affection. *Affection? Is that what it is? Or is this how a man behaves after bedding a woman?* Adrianna didn't have a clue, since this was her first clandestine affair.

"Blast it, there should be an instruction manual for handling affairs properly," she grumbled to Buckshot as she stuffed her booted foot in the stirrup.

She could name on two hands various women in Boston who flitted from one tryst to another, while juggling their loveless marriages. It was all so pretentious. Adrianna was glad her Western-style affair with Quin was uncomplicated. Especially considering the complications life kept tossing in her path while she faced the challenges of establishing herself as a credible and successful female rancher.

"Rocky?" she called to her new foreman. "Will you ride north with me to check the herds?"

The cowboy, who was about Quin's age, set aside the block of hay he was tossing to the penned Herefords. He ambled over to mount his horse. Then he raked his hand through his sandy-blond hair and set his straw hat in place.

"Are we looking for anything in particular, ma'am?"

"Counting heads to see if someone stole a few cattle while we were distracted by dousing the fire."

His pale blue eyes narrowed in self-deprecation. "I should've thought of that early this morning." He waited a beat, then glanced questioningly at her. "Is Cahill upset with me for taking this job? He was always fair with me. Don't want hard feelings if I can help it."

"No, he got Elda in the swap." Adrianna grinned broadly. "Cahill is in culinary paradise and I acquired the best foremen in the state."

The cowboy blushed, chuckled, then said. "And I have the prettiest boss in the whole country. You'll hear no complaints about the good deal I got."

Although Adrianna was sensitive to comments about being known for her looks and wealth rather than her intelligence, she decided not to call him out. She wasn't about to lose the best foreman a rancher could have. Quin would have to make do with second best because she needed Rocky's expertise to make a good start.

Quin swore two blue streaks when he counted the calves in the pasture near the place called Comanche Bluff, a former Comanche campground—the site Lucas Burnett had tried to buy because of its sentimental value to him. Although Quin had told Burnett he could visit the site any time he pleased, he knew his friend hadn't rustled his cattle. But *someone* had taken advantage during the town party and the fire.

When he returned to headquarters, it was time for supper and Boston's long-legged, dapple-gray gelding wasn't in the barn. His first impulse was to race off to locate her. The recent rustling, the butchered calf and the fires were making him edgy and suspicious. However, he hesitated in thundering off to check on

Boston and risk offending her independent streak. Of all the women he knew, she was the only one who didn't appreciate being fussed over.

Too bad he hadn't noticed how independent his kid sister had become while underfoot, he mused regretfully. Maybe she wouldn't have gotten into trouble by trying to prove she could survive in the world without him standing over her. Now she was in Deadwood—of all places!—raising a child alone, if that obnoxious Preston Van Slyck was to be believed.

Quin intended to drive his cattle to the railhead in Dodge—if rustlers didn't steal the rest of his herd—then ride north to check on Leanna. He was going to drag her home, kicking and screaming if he had to.

"Cahill, a word, please."

Quin glanced over to see Hiram Butler standing on the stoop. He jogged to the house to stare quizzically at Boston's man of affairs. "What's wrong now?"

"At the moment? Nothing that I know of," Butler replied. "I wondered if I might place my employers' money and important papers in your safe. I refused to leave it at the abandoned house for someone to swipe while we were away."

"Certainly. Glad to help."

Quin strode swiftly to the office to open the cabinet that held the safe. He frowned, bemused, when Butler entered the office carrying Adrianna's hatbox.

"Boston has a money *hat?* I thought most heiresses had money *trees.*"

Hazel eyes drilled into him, clearly unamused by the teasing comment. "Why do you insist on calling Adrianna 'Boston'?" Butler demanded grouchily.

"Because it amuses me."

"You have a peculiar sense of humor, Cahill."

"Why do you go by Butler, *Hiram?* You know everyone assumes you *are* the butler."

The older man retrieved several stacks of banknotes from the box, along with cashbooks and ledgers he handled as if they were solid gold. "You can tell a great deal about a man's depth of character when he thinks you're a servant," Butler replied. "I used the tactic constantly while interviewing agents who wanted the McKnights to invest with them."

"Subtle," Quin remarked. "I like it."

After Quin locked away the banknotes, ledgers and official-looking papers, he heard the front door open and shut. For the first time in two years, he wasn't the only one going in and out of it, he realized. *Temporarily,* he qualified. When Boston's home aired out she and her entourage—Elda included—would ride off. Quin would rattle around in silence again. It was a dispiriting thought.

"Cahill!" Boston called from the foyer.

"In the office," he called back. When she breezed through the door he raised a curious brow. "Did you have cattle stolen, just as I did?"

She nodded her disheveled head. "A dozen longhorns. We found them in a box canyon, waiting to be driven away. Did you find yours?"

Quin shook his head. "I'll make a thorough search tomorrow. Hopefully, I can recover them."

He noticed the folded paper in her hand. "What's this, an invitation to another party? Ca-Cross must be the new social hub of the state. Imagine that."

Butler rolled his eyes and said, "Ah, another attempt at humor. It, too, failed, I see."

"A young Mexican boy, riding a mule, came to the house the same time I did," Boston explained as she extended her hand. "He asked me to deliver this note to you."

He absently took the note while Butler informed Boston that her ready cash and documents were secure in the safe. Quin unfolded the paper, then cursed in disbelief when he read the hastily scrawled, unsigned message.

"Now what's happened?" Boston asked worriedly.

Quin sat down at his desk before he fell down in stunned amazement. He felt as if someone had kicked him in the chest, for he could barely catch his breath and his mind was spinning like a pinwheel. Dazed, he handed the message to Boston.

"It can't be!" she howled.

"What in the blazes…?" Butler hooted as he looked over her shoulder to read the missive.

The room spun and Quin struggled to wrap his thoughts around the shocking claim mentioned in the note.

Your parents' wagon wreck was no accident. Come alone to Phantom Springs at eight o'clock tonight. Bring two thousand dollars and you will have the information you need.

"No accident?" Quin wheezed unsteadily. "What does that mean? Murder? Manslaughter? How? Why?"

Boston and Butler shrugged helplessly while Quin reread the note—three times.

"Why send this note two years later?" Boston questioned warily.

"This might be a cunning scheme to prey on your emotions and extort money," the accountant speculated.

Boston eased a hip onto the edge of the desk, then leaned toward him, forcing him to raise his downcast head and acknowledge her. "I don't think you should go, Cahill," she advised. "This note has *disaster* written all over it."

"I agree with her," Butler chimed in. "Given the rustling, butchering and fires in this area, this note is too suspicious. Just another way to separate you from your money."

Anger and frustration roiled inside Quin. "What if it was a robbery turned disaster, not a hapless accident? My parents might still be alive and nothing would have changed on the 4C," he said, more to himself than anyone else. "There wouldn't be a rift between my brothers and sister and me. Although Bowie had already left home to tame the rough towns in Deer County, Chance and Leanna might have delayed their departure, instead of flying off on the wings of an argument."

Boston laid her hand on his rigid shoulder. "Quin, are you all right?"

"Hell, no!" he burst out. He stared into space, reliving the anguish of losing both parents suddenly and the torment of the angry argument with his surviving family. Not to mention the grief and guilt that constantly plagued him because he had waylaid on the cattle drive to indulge in selfish pleasure.

A robbery attempt on his parents might not have been so easy if *he* had been on hand that fateful evening. Or the outcome might have turned out differently if *Bowie* or *Chance* had accompanied their parents to Wolf Grove that day. Another set of eyes and ears and an expert shooter might have made a difference between life and death.

"If it was a robbery attempt gone wrong, then I want to know the details," he muttered harshly. "I want to know who was responsible for killing my parents."

Boston clasped her hands around Quin's and got right in his face. "You go traipsing off to Phantom Springs, carrying that much money to meet who knows how many thieves that might set upon you, you'll end up dead."

"She's right, you know," Butler chimed in, his expression grim. "This might be a clever trap designed specifically to plot *your* murder. You have no way of knowing if there is one or five scoundrels waiting to attack."

Quin pulled his hands from Boston's grasp, then scraped his fingers through his tousled hair. He tried to think logically. Boston and Butler were right, of course. There were all sorts of potential pitfalls awaiting him. But if his parents had been a target of robbery, because they were driving a wagon heaped with supplies, then Quin had to know. He wanted justice and he wanted revenge for the way his family had been torn apart and for depriving his parents of years of life!

When Quin bolted to his feet, Boston blew out an agitated breath. "Do not do this, Cahill."

He stared at her somberly for a long moment. "If the situation were reversed and you learned one or both of your parents had been victims of a fatal crime, would you want to know?"

"Of course." She met his gaze head-on. "But racing off in the dark, with a fistful of money, doesn't guarantee you'll receive any valuable information." She flung out her hand in frustration. "What if I received a note offering information about who stole my Herefords and planted them in your pasture? What if the sender named *you* as the guilty party? That wouldn't make it necessarily so, would it? We are discussing *outlaws,* Cahill. They have no credibility."

"Unless this unidentified informant saw or overheard what happened to my parents and wants traveling money so he can hightail it out of the county before he's hunted down and silenced," Quin speculated.

"He makes a valid point," Butler said to Boston.

"Valid or not, I still don't like it," she grumbled.

"Neither do I," Butler admitted. "It's too dangerous."

Boston crossed her arms over her chest and stared unblinkingly at Quin. "Then it's settled. You are not going."

"You and Butler don't get a vote," he said dictatorially.

He lurched toward the cabinet, then hunkered down to retrieve the money from the safe.

"Be careful that you don't take Adrianna's money for this foolhardy crusade of yours," Butler said, and scowled.

Quin glanced over his shoulder and smiled faintly. "I have plenty on hand since I withdrew money from the bank last week to make payroll. Not to worry, Hiram."

"Dinner is served," Beatrice announced from the hall. "It's one of Elda's mouthwatering specialties."

"Tell Elda we'll be there directly." Boston turned back to Quin. "If you insist on this dangerous folly, then I'm going with you."

Quin stared her down. "No, you aren't," he said slowly and succinctly. "I expressly forbid it. This is not your concern, Boston."

She tilted her chin to a defiant angle. "Yes, it is. You are our gracious host. If you get yourself robbed and killed, then where are we supposed to go? My house hasn't aired out completely. And I'm not going to ride back and forth from town to see how many cattle were rustled during the night. You do not invite guests to your home, then get yourself ambushed. If you had proper Eastern manners you would know that."

He almost smiled at her sassy retort, but the possibility of his parents being senselessly killed for money and a wagonload of supplies weighed heavily on his disposition.

"Think it over during supper," she insisted as she whirled toward the hall. "Maybe delicious food and time will bring you back to your senses."

When Butler turned to leave, Quin said, "Hiram, I know you don't like me much but I need a favor."

Butler pivoted around to give Quin the evil eye. "I wouldn't like any man who slept with Adrianna, especially one who wasn't married to her."

Quin shifted uncomfortably beneath Butler's narrow-eyed glare. Then a thought occurred to him and he smiled wryly. "But you're going to keep silent and grant my favor because you are sleeping with Bea. You don't want me to throw it in your face, do you?"

Butler scowled. "What's the favor, Cahill?"

"Make sure Boston doesn't follow me tonight."

Butler nodded, then headed for the door. "I had planned to do that without a prompt from you, Cahill. Consider it done."

When Butler exited, Quin tucked the stack of money in the bottom desk drawer for safekeeping. He was going to meet the mysterious informant tonight, come hell or high water—or both.

There was nothing Boston could do to stop him, short of shooting him down, before someone else beat her to it.

Chapter Nine

Adrianna had a bad feeling about Cahill's evening excursion. Blast it, too many things could go wrong. There were enough problems with the rustling and arson that plagued both ranches. True, other ranchers had been targeted—Womack, Fitzgerald and Burnett, to name only a few. But it seemed to Adrianna that the most frequent criminal activity centered on Cahill and her and was written off to the supposed feud between them.

She had no idea what that implied—maybe nothing. Yet, she wondered if someone was using the feud to explain the rustling and fires, and letting the "curse" take the blame. If someone might have upped the ante to extort more money by preying on Quin's emotions concerning his parents' deaths.

What better way to get a man to do your bidding than to suggest the family wagon wreck was no accident? Adrianna didn't trust this mysterious informant. Unfortunately, Quin was personally involved and burdened with grief and guilt. He was risking peril by venturing out alone at night, carrying money. His family had imploded after the untimely deaths. He *wanted* to believe someone else was to blame for the tragedy.

But why now? Why two years after the wagon wreck? she asked herself repeatedly. It was too suspicious not to raise concern and doubt.

Bearing that in mind, Adrianna pocketed her pistol in her jacket, then exited Quin's former bedroom. She nearly jumped out of her own skin when a shadowy silhouette pounced on her.

"I knew it," Quin muttered sourly. "I told you that you aren't invited to this meeting tonight and I damn well mean it, Boston!"

"You are not my boss, my father or my husband," she sniped as she jerked her arm from his grasp.

"Butler!" Quin called out loudly.

"Tattletale," Adrianna snapped at Quin.

Hiram Butler—the traitor—stepped around the corner. Adrianna glowered mutinously at him, then glared pitchforks at Quin. "What did you do? *Pay* him to side with you?"

"No, that's your tactic." Quin smirked. "I lost my foreman to that trick, as you well know."

Adrianna stared down Butler when he walked up beside her. "I thought you were my loyal friend and part of my family," she said, trying to shame him.

"I am," Butler affirmed. "Which is why I have no choice but to stand guard over you while Cahill rides off on his foolhardy errand." He glanced meaningfully at Quin, then Adrianna. "No sense both of you walking into a death trap."

Quin clasped her shoulders, turned her around, then

gave her a nudge over the threshold of his former bedroom. No doubt, he didn't want Butler to know she and Quin had become intimate in the master suite. She should tell her overprotective accountant about last evening's escapade so he would be tempted to shoot Quin, she thought spitefully. And she would be happy to load Butler's gun for him.

"And stay there," Quin barked sharply. "Butler will be sitting outside the door until I get back."

She glowered at Quin. "What if you don't come back? Am I supposed to stay here forever?"

"If the news of my demise arrives in a day or two, then take over the house and run the ranch as you see fit," he offered generously.

"And deal with your wayward family?" She scoffed in annoyance. "They might swoop in like vultures after you're gone. No, thank you. I have my own problems so I have no need of yours, Cahill."

She *did* have a serious problem. She was very much afraid that she was in love with Cahill. She must be, because the thought of him walking into a trap and never coming home terrified her. She had never felt so protective of a man, never felt so content with a man. Cahill challenged her, amused and aroused her. She didn't want to lose him.

When Quin shut the door—slammed it was more accurate—Adrianna flounced on the bed. "Butler, you are not going to hear the end of this!" she shouted at her turncoat of an accountant.

"I didn't expect to, my dear," Butler said from the other side of the door. "But it's for your own well-being."

Adrianna blew out an exasperated breath when she

heard Quin's footsteps recede in the hall. Taking advantage of the noise Butler made by scooting a chair in front of the door to block her exit, she opened the window. She glanced speculatively at the private balcony outside the master suite, then she surveyed the sloped roof outside Quin's former room.

Back in the day at her country estate, she and Rosa had performed disappearing acts and acrobatic maneuvers so they could sneak from the house for midnight rides and walks along the river. The only difference between now and then was Adrianna was inspired by the noble purpose of saving Quin from disaster.

Quietly, she straddled the windowsill, then eased onto the steep roof. She made as little noise as possible, so as not to alert Bea and Elda, who might be part of the conspiracy with Butler. It wouldn't surprise her, considering their loyalty and affection. She loved her overprotective, adopted family despite their misguided intentions, she mused as she inched along the wooden shingles to reach the balcony. She slung a leg over the railing, then glanced around, trying to decide how best to descend to the ground without breaking her neck.

The only sensible escape route was to crawl along the overhanging tree branch that was a few feet beyond the railing. She pulled off her boots, then tucked them in the waistband of her breeches. Apprehension sizzled through her as she balanced on the railing and extended herself to grasp the branch. It was a long way to the ground, she noticed. One misstep and she would nosedive to the lawn. She would do Quin no good whatsoever if he became the victim of an ambush and she landed in a broken heap.

Adrianna inhaled a bolstering breath, then sprang forward to grab the limb. Reverting to her hoyden days, she crawled along the branch, then picked her way down to the tree bough. She cursed sourly when she saw Quin trotting the bloodred bay gelding from the barn. If she didn't quicken her pace, she would be too far behind to follow his trail to the place called Phantom Springs.

She hopped lightly to the ground, then darted from one tree to the next to prevent being seen. She cast an occasional glance toward the window of the room where Quin had imprisoned her, hoping her well-meaning guard had yet to realize she had snuck out. Adrianna couldn't spare the time to saddle Buckshot. She dashed toward the bunkhouse where two saddle horses—a strawberry roan and a brown gelding with three white stockings—were tied to the hitching post. She borrowed the closest one to her. She'd explain later, she decided as she mounted up and raced off in the darkness.

Quin trotted Cactus through the shadows, headed toward the wooded hillside where the cool springs bubbled from a jumble of rocks to flow across a rapid-filled stream. The creek meandered southeast, eventually providing the water supply for Cahill Crossing.

Anticipation crackled through him as he glanced this way and that, searching the swaying shadows in the trees. Boston's objections rang in his ears, but the prospect of discovering what happened the evening Ruby and Earl Cahill died overrode the possibility of personal danger. True, there was the dangerous curve that overlooked a rock-filled ravine on the road to Wolf Grove. But if his parents had been *chased* by thieves and were driving too fast in the overloaded wagon, Quin wanted to know. His father, who had been nursing an injured wrist, could have oversteered the wagon in his attempt to beat the outlaws back to town. The robbery could have caused the disaster.

Damnation, Quin and his family had been through hell after their parents' sudden deaths. He just had to find out what had happened at the site the locals had named Ghost Canyon after the accident. The *incident,* Quin hastily corrected. By the time he had returned from Kansas, Marshal Hobbs had investigated the site and removed the bodies. Quin had stood on the cliff at the bend of the road, listening to the Texas wind whisper through the canyon like voices calling from the Great Beyond.

The thought gave him cold chills, especially when he was headed for Phantom Springs where the murmur of water rushing over the rapids created a sound similar to the wind whipping through Ghost Canyon. Quin didn't want to end up dead during his crusade to discover the truth.

Just to be on the safe side, Quin retrieved one of his six-shooters, then dismounted. He had dealt with plenty of dangerous situations during trail drives and he was accustomed to proceeding with caution. Tonight was no different. There were plenty of trees and boulders in the area to conceal bushwhackers. He did not intend to ride up to the site, making a racket to invite an ambush.

Guided by dappled moonlight, Quin crept forward. A dozen questions chased one another around his mind as he sought out the mysterious informant. *Why now? How did you come by this information? Who was involved?*

How can I contact you later to serve as a witness at a trial?

The sound of twigs snapping in the darkness brought Quin to high alert. He aimed his pistol toward the sound, then tethered Cactus on the lower limb of a nearby tree. As a precaution, he left the money in the saddlebag, in case this was a hoax and he stumbled into a trap, as Boston predicted.

Cautiously, he crept toward the springs. He blinked in surprise when he saw a man lying facedown, his head dangling in the water. There was a bullet hole in his back.

"Damn it," Quin muttered as he squatted down to grab the man by the shoulder and ease him to his back. The would-be informant—or bushwhacker, Quin wasn't sure which—had sandy-blond hair, bowed legs and a skinny physique. The dead man was in no condition to convey information.

Quin studied the man's features closely, then recalled that he had brushed shoulders with this character at the wedding party. He hadn't recognized the man as a local and he hadn't given him another thought—until now.

Setting aside his pistol, Quin dug into the pockets of the dead man's wet jacket, breeches and shirt. He found a few coins but no identification.

"Damnation!" he growled irritably.

Quin was about to rise to his feet when he felt a presence behind him. He made a grab for the pistol but someone clobbered him over the head. He swayed on his knees when stars exploded in front of his eyes. He took a blind swing at whoever had snuck up behind him but he received another blow to the skull for his effort. A boot heel slammed between his shoulder blades, sending him sprawling beside the dead man.

His last thought, before he blacked out, was that if he wound up with a bullet in *his* back his last memory would be Boston's voice ringing in his ears, reminding him that she'd told him so....

Adrianna heard the gunshot in the distance and felt her heart shrivel in her chest. Blast it, she should have pushed the borrowed horse to a swifter pace so she could keep a closer eye on Quin. Now he was likely dead and she was no use to him whatsoever.

Damn him, why hadn't he listened to reason? If she had been nearby, things might have turned out differently.

She winced, remembering what Quin had said about feeling guilty because he hadn't been home the fateful day his parents drove to Wolf Grove—and never made it back alive. Now she knew how he felt—angry, guilty and full of regret. She should have pitched a royal fit until he agreed to let her accompany him. She should have descended the tree faster so she could have been on hand to help him spot the bushwhacker....

Her wild, tormenting thoughts trailed off when she heard the thunder of hooves racing to the east. She gouged her horse, then jerked back on the reins when a second horse galloped hell-for-leather to the west in the darkness.

As anxious as she was to locate Quin—to see him, touch him and know he was safe, she forced herself to wait another beat. Sure enough, a third rider headed south. No doubt, there was a gang involved. They had split up to avoid capture—in case Quin hadn't come alone as instructed.

Once she was reasonably certain the danger had passed, Adrianna nudged her horse, unsure where she was going. In the near distance, she heard murmurs. Alarmed, she halted and pricked her ears. She realized the sound she heard was water rushing over rocks. Phantom Springs, no doubt.

She nudged the horse forward, then swore sourly when she spotted Cactus tethered to a tree. She dismounted in a single bound to rush toward the sound of gurgling water. Her thudding heart ceased beating the moment when she saw Quin sprawled facedown beside another lifeless body that was faceup.

"Quin?" she choked out as she skidded onto her knees beside him. "Quin, can you hear me?"

Nothing. He didn't respond or move, just lay motionless beside the other man—who looked vaguely familiar. She was too distressed to recall where she might have seen him.

Desperate, Adrianna ripped off the hem of her blouse to dip in the water. Since she didn't see a bloody wound on Quin's back she rolled him over, then frowned, bemused. There was no pool of blood or seeping stain on his chest or torso. But she knew for a fact that she had heard a gunshot.

Confused, she rolled over the other man and found the fatal wound on his back. Surely Quin hadn't shot this man in the back—it wasn't his style. But why did Quin look as dead as his companion when he wasn't lying in a pool of his own blood?

Muffling a sniff, she wiped the tears from her eyes,

then pressed shaky fingertips to the side of Quin's neck. She half collapsed in relief when she noted he still had a pulse. Frantic to determine why he wasn't moving, she ran her hand over his scalp. There were two goose-egg-size knots on the back of his head.

Why didn't I notice them when I rolled him to his back before? she asked herself. Because she had been expecting to see bullet holes. Thank goodness, she hadn't found any.

Adrianna grabbed her makeshift rag and blotted the knots on his head. Then she eased Quin to his back to sprinkle water on his pallid face. When that didn't work, she cupped her hands and dribbled more water on his face.

Finally, he stirred, grimaced uncomfortably, then exhaled a wobbly sigh. He looked incredibly vulnerable. Compassion squeezed Adrianna's chest. Impulsively, she pressed her lips to his, wishing her kiss would revive Quin and restore him to the energetic, commanding— and sometimes maddening—man he usually was.

Eventually he opened his eyes, but he looked so dazed that she wondered if he recognized her. "Quin, it's me. Boston."

"What the hell are you doing here?" he grumbled sluggishly.

"I came to tell you I told you so, of course," she muttered caustically, her fear transforming into annoyance.

"What hit me?" he asked dazedly.

"I don't know, but *I'd* like to hit you. You scared me half to death," she snapped, even as she cradled his injured head on her lap and held the cold compress against his skull.

Quin pried open one eye and squinted up at her. "My brain might be scrambled but I remember telling you to stay put," he mumbled. "Did you bribe Butler to let you follow me?"

"No." She offered no explanation. "What happened here?"

Quin tried to lever himself onto an elbow, then wilted back to the ground. "The world is spinning and my skull feels like it split wide-open. It's making me nauseous."

"I'm sorry...now tell me what happened," she demanded as she cast the dead man a hasty glance. "Your friend has a hole in his back. Any idea how it got there? It wasn't your work, was it? I can't picture you gunning down someone in that cowardly fashion. *Me*, maybe, but no one else."

Quin gingerly inspected the twin knots on his head, then grimaced in pain. "All I know is I crept in here and found this man with his head draped in the spring. He had a bullet hole in his back."

He dragged in a restorative breath but Adrianna thought he still looked pale and shaky so she refused to let him stand until he regained a bit more color.

"I turned the man over and remembered that I saw him at the party," he went on to say. "I don't think he's a local, which strikes me as odd. I was hoping he was still alive, but he was long past telling me what I wanted to know. Then someone clubbed me from behind. I tried to spin around but he hit me again. That's the last thing I remember. Except your voice in my head saying, *I told you so.*"

"Next time listen to *my* voice in *your* head, Cahill," she advised. "Now what about the other three men?"

Quin frowned. "What are you talking about?"

"I heard a gunshot. Then three men rode off in different directions," she reported. "One went east, one west and one south. I was unable to identify any of the men or describe their horses in the darkness."

"Three?" he croaked. "Are you sure about that, Boston?"

"Of course I'm sure. I'm not the one with two knots on my head.... Do you think you can stand up yet?"

Quin pushed upright and leaned heavily against her. He waited a moment, inhaled a few deep breaths, then tried again—and failed.

"You wait here while I fetch Cactus," she ordered as she scrambled to her feet.

When she returned a minute later, leading Cactus, Quin said, "Check the saddlebags to see if the money is where I left it."

She did as he asked. "There's nothing here."

"Hell and damnation," Quin bit out as he rolled onto all fours, then tried to stand.

Adrianna darted over to lend support. She felt a sentimental tug at her heartstrings when Quin draped his arm around her shoulder, then kissed her on the cheek.

"I'm sorry I got you into this mess," he murmured. "I want to make double damn certain that everyone around here knows you can't identify the other men involved. As far as anyone knows, you weren't here. Understand, Boston?"

"Fine. We'll play it your way for the time being, at least." She glanced down at the dead man. "My guess is that whoever dreamed up this extortion scheme decided to split the money three ways instead of four. Worse, we still don't know if there is any truth to the possibility of foul play in your parents' death."

Quin muttered a string of expletives as Adrianna assisted him into the saddle. She frowned in concern when Quin doubled over Cactus's neck, then groaned miserably. She was no doctor, but she suspected he was suffering from a concussion. She needed to get him home so he could rest.

She glanced back at the dead man. He wasn't going anywhere so he could wait until she had tended to Quin.

Leading Cactus back to the borrowed horse, Adrianna mounted up and kept a watchful eye on Quin, who faded in and out of consciousness during the ride. When they reached the house, she shouted for help. Bea, Butler and Elda appeared on the porch. Three sets of eyes rounded in concern when they spotted Quin.

As expected, Butler's disapproving gaze zeroed in on her. "You'd better be all right," he huffed. "And do not pull a prank like that again! I thought you had passed that hoyden stage a decade ago. Your father would not approve."

"He didn't approve of anything unladylike that I did," she countered, then directed everyone's attention to Quin. "Someone pounded Cahill over the head twice and took the money." She bounded from the saddle, then rushed over to Quin. "Help me get him upstairs." She glanced hastily at Bea. "Bring your needle and thread. I think he's going to need stitches."

"Where am I?" Quin mumbled when the foursome jostled him off the horse.

"In hell, Cahill," Adrianna told him. "I'm in charge now. You cannot rise from bed without my permission."

"Damn, my worst nightmare," he groaned.

Adrianna wasn't sure but she thought she saw the smallest hint of a smile pass his ashen lips before he collapsed again.

Quin awoke to find himself tucked in the over-size bed in the master suite. His stomach pitched and rolled like a ship at the mercy of a storm-ravaged sea. His head pounded in rhythm with his pulse. His eyes blurred when he kept them open too long at a time. It hurt to think but he tried to remember what had happened after someone clobbered him the previous night. Unfortunately, bits and pieces of the incident kept flitting through his mind, then shattering like glass.

What he recalled clearly was that Boston had defied his orders and followed him. "The damn fool woman," he grumbled crankily.

"I do hope you aren't referring to me, Cahill," came Boston's familiar voice from somewhere behind him. "The only *damn fool* in this room is *you*. And you have three stitches on your scalp to prove it."

The moment Quin levered himself up on his elbows to settle into a half-inclined position nausea pelted him. Boston was there in a flash to assist him. He sighed heavily as he leaned against the pillow she propped behind his tender head.

"Elda brought up some broth and crackers," she informed him. "You are going to eat them."

"I'm not hun—"

She crammed a spoonful of tasty broth in his open mouth, then said, "Do as you're told. Dr. Lewis will be here soon. We'll see what he has to say about your condition."

He narrowed his eyes at her. "You are a mean, bossy tyrant, Boston," he complained, but his voice held no censure.

"Thank you, Cahill. I love you, too."

That'd be the day, he predicted. He'd made Boston irate the first time they met because he'd opened his big mouth and spouted off about how she was out of her element in Texas and she should go home. Then they had engaged in a feud to annoy each other and someone had used their conflict as an explanation for rustled cattle and destructive fires. Now she was a witness to murder and she could find herself in jeopardy.

He frowned, bemused. "How many riders did you say you heard racing away from Phantom Springs?"

"Three." She shoved a cracker in his mouth to ease his nausea. Surprisingly it helped. "They left one at a time," she continued. "That was *after* someone fired a single shot."

Quin munched on the cracker pensively. "I didn't hear the shot so I must have been unconscious when it happened."

"I thought *you* shot someone or someone shot you. It was very disconcerting."

He sent her a discreet glance, wondering if she liked him well enough to worry about him. "Careful, Boston, you keep saying things like that and I'll start thinking you care."

She shrugged nonchalantly and stuffed a spoonful of broth in his mouth again. "I'm returning a favor. You allowed me and my family to stay at your house after the fire." She bent to graze her lush lips over his and he felt better immediately…until she added, "Now hush up and eat. I have better things to do besides mollycoddle you, Cahill."

"Boston?" he said when she rose from the edge of the bed.

"Yes?"

"Um, thank you…" He wasn't accustomed to having to depend on others and it injured his pride. When his brothers and sister abandoned him, he had vowed to manage without anyone. For the most part, he had, though he had practically worked himself to death doing it.

She braced her hands on either side of him, then leaned down to kiss him again. "You're welcome, Cahill. Now get better. That's an order."

When she walked away, he swallowed a smile and decided a few dozen of Boston's kisses were the only remedy he needed to get back on his feet.

Chapter Ten

Adrianna was greatly relieved when the doctor arrived to check on Quin. Dr. Lewis was a slight, fair-haired man who was an inch or two under six feet. He was thirty—or thereabouts—had kind brown eyes and a reassuring smile. The physician's examination revealed Quin had suffered a mild concussion.

She figured his hardheadedness was the reason he wasn't comatose. If any other man had endured repetitive blows, he probably would have been dead.

Dr. Lewis prescribed plenty of rest for Quin, then questioned her about the dead man they had found last night by the springs. As Quin had cautioned, Adrianna didn't volunteer any information other than she had gone looking for Quin when he didn't return home promptly.

The young doctor left the house in his buggy, promising to notify the city marshal as Adrianna had requested. Surprisingly, Tobias Hobbs, the city marshal, arrived twenty minutes later. Hobbs was mid-thirties, six foot tall with dark hair and a mustache. He was an attractive man who wore a stylish bowler hat, vest and suit.

Of course, he didn't compare to Quin Cahill in size and stature, but then Adrianna had developed a sentimental attachment to cowboys—one in particular. However, she tried exceptionally hard not to let Cahill know she was in danger of losing her heart to him.

It would humiliate her to no end to confide the truth and have him remind her that he didn't have time in his life for lasting attachments. So Adrianna behaved as nonchalantly as she knew how and kept her growing affection for Cahill a carefully guarded secret.

"That was fast," Adrianna commented as Marshal Hobbs dismounted from his horse. "I didn't think Dr. Lewis had time to contact you so you could ride out."

"I was already on my way out here," Hobbs explained, his expression serious as he tipped his hat politely to her. "We met briefly at your town party, Miz McKnight. Remember?"

"I remember," she replied. Hobbs had gone through the receiving line but Adrianna had only had time to say hello and welcome him before he'd ambled off.

"I was told you had a fire at your ranch recently. Sorry to hear it."

She nodded. "Cahill was kind enough to offer us shelter temporarily." She opened the door to invite Hobbs inside.

"Half the people in town wager Cahill started your fire to drive you away. The other half suspects it's a scheme to get you into his house so he can romance you out of your ranch." Hobbs stared pointedly at her. "Apparently, it worked."

"That is preposterous," she scoffed. "I want those rumors quelled immediately."

Hobbs lifted his shoulder in a casual shrug. "You and Cahill are wealthy and high profile. The rest of us are ordinary folks. Some people thrive on gossip about the activities and woes of the rich."

"The fact is, Cahill helped douse the fire. Then he generously allowed my employees and me a place to stay until my home airs out," she explained irritably.

"Whatever you say," he patronized, annoying her further. "I'm not sitting in judgment. My job is to enforce the law."

"And to investigate crimes," she reminded him crisply. "I sent for you to investigate a shooting death last night. We didn't move the body so you can survey the area."

"I already looked around the site." Hobbs was all business as he stared at her. "I received an anonymous note this morning that said there was a dead body at Phantom Springs on 4C Ranch. It also said Cahill was the cause of death."

"What?" Adrianna hooted in disbelief. "That is absurd. Cahill had nothing to do with the killing. It's a wonder he isn't dead himself!"

The marshal's dark eyes narrowed skeptically. "How do you know for certain that he *wasn't* involved?"

Adrianna heeded Quin's warning not to mention her involvement to anyone, in case she became a witness who needed to be silenced. "Because Cahill told me what happened. He arrived on the scene to find a man shot in the back."

Hobbs glanced toward the parlor. "Is Cahill here? I'd like to speak to him."

"He's in bed, recovering from two blows to the head."

"So that's why Doc was here?"

"Precisely. Cahill has a concussion." Adrianna led the way upstairs. "You may speak to him if he is awake and coherent. If not, you can question him after he has recovered."

"Miz McKnight, might I remind you that I am the marshal of Cahill Crossing and I handle investigations as I see fit?" he said authoritatively.

Adrianna pivoted two steps above him and relied upon the lofty tone she'd heard her father employ when he put someone in his place. "Might I remind you, Mr. Hobbs," she countered, purposely omitting his title, "that Cahill is injured. You will wait until he can answer your questions accurately. If he is still confused about what happened, then you will wait another day. If you have a problem with that, speak to Dr. Lewis and he will advise the same thing."

They exchanged squinty-eyed stares for a long moment. Then Hobbs inclined his dark head ever so slightly. "Lead the way, ma'am. Let's see how your patient is feeling, shall we?"

Annoyed by the lawman's unyielding attitude, she strode toward the master suite. To her dismay, Quin was awake, so she couldn't shoo away the marshal.

"Cahill," Hobbs greeted as he came to stand at the foot of the bed. "I'm hoping you can answer some questions. As I told your...*nurse*—" he cut Adrianna a wry glance "—I received an anonymous tip that someone died on your ranch last night and that you are the one who killed him. Mind telling me what that was all about?"

Quin combed his fingers through his tousled hair and tried to look alert but he couldn't pull it off. Adrianna thought he should wait to have this discussion but his expression indicated he wanted to clear the air immediately.

"I received an anonymous letter also," Quin reported. "It arrived at supper time last night. According to the note, my parents' deaths were not the result of the common kind of accident on a dangerous curve. If I brought money to the meeting site I could trade it for information."

"Are we talking *robbery? Manslaughter? Murder?*" Hobbs choked out. "I investigated the wreck at Ghost Canyon myself. There were no tracks nearby to indicate an attack. The broken debris from the wagon and its cargo were strewn over the rocks and underbrush."

"That doesn't mean someone didn't wipe the area clean to conceal his guilt," Boston interjected.

Hobbs sent her a silencing glance—as if that would shut her up, thought Quin.

"If anything, a wagon wheel or hub gave way at the worst of all possible times," the marshal continued. "You read my report yourself, Cahill. Your whole family did."

Quin snorted. "Of course, it would look bad if it turned out you had botched the investigation, wouldn't it? I can see why you might be reluctant and skeptical."

Hobbs snapped up his dark head and his brown eyes flashed indignation. "Now see here, Cahill, no one has questioned my ability to do my job in the past. I can understand that you are upset about the loss of your parents. But accidental manslaughter or *murder?* Why would an informant contact you two years after the fact?"

"That's what I wanted to know, Hobbs. Which is why I rode out to Phantom Springs, as the note instructed. Unfortunately, the supposed informant was already dead," Quin replied.

"And you can prove that?" Hobbs challenged doubtfully.

"Oh, for heaven's sake, be sensible," Boston interjected. "Why would Cahill want to shoot a man who might have vital information about his parents' deaths?"

Hobbs cut Boston an annoyed glance. "If rumors are to be believed, you and Cahill were involved in a feud. Suddenly you reconciled. Or at least that's what some folks presumed…until someone burned down the new addition on your house. Now here you are in Cahill's home and no one knows what to believe."

"And what does any of that have to do with a dead man at Phantom Springs?" she countered sharply. "Let's stick to one investigation at a time, shall we?"

"I'm wondering if whoever deliberately set the fire during the party was under orders. Perhaps the mastermind decided to silence the arsonist permanently to avoid being blackmailed." Hobbs glanced accusingly at Quin.

Quin was tempted to leap off the bed and sock the marshal in the jaw for voicing such ridiculous suspicions. Who was spreading rumors to make him look bad? Quin wondered. Damn it, someone was spreading incriminating explanations for everything he and Boston did these days.

"That is the most ridiculous speculation I ever heard," Boston sputtered, giving Hobbs another glimpse of her fiery spirit. "Cahill didn't shoot that poor man to keep him silent about a fire, because it was likely set by a *lightning* bolt." She glanced briefly at Quin. "As for the anonymous note that foul play might have been involved in Ruby's and Earl's deaths, Cahill had no reason to kill the messenger. He wanted information."

Quin had to hand it to Boston. She could go toe to toe with the marshal, who had obviously heard all sorts of wild conjectures from the locals.

He was grateful for her assistance because his head hurt like hell and it was difficult to keep up with the rapid-fire conversation when he couldn't think straight. She distracted Hobbs by coming on like an attack dog, taking the focus off Quin while he was dazed. No one ever protected him like that. Except Boston.

Hobbs smirked and focused directly on Boston. "If you weren't there you can't know what was said and what happened. It is possible the supposed informant had nothing to offer and Cahill was furious enough to shoot him for his deception. In fact, considering the scandalous gossip circulating about Leanna during the party, I expect Cahill was in the worst of all possible moods by the time he rode off last night."

Quin gnashed his teeth. There were so many rumors buzzing about his family that they had become tangled and cast suspicion and unfavorable light on all of them.

"*You* weren't there, either," Boston retaliated, lifting her chin defiantly. "You can't speculate on what happened, can you? You have Quin's testimony and since he has no prior record of criminal activity you have no reason to doubt him."

Hobbs muttered something under his breath, then shot Quin a hard glance. He walked over to the double holsters draped over the back of the chair. He removed both pistols and sniffed the barrels before checking the chambers.

His dark eyes settled accusingly on Quin. "Do you plan to deny this pistol has been fired recently?"

"Not by me it wasn't," Quin maintained.

"Then by whom?" Hobbs demanded gruffly. "Cahill, I know you claim to be injured but it is my duty to take you to jail for suspicion of murder."

"Because of an anonymous tip?" Boston spewed in outrage.

Hobbs held up the six-shooter. "This is a possible murder weapon found in Cahill's possession, ma'am. I can't disregard the possibility of Cahill's involvement in the death just because he runs the largest spread in the area. If he is innocent, my investigation will clear him."

He spun on his heels, then halted at the door. "I'll wait for you downstairs, Cahill. I expect you are as anxious to follow proper protocol as I am. Otherwise, the locals will speculate that you bribed me to dismiss any charges of wrongdoing. Time will tell if you are innocent."

"Of course he's innocent," Boston burst out angrily. "A stint in jail will only invite more offensive rumors about this absurd curse the spiteful locals delight in nurturing."

Hobbs waved the pistol in her fuming face and said,

"Best not to argue with a smoking gun, ma'am. You might want to consider the possibility that Cahill is trying to use *you* to corroborate his story so he can go free."

When Hobbs walked out, Boston lurched toward Quin. "This is outrageous! I am going to tell Hobbs that I was on hand and that I heard——"

"No," he interrupted sharply, then winced when his raised voice sent a stab of pain rippling through his tender skull. "Stay out of this, Boston. We will sort it out without involving you. After I convince Hobbs to see reason, we'll investigate discreetly to disprove these infuriating rumors that put a negative slant on everything we say or do."

She blew out an agitated breath, then dashed over to assist Quin when he tried to sit up on the edge of the bed. "I'm going to consult a lawyer. There is a reputable one in town, isn't there? If not, I'll send Butler to Wolf Grove to fetch one," she insisted. "You are not going to spend unnecessary time in jail and invite another avalanche of damaging gossip!"

"I'll be fine," he assured her—and negated his claim by wobbling when he stood.

"You are nowhere near fine, Cahill," she grumbled as she handed him a clean shirt. "Now sit down so I can help you with your boots."

Dutifully, he sat down. Quin was not looking forward to the horseback ride to town. However, he was anxious to clear up the misunderstanding about what happened at Phantom Springs and convince Hobbs to reopen the investigation deemed an accident two years earlier. Quin was convinced his parents' wreck was more than an accident. Naturally, Hobbs wasn't enthusiastic about reviewing the case and risking speculation that he hadn't done his job right the first time.

Quin wondered if the guilty party responsible for the deaths of his parents might have consisted of *four* outlaws who wiped away their tracks after the wagon plummeted over the edge of the cliff. They might have stolen money and supplies without the Cahills being aware. Quin had no clue how much money his parents had carried with them to Wolf Grove. Plus, Quin had never itemized the supplies to determine if the receipt of purchased goods matched the items carted away from the wreckage.

Quin had been too busy planning a double funeral and suffering from overwhelming grief, guilt and torment. Not to mention the distraction and anguish he had suffered when his family walked out when he had needed them most. He had been too upset to ask the right questions about the accident.

Quin glanced down at Boston, who knelt in front of him to help him with his boots. Only one person had stood *up* for him, *with* him and *because* of him in the past two years, he reminded himself again. It was this feisty, quick-minded firebrand who he was desperate to protect from involvement in this recent murder. If something happened to Boston, Quin could never forgive himself.

Hell, he was having enough trouble forgiving himself for failing his parents, especially now that he suspected they had been victims of an attack he might have prevented if he'd been home as he should have been.

Same as his brothers should have been around to

lend a hand that fateful day, he thought resentfully. They were as guilty of neglect as he was and they had been a helluva lot closer to home.

When Boston stood in front of him, Quin's tormented thoughts trailed off and he grasped her hand to detain her. "Promise me you'll keep quiet about following me to the springs last night," he demanded.

"I am not letting you rot in jail," she stated resolutely. "You need to be home recuperating."

He squeezed her hand and managed a faint smile as he rose slowly to his feet, then waited for the room to stop spinning around him. *"Promise me,"* he repeated emphatically. "I'll never ask anything else of you if you'll do this, Boston."

She exhaled audibly, then regarded him from beneath a long fringe of black lashes. Eventually she bobbed her head, causing the thick chestnut-colored braid to ripple over her shoulder. "All right, but you have only one day to convince Marshal Hobbs that he needs to look elsewhere for a murderer."

"I'm sure I can talk sense into him, man to man, when you aren't gnawing on his ear and his ankles," Quin said teasingly.

Boston rolled her eyes as she assisted him across the room. "Men," she said, then sniffed.

Quin wasn't sure what that meant but he was pretty sure it wasn't a compliment.

By the time Quin reached town, he had a splitting headache. He noticed the crowd gathering around the jail, as if Hobbs had arrested the worst offender on the Most Wanted list. Heavens above! Whoever was spewing gossip to ruin the Cahill reputation and fuel superstitious nonsense about a curse was doing a bang-up job.

Quin growled under his breath when he saw Preston Van Slyck standing in front of the bank, wearing a ridiculing smile. Whether or not that bastard had anything to do with the would-be informant's death, he was enjoying Quin's public humiliation.

Just as Preston had delighted in spreading scandal about Leanna at the party. Damn him.

Somebody should string up Preston Van Slyck on general principles, Quin mused as he dismounted—and clung to his horse for support. Preston was a womanizer of the worst sort and a sorry excuse for a man. Yep, thought Quin, that "gentleman" deserved to be the honored guest at a necktie party. Unfortunately, *Quin* was the one under arrest for murder and facing the possibility of a lynching.

He grimaced when he met the accusing stares of townsfolk who apparently had been swayed by gossip. The public consensus was that he deserved to suffer. He wondered if folks would be mollified if they knew how lousy he felt already.

"Come on, Cahill," Marshal Hobbs prompted as he urged Quin up the steps to the pinewood office. Then he turned to the crowd gathered on Town Square. "Go on about your business and let me do my job."

Serenaded by mumbling and grumbling from the crowd of saddle tramps, tracklayers and other ne'er-do-wells from the wrong side of the tracks, Quin wobbled into the office. He wasn't looking forward to camping out on the lumpy cot behind bars. The sooner he convinced Hobbs he was barking up the wrong tree, the better.

Quin removed his hat and directed the marshal's attention to the stitches on the back of his head. "I didn't get these brain-scrambling blows from a dead man," he insisted. "I was hunkered over the would-be informant and I was attacked from my blind side."

Hobbs spared a cursory glance at the injury as he marched Quin across the office to the back room. He opened the cell door, then gestured for Quin to enter. "How am I supposed to know if the man at the springs clubbed *you,* then tried to make a getaway with the money before *you* shot him in the back?"

"Then I would be claiming self-defense against a brutal attack," Quin said reasonably. "That is not what happened."

Hobbs narrowed his dark eyes as he shut the barred door with a clank. "Did you shoot the man you hired to set the fire to shut him up permanently? Was he trying to blackmail you?"

"For God's sake, Hobbs, you heard what Boston, er, Adrianna said. Lightning started the fire at her ranch."

Hobbs ambled back to his office to hang his bowler hat on the hook by the door. Then he strode to the potbelly stove to pour himself a cup of coffee. He didn't offer Quin a cup. Apparently, prisoners received no kindness whatsoever.

"What do you know about the dead man at Phantom Springs?" the marshal asked intently as he stood in the doorway.

"I never saw him until the night of Rosa and Lucas's wedding celebration. He brushed past me on his way to the refreshment table but he didn't speak or try to draw my attention. Adrianna remembers him vaguely, as well. But we have no idea who he is...was."

"Yet you claim he knew something about the supposed deaths of your parents?" Hobbs asked skeptically, then sipped his coffee. "Sorry, Cahill, but too many things are going on around here and most of them have to do with you, one way or another. If you are lying to me about this unidentified dead man you are headed straight to court for trial."

Quin tried not to lose his temper but it was damn hard when he felt miserable and frustrated—to the extreme. Never in his life had he had to work so hard to be believed. These days, his name and reputation counted for nothing and a constant fog of suspicion surrounded him. And damn it, just when he thought he had begun to heal from the remorse and anguish of two years past and move on with his life, another obstacle stood in his path.

Too bad his family wasn't around to help him bear the burden and uncover the truth, he thought resentfully. His one champion was Boston, and he didn't want her sucked into the vortex of this exasperating turmoil.

Quin sighed heavily. "Look, Hobbs, I have no reason to lie. I received the note last night and Adrianna and Hiram Butler saw it. They tried to persuade me not to go alone to that rendezvous site with money in hand. They thought I was walking into a trap. Turns out they were right."

Hobbs came to stand by the cell. "Where is the note?"

"At home."

"And the money? How much money are we discussing?"

"Two thousand dollars."

"Two thousand dollars?" Hobbs hooted. "Where's the money now? Did you exchange it for *supposed* information?"

His skeptical comment prompted Quin to clench his fists around the iron bars. "Whoever hit me from behind must have taken it. As a precaution, I left it in my saddlebags and went to meet the man who was *dead* when I arrived."

"But you didn't see this second supposed assailant?" Hobbs questioned doubtfully.

"No. When I tried to turn on him after he delivered the first blow to the back of my head he hit me a second time. I blacked out." Quin waited a beat and decided to twist the truth, in hopes of protecting Boston and convincing Hobbs to believe his side of the story. "I didn't hear the shot being fired from my pistol while I was unconscious. I don't know who fired at whom or why. I came to in time to hear three riders racing away in three different directions."

Hobbs glanced up with sudden interest. *"Three* men? They rode off in *three* different directions?"

Quin bobbed his aching head. "It was a gang, obviously."

Hobbs took several swallows of coffee, frowned pensively, then set aside the cup. "I'd better check the site again and bring in the body. I also want to see this supposed note you received. I'll swing by to question Adrianna and Butler."

"And I'd like to see the note *you* received about the

dead man," Quin insisted. "I wonder if the handwriting matches."

Hobbs strode to his desk, then returned with the note.

Quin squinted at the handwriting. "It doesn't look the same. One of the other gang members must have written it."

Hobbs sent him another dubious glance, then replaced the note in his desk drawer. He craned his neck around the corner to the room with the cells. "Sit tight, Cahill. I'm locking up this office while I investigate."

Quin plunked down on the cot to rest. So much for the man-to-man discussion to clear his name quickly. It looked as if he would be sleeping off this hellish head-ache on a lumpy cot in jail.

He wondered if his brothers and sister would delight in knowing Quin was in misery. They, like some of the spiteful locals who chose to believe the gossip and scandal, probably thought Quin was exactly where he belonged. As for the envious and resentful folks here-about, they probably wanted him to sit here and rot.

Chapter Eleven

After Cahill and Hobbs left, Adrianna rode to her ranch. She walked into the foyer of her house and took a whiff of the air. Although she had opened all the windows after the rainstorm doused the fire, a hint of smoke still clung to the fabric of the furniture and drapes.

Not enough to use as an excuse to stay with Quin much longer, she mused as she ascended the staircase. Tonight she would be in his bed—without him. Since Quin hadn't returned home, she presumed he hadn't convinced Marshal Hobbs of innocence in the unidentified man's death. Surely someone around town knew who he was. If no one claimed to know him, did that suggest he knew nothing about Ruby and Earl Cahill's wagon wreck and he was attempting to extort money?

Adrianna expelled an exasperated breath as she stared out the upstairs window. Her troubled thoughts trailed off when she noticed the brown saddle horse with three white stockings grazing in her pasture with the remuda. She snapped to attention. That was the very same horse she had commandeered the previous night to follow Quin when he rode to Phantom Springs—and received two knots on his hard head and become a murder suspect.

Who had tethered that horse in front of Quin's bunkhouse one night and why was it grazing in her pasture this afternoon? And where was the strawberry roan horse that had been tethered beside it?

Adrianna lurched toward the door. Too many unexplainable and suspicious incidents were occurring at her ranch and the 4C. Someone was exploiting the rumors of her personal feud and the supposed Cahill Curse to explain rustling, butchering and arson. That someone was making a profit from the ranch losses. Adrianna was determined to find out who that someone was.

She flew down the steps and breezed out the door to take a head count of the cowhands in charge of the chores at headquarters. Everyone who was supposed to be on the premises appeared to be working. As for the hired hands in charge of riding fences and checking herds, Adrianna couldn't say if they were on duty. But she was going to ride around the pastures to make certain her cowboys were doing what they were supposed to be doing.

Furthermore, she wasn't going to voice any suspicions to anyone except Cahill because she wasn't sure whom she could trust. Her disgruntled ex-foreman was only goodness knew where. Even her new foreman wasn't exempt from suspicion, she mused as she strode off swiftly to retrieve Buckshot. Rocky Rhodes was familiar with her ranch and with the 4C, she reminded herself warily. He had access to both places and might be making extra money for himself.

Rocky seemed to be an honest man but Adrianna had encountered several charlatans in her time. She wasn't looking past the possible motives of anyone in her quest to ferret out the rustlers, arsonists and murderers.

"Where ya headed, Miz McKnight?"

Speak of the devil, Adrianna thought when she heard Rocky's drawling voice behind her. She pasted on a pleasant smile, then pivoted to face the blond-haired, blue-eyed foreman. "I'm going to ride out and check the herds."

"Want some company?"

"Thanks for the offer, but I'll be fine." She tossed him a casual smile that concealed her wary suspicion.

"Sure was a good party you hosted for Rosa and Lucas." He glanced toward the charred remains of her new house addition. "Too bad that fire spoiled the evening."

Adrianna tried to recall if she had seen Rocky in town before he had showed up to help douse the fire. To be honest, she had been so busy with party arrangements and meeting new acquaintances that she couldn't recall seeing Rocky or any other cowhands from her ranch. She didn't know who'd had the night off and who had remained behind.

She wondered if she was suffering paranoia, wondered if she could trust anyone but Cahill and her adopted family. With all that was going on, she was mistrustful of everyone because she didn't know who was out to get her and Cahill—and why.

Adrianna rode off to see if other cattle had been corralled in the box canyon where she and Rock had found part of the stolen herd.

Several hours later, Adrianna returned to 4C, disappointed that her extended ride had turned up nothing. She still didn't know who on her ranch favored the horse she had commandeered from Quin's bunkhouse. But she was going to keep a watchful eye, she vowed. That horse had been out of place. Rocky could have ridden over to visit his former coworkers at 4C, she supposed, but she wasn't going to fire out questions to make hired hands cautious until she acquired more facts.

Nevertheless, she had the niggling feeling something was going on behind the scenes at both ranches. She would be discreet, but she was going to track down the rustlers, arsonists and murderers—somehow or other.

Leaving Buckshot for Skeeter Gregory, Quin's right-hand man, to unsaddle, she headed for the house. The scent of Elda's delicious meal met her at the front door, reminding her that she had skipped lunch. She was on her way to the kitchen when Butler flagged her down and directed her into Quin's office.

"Is he back yet?" she asked hopefully. He hadn't been gone a full day and she missed him terribly.

Butler shook his head. "No, but Marshal Hobbs was here earlier. He wanted to see the note Quin received from the supposed informant."

"Did Hobbs take it with him as evidence?"

"No, because I didn't give it to him." Butler pulled the missive from the pocket of his vest.

Adrianna frowned, bemused. "Why not?"

"Because this is the only conclusive evidence we have that Cahill was lured to Phantom Springs," he replied. "We are keeping it, in case we have to consult a lawyer to defend Cahill in court."

Adrianna walked over to give Butler a hug. "You are brilliant, Hiram. Thank you."

He hugged her back. "You do not pay me to be stupid…but I have to ask if you'd prefer to be rid of Cahill."

She reared back in his arms to meet his searching hazel-eyed gaze. She had the inescapable feeling Butler knew she had become intimate with Cahill. He was asking the silent question about whether Quin was like the annoying, unwanted suitors from her past.

Feeling awkward and embarrassed, she stared at the air over his left shoulder. "I like Cahill the way you like Beatrice," she admitted quietly.

Butler nodded somberly. "I thought so. But you should know that if he hurts you, he will pay dearly."

She chuckled. "Elda will poison his food?"

Butler grinned. "For starters. Then Bea will wallop him a few times with her broom and dustpan and I will doctor his financial ledgers to make him look corrupt. The scandal circulating now will be child's play in comparison."

"If he isn't home by bedtime I'm barnstorming the marshal's office first thing in the morning," she insisted on the way to the dining room. "I'm taking that note as evidence but I won't turn it over to Hobbs. Smoking gun aside, Cahill wouldn't shoot a man in the back and I know it. I suspect one of the three men at the springs set him up. I will *refuse* to leave the office until Hobbs agrees with my conclusions."

Butler snickered. "I pity the marshal. He'll likely

release Cahill, if only to get you out of his hair and stop you from barking in his ear, Addie K."

"I'm counting on it," Adrianna murmured before she sat down to Elda's mouthwatering meal—and wondered what jailers served their prisoners for supper in Ca-Cross.

Early the next morning Adrianna rode into town with the note Quin had received. Her first stop was Rosa's Boutique, which sat across the square from the marshal's office. When she entered the shop, Rosa poked her silver-blond head around the corner of the sewing room. A concerned frown replaced her usual smile.

"Glad you're here, Addie K. I've been worried about Quin." She rushed forward to clasp Adrianna's hands in her own. "I went to check on him twice yesterday but Marshal Hobbs had the place locked up tight while he was investigating. Rumors about Quin killing a man hired to start the fire at your house are flying all over town."

"Blast it, people can be so gullible and foolish. Why are they so quick to believe the worst?" Adrianna muttered under her breath. "Whoever killed that man at Phantom Springs set up Quin. He received a message suggesting his parents' deaths weren't accidental."

Rosa's lavender-colored eyes nearly popped from their sockets. "What? You mean it was murder? Heavens!"

"We don't know if the wreck resulted from a robbery gone bad or if the note Cahill received was an extortion attempt. The would-be informant was dead when Cahill arrived."

"It does make you wonder, when it's been two years since the incident," Rosa said pensively.

"Personally, I think this is an attempt to swindle money from Cahill, same as the horses and cattle stolen from both our ranches. This time Quin received two knots on his head while trying to seek the truth. Plus, the extortion money was taken while Quin was unconscious."

Rosa flung up her arms. "What the blazes is going on around here? Rumors are buzzing about Quin committing murder and about his sister raising her illegitimate child while working as a… Well, you know. Why would anyone want to drag the Cahill name through the mud?"

Adrianna shrugged. "I suppose for the same reason the Greers and McKnights were accused of all sorts of unethical corruption to explain our families' business success."

Rosa nodded, disgruntled. "Ah, yes, the backstabbers of the world spend more time slandering others who are more fortunate than devising ways to ensure their own prosperity."

Adrianna glanced sideways to see a crowd gathering on the square. "Uh-oh, that doesn't bode well for Quin."

"Just what we need," Rosa grumbled. "The drunken mob spouting threats of hanging the town founder."

Adrianna swallowed hard at the disturbing prospect. "I need to talk to the marshal…now."

"Do you need Lucas and me as character witnesses for Quin?" Rosa asked.

"Thanks, but I hope it won't come to that."

Adrianna spun on her heel, then jogged across the square. She veered around the crowd of scraggly-looking men from Wrong Side who were discussing when and where to lynch Cahill. She glanced at the cocky Preston Van Slyck, who was propped against the supporting beam of the bank, grinning from ear to ear.

Hmm, she thought suspiciously. *I wonder who egged on the local riffraff to form a spiteful mob?*

Adrianna couldn't explain a connection between Preston and the unidentified dead man, but she knew Preston's type. The banker's son was ecstatic when others were miserable, especially if he felt he'd been wronged and wanted to enjoy spiteful revenge. If Leanna Cahill had rejected Preston, he would delight in getting even—every way possible.

Her thoughts scattered as she scurried across the boardwalk to reach the marshal's pinewood office before the mob decided it was a grand day for a necktie party. She burst inside to see Hobbs sipping coffee. His booted feet were stacked on the corner of his scarred desk. Her gaze flew immediately to the open door leading to the cells. Quin craned his neck around the corner. He looked rather the worse for wear. There were dark circles under his eyes and strained lines bracketed his mouth.

Her temper boiled in nothing flat and she wheeled toward the marshal to slap down the missive on his desk. "Here's proof enough that Cahill was lured to Phantom Springs and set up to take blame for the murder."

Hobbs put his feet on the floor, then assessed the note. "It says nothing about being set up for murder," he remarked caustically. "Oh, wait, there it is between the lines."

When he tried to pick up the note, Adrianna snatched it away and tucked it in the pocket of her breeches.

"This evidence will be in our lawyer's possession for safekeeping. Now where is the note *you* supposedly received?" she countered in the same sarcastic tone he'd used on her.

His dark eyes glittered. "I don't have to show you evidence. The judge will review it in court."

Adrianna wanted to strangle the hard-nosed, by-the-book lawman who apparently didn't believe in benefit of the doubt. She planted her hands on his desk and leaned down to get right in his face. "Did you find evidence of three other horses at the murder scene?" she demanded sharply.

"No," he snapped at her. "Parts of that area are piles of rock and pebbles. I did find a horse I assume belonged to the dead man. I used it to cart the body to the undertaker." He tried to stare her down, but she refused to be intimidated. "Now why don't you run along, Miz McKnight. I need to write up my report."

Adrianna glanced out the window to see the mob moving in the direction of the jail. She was angry and desperate. She needed Hobbs's cooperation—and fast.

"There is no need to write a report because you don't have the dead man's murderer in custody," she said through gritted teeth. "You saw the note we received and there are two witnesses to verify its existence as the reason Cahill went to the rendezvous site."

When Hobbs glared at her, then opened his mouth to interject a comment, Adrianna slapped her hand against his desk to demand his full attention. "I know for a fact there were three riders that left Phantom Springs that night."

"Damn it, Boston!" Quin snapped from the cell room.

He bounded to his feet, then clamped his fists around the iron bars. "Leave it alone."

Hobbs swiveled his dark head toward the cell. "You said *you* heard them when you came to."

"We *both* heard them," Quin insisted.

Adrianna realized Cahill must have felt the need to argue the point, in hopes of gaining his freedom and protecting her. That was fine, well and noble, but unnecessary.

"You were there?" Hobbs demanded intently.

"That's right," she declared. "I followed Cahill because I thought he was riding into a trap. Before I could move in closer, I heard the shot, then I saw three men ride off in three different directions."

"And you can identify these men?" he questioned.

"No, she can't," Quin called out quickly.

"Have you discovered the name of the deceased?" she interrogated Hobbs, then she cast a wary glance at the approaching mob.

"Not yet."

"I demand that you release Cahill immediately. You have no solid evidence. Even your so-called smoking gun could have been fired by the real killer or one of his cohorts to make Cahill look guilty...*and you know it*," she said emphatically.

"I know nothing of the kind—"

"Then I'm hiring Lucas Burnett and Dog to investigate the scene of the crime," Adrianna interrupted in a sharp tone. "I'm willing to bet a part-Comanche, ex–Texas Ranger and Dog can find a trail that indicates there were *three* riders, just as Cahill and I claim. What do you want to bet, Hobbs?"

The marshal muttered, shifted in his chair, then glanced out the window at the lurking crowd.

"Do you know how bad you're going to look at election time when I support whoever runs for office *against* you? I will mention the evidence I know Burnett and Dog will find at the scene that *you* didn't find. I'll make you look bad, Hobbs. Count on it."

Hobbs's back went ramrod stiff. His brows swooped down over his slitted eyes. "Are you trying to blackmail me?" he challenged in a low growl.

"No. I'm hiring Burnett as my private investigator," she assured him sternly. "Release Cahill, turn over his pistol and tell the mob the truth. There is no evidence that Cahill had anything to do with the murder. He arrived too late to stop the shooting and he is an injured victim of the crime."

Quin craned his neck around the corner of the cell room to watch the glaring contest between Boston and Hobbs. She was magnificent, he mused. He admired her keen intelligence and fiery spirit—especially when it wasn't directed at him.

To Quin's everlasting relief, Hobbs blew out an agitated breath, then pushed away from his desk.

"All right, I'll release Cahill and assure the mob there is no evidence of his involvement. But if you think that will quell the rumors floating around town, you are mistaken, Miz McKnight."

"I'm still sending out Burnett to canvass the springs," she vowed resolutely. "We'll let you know our findings." She looked down her pert nose and Quin silently applauded her ability to portray the power-wielding heiress from Boston. He wondered if she was mimicking her father—and decided it was likely. Quin had picked up several mannerisms from *his* father over the years and he used them when necessary.

Muttering under his breath, Hobbs stepped around the corner to unlock the cell and return the six-shooter. He moved aside to let Quin pass. "If anyone else turns up dead around here, don't expect me to look the other way," he warned. "The Cahills and McKnights are not above the law."

"Truth and justice will prevail, Marshal," Boston retorted, refusing to back down an inch. "A murderer is running loose. I trust you'll do all within your power to find him. Or rather the *three* of them." She stared pointedly at the pot on the stove. "You don't have time to lounge around your office, drinking coffee and propping your feet on your desk."

Hobbs glared at her, then stalked outside to confront the mob before they reached the boardwalk.

"I don't think Hobbs likes me much," Boston commented, then smiled wickedly. "I wonder why?"

"Can't imagine. But don't take it too hard. He doesn't like me, either." Quin dropped a kiss to her dewy lips. "Thanks for coming to my defense. That lumpy cot and drafty cell were getting old real quick."

"I missed having you in bed last night," she whispered.

Desire pummeled him below the belt buckle in the time it took to blink. Funny how quickly one word or thought aroused him these days. No other woman had that ability. But then, there was only one Boston in the world.

And that was probably a good thing.

When Quin opened the door, all eyes darted past Hobbs to zero in on him and Boston. Quin maintained a deadpan expression long after Hobbs said, "Break it up, men. The real murderer is on the loose. If anybody can identify the dead man at the undertaker's I want to know immediately."

When Quin veered toward Preston, Boston tugged on his arm. "Don't kill that arrogant bastard in front of the mob. I refuse to attend your necktie party today since I'm not dressed properly for the occasion."

"Van Slyck deserves to have his head bashed in for what he said about my sister," Quin grumbled resentfully.

"I agree, but people are watching every move you make. Don't provide fodder for gossip." She squeezed his hand, then veered away. "I'll catch up with you later. I'm going to ask Rosa to fetch Lucas and Dog to investigate."

When she strode off, Quin ambled toward Preston, who smiled tauntingly. "Oh, dear, you aren't planning to kill me, too, are you, Cahill?"

"For what? Being a lecherous ass?" Quin replied, flashing an identical smile. "I didn't think to ask the other night, Van Slyck. What were you doing in Deadwood, crawling to Leanna on your knees, begging her to give you another chance? She rejected you again, didn't she? As I recall, it didn't take her long the first time you came sniffing around to realize how worthless you are."

To Quin's amusement, Preston's face turned purple with rage. The color looked good on him.

"Go to hell, Cahill," he sneered viciously.

"Can't. It's *your* future address, Van Slyck. And why'd you kill that man on my property?"

"I didn't. If I wanted to kill someone I'd start with *you*," he snarled in a hateful tone.

Quin couldn't prove Preston had anything to do with the murder. But for certain, Preston was spiteful, vindictive, and he delighted in rubbing Quin's face in scandal every chance he got. Preston was a cheapjack, after all.

Adrianna was thrilled that Rosa offered Lucas and Dog's services to scout the site of the shooting. She was also greatly relieved that Quin had resisted pounding Preston flat and mailing him to the end of the earth.

The minute they returned to 4C, she ordered Quin to bed and, surprisingly, he didn't object. He teased her by saying, "I saw the way you worked over Hobbs so I don't dare argue with you."

Adrianna had to admit that she felt physically and emotionally wrung out herself. The past week of party planning, destructive fires, an unsolved murder and Quin's stint in jail had worn her out.

Leaving Butler in charge of whatever problems arose, Adrianna collapsed in Quin's former bedroom. Three hours later, she awoke to rake her tangled hair from her face. She sat up on the edge of the bed to work the tension from her neck and back, then expelled a heavy sigh. It was time to move home, she told herself sensibly. An extended stay at 4C would invite more gossip. Heaven knew there was too much of that floating around Ca-Cross!

Adrianna went downstairs to see Butler in the office, entering expenses from their ranch into his ledger. Bea was flitting around, dusting everything that didn't move. Elda was in the kitchen putting together a gourmet meal for supper.

Their last meal at 4C, she mused. She and her adopted family would leave in the morning. She would divide her time between overseeing her cattle and horse operation and checking to see what Lucas and Dog's search turned up. In addition, she was going to keep a watchful eye on her cowboys. She wanted to know who favored that brown gelding with three white stockings she had commandeered the night of the murder.

"Leaving?" Elda chirped after Adrianna made the announcement to go home. "But I like it here. There's more room and this kitchen is spacious so I don't bump into myself when I turn around. Plus, the cowhands are so kind and courteous that I prepare them snacks to take to the bunkhouse."

"You can stay if you prefer," Adrianna told the plump cook. "I'm sure Cahill would be delighted."

"I'd be delighted about what?"

Adrianna pivoted to see Cahill leaning against the doorjamb of the parlor. His clothing was wrinkled, his hair was mussed from sleep and a five-o'clock shadow that was two days old lined his jaw. Still, the sight of him squeezed at her heart and desire coiled deep inside her. It amazed her that she could look at this ruggedly handsome rancher and want him with every fiber of her being.

"I said you would prefer Elda remained behind when we leave tomorrow," she said belatedly.

His thick, dark brows furrowed. "You're leaving?"

She was pleased that he looked and sounded disappointed. She would feel ever so much better if he'd miss her half as much as she was going to miss being with him.

She sent her employees dismissive glances and they took their cues to grant her privacy. "We both know my staying here fuels gossip."

He scoffed caustically. "It won't matter, Boston. Gossip will claim we had a spat and you left me. I told you, it makes no difference what we do. Wagging tongues will put an unflattering spin on everything."

"Regardless, it's best for me to leave and we both know it," she said as she stared out the window, watching the hired hands tend their evening chores.

When he moved up behind her, his warm breath fanned her neck, leaving erotic fires burning in its wake. Adrianna closed her eyes and marshaled her failing willpower.

"Don't go, Boston," he murmured, then skimmed his lips over the column of her throat. "I like having you here."

For how long? she wondered. Until the demands of the ranch occupied all his time? Before he left on the spring cattle drive and never gave her another thought?

How long would it take him to forget his interest in her while he was on the trail, visiting cow towns where ladies of the evening entertained drovers and cowhands? She'd become a half-forgotten memory and she would be pining away for him like a brokenhearted fool.

"I can't stay," she replied, trying to ignore the reckless desire spiraling inside her.

He stepped away, and when she turned to face him, his expression was impersonal. "Whatever you want,

Boston. But before you go, I want to thank you for pressuring Hobbs to release me." He held out his hand. "And before I forget, I'll need that note you waved in the marshal's face this morning. It's all I have to prove I was lured to Phantom Springs."

Adrianna retrieved the note, then handed it to him. She pasted on a cheery smile. "You're welcome, Cahill. I enjoyed telling that stubborn, by-the-book marshal what was what."

"Good, I'll be sure to call on you next time I'm arrested."

"There will be a next time?" she asked flippantly.

"Sure, once you're arrested for murder you become everybody's favorite scapegoat and prime suspect."

"Supper is served," Butler announced formally, then took his leave in his usual stoic manner.

Cahill smiled dryly. "I still say your man of affairs enjoys acting like a stuffy butler. I think he missed his true calling."

"No, his calling is numbers, investments and balancing financial ledgers," she assured him on the way to the dining room. "It's a game he plays to keep others off guard and to amuse himself."

Just as Cahill amused himself temporarily—at her expense, she told herself. Cahill needed her to be his fast-talking champion this morning to spring him from jail, but any woman could satisfy him in bed. If he couldn't love Adrianna for who and what she was, then she didn't need him.

Men had wanted her for the wrong reasons all of her adult life. Quin Cahill was the only man she wanted to love her for all the right reasons. But if he couldn't voice the heartfelt words she ached to hear she wouldn't take the humiliating risk of baring her soul to him.

She had her new life in Texas and her unlimited independence, she consoled herself. It would have to be enough.

Chapter Twelve

Quin tossed, turned and cursed because he couldn't fall asleep. He knew it didn't have a damn thing to do with the long nap he'd had after he'd been released from jail.

She was leaving. The words took hold of his thoughts and twisted his heart out of shape. The only enjoyment he'd experienced the past two years was being with Boston. She'd touched off emotions he'd placed in cold storage after his traitorous family had walked out on him. Boston's quick wit and courage impressed him. She brightened his life and touched his soul. Not to mention that she set his body on fire in the heat of passion.

And she was leaving.

Scowling, Quin rolled off the bed in the master suite and stared out the window. He considered traipsing downstairs to pour himself a drink, but he knew that wouldn't appease him. What he wanted was sleeping in his former bedroom.

Admitting defeat, he wrapped a towel around his naked hips and headed for the door. He tiptoed down the hall to let himself into Boston's room. He inwardly groaned when a shaft of moonlight slanted across the bed, illuminating her curly dark hair and enchanting face.

"Cahill? Are you all right? Is your head hurting again?"

"No, just the rest of me," he murmured as he eased the door shut, locked it behind him, then went to stand over her.

"Is there something I can do to make you feel better?"

"Yes, you can give me *you*," he whispered as he eased down on the edge of the bed.

Her soft snicker turned his heart wrong side out. The touch of her hand on his bare chest made him burn with feverish desire in the space of a breath. And when she levered herself up to press her lush lips to his, Quin drowned in the heady sensations she never failed to arouse in him.

"I'm gonna miss you like crazy, Boston," he rumbled as he discarded the towel and stretched out beside her.

"But I'm here now," she whispered throatily. "We have tonight."

Yes, they did, Quin mused as he tunneled his hand beneath her silky nightgown. "One of Rosa's creations?" he mumbled against her parted lips.

"Of course. One of a kind."

"I'd like it even better if you weren't wearing it," he insisted as he drew the shimmering fabric over her head and tossed it in the same direction as the towel. "You look best wearing nothing but me...."

When he lowered his head to blaze a path of kisses down the slender curve of her throat to the beaded peaks of her breasts, she moaned softly. Quin loved that sound. He enjoyed pleasuring her and he ached to have her want him to the same mindless extreme that he wanted her.

When he teased her nipples with thumb and forefinger, he heard her breath catch and felt her body melt against him. A coil of heat scorched him as she brought his mouth back to hers. Her arms came around his neck and she kissed him as if the world was ending and they had only one breath left.

Quin swore his eyes had rolled back in his head and he was on the brink of passing out when her adventurous fingertips moved hither and yon, investigating the various textures of his flesh. He held his breath when her caresses descended across his belly, then stroked him from base to tip.

He lost the ability to breathe or think. He could do nothing more than feel the intense pleasure building with each unhurried caress of her hand. Pulsating awareness pelted him as she eased him onto his back, then hovered above him.

When she smiled down at him, her cedar-tree-green eyes sparkling in the shaft of moonlight, he marveled at her incredible beauty. He tried to conjure up the face of any other woman who compared to Boston's striking beauty and irrepressible spirit. No one came to mind. She mystified him. Knowing she wanted nothing more from him than another night of splendor they could provide for each other tormented him. He, who had been too busy managing the 4C alone, wanted Boston to need him to the same degree that he'd come to need her....

His thoughts fizzled out when her curly hair glided

over his laboring chest like a provocative caress. She skimmed her warm mouth over the length of his hard shaft and he groaned in unholy torment. When she took him into her mouth and measured him with her tongue and teeth Quin swore she was going to kill him with pleasure—and he wasn't going to protest.

His lungs practically collapsed when he tried to drag in a shaky breath. His heart hammered hard enough in his chest to crack ribs. She shattered his self-control and made him a willing slave to each lingering touch of her hands and lips—and he loved every minute of it.

Quin swore she had dragged him to the crumbling edge and he was on the verge of a mindless fall into rapturous oblivion. But then she pulled him back to seduce him again—one intimate kiss and caress at a time—and he moaned achingly.

It was unsettling to have one's emotions strung out like laundry on a clothesline for someone else to see. But Boston laid his body and soul bare and he suddenly didn't care about anything except being with her....

Indescribable sensations sizzled through him and a wild burst of pleasure crashed over him like a wave, towing him into an undercurrent of passion so wide and deep he couldn't find his way back to the surface.

"Enough," he croaked, surprised he could speak at all. "You're killing me, Boston. I need you…now."

She raised her head where she lay between his legs and smiled impishly. "You don't need me enough yet, Cahill."

When she glided her hands up and down his throbbing length, then nibbled at him again, Quin swore he was going to explode. He couldn't endure another moment of this intense pleasure without shattering in a million pieces. He rolled sideways, taking Boston to her back. Only then could he drag in a restorative breath and grasp the flying reins of his self-restraint.

"You are going to pay for that, vixen," he promised wickedly. "We'll see when enough is enough…."

Adrianna sorely wished she hadn't tormented Quin with erotic seduction because he turned it back upon her. Yet, she had been fascinated by the power she seemed to hold over him. She delighted in the husky sounds of his pleasure and savored the feel of his masculine body tensing, then melting, beneath her intimate touch.

Her thoughts scattered like ashes in a storm when Quin worked his way down her body one inch at a time. Each kiss, each caress, was an aphrodisiac that left her head spinning like a windmill and her body quivering with inexpressible sensations that burned her alive. Even when she swore she couldn't survive another moment of the fiery pleasure, her body cried out for more of the soul-shattering ecstasy bursting inside her.

Then he pressed his mouth against her in the most intimate of kisses and tasted her desire for him. Spasms of passion uncoiled inside her, consuming her very being. Desperate, she grabbed Quin by the hair and pulled him upward. She wrapped her hand around his rigid length and guided him exactly to her. Then she looked up to see those mercury-colored eyes shimmering in the moonlight and she knew she was gazing into the face of the man she loved. She must love him because the feeling of his powerful body surging into hers made her feel whole, alive and content.

He angled his ruffled head to kiss her as he plunged

deeper and Adrianna knew he had taken her body, heart and soul into his possession....

And she was going to leave him in the morning and pretend tonight was only about lust because that's the way Quin Cahill wanted it. The 4C came first and foremost and he indulged in passionate trysts when it was convenient.

"Adrianna—" Her name tumbled off his tongue in a husky drawl and she arched helplessly against him, giving all she was and demanding all he had to give.

He shuddered against her and she clamped her arms around his shoulders and her legs around his muscled hips. She held on tightly because her world was tumbling helter-skelter in incredible sensations. Pleasure burst inside her like fireworks on the Fourth of July and she nearly passed out from the overwhelming pleasure of it all.

Adrianna held him close until they could breathe normally again. She thought their first night together had been nothing short of phenomenal but tonight defied description. She wondered what it would be like to make love with him for the rest of her life....

When he pressed a gentle kiss to her cheek, then eased down beside her, she tossed aside her whimsical thoughts and snuggled up beside him. She knew he'd be gone by first light to keep up appearances in the household.

At least she had the rest of the night. Adrianna didn't care how much—or how little—sleep she got because she could catch up during the lonely nights ahead. With that in mind, she kissed Quin and let go of every inhibition. She showed him without words that she was helplessly, madly in love with him....

The next morning Quin was sitting at the dining table, sampling Elda's special-brewed coffee, when Boston ambled into the room. He wanted to draw her down on his lap and hold her possessively. Unfortunately, Elda whizzed through the door, carrying a stack of pancakes and bacon that made his mouth water. When she set the plates on the table, then turned away, Quin reached out impulsively to give Boston a pat on the derriere when she walked by.

She arched a brow and looked down at him, surprised.

No more surprised by that display than I am, thought Quin. He wasn't one for affectionate gestures, but with Boston, it was different. *He* was different....

And she was leaving him.... Gawd, he hated the thought.

"Did you sleep well, Boston?" he asked teasingly.

She peered at him over the rim of her coffee cup. "Well enough, I suppose." Her green eyes sparkled with playful mischief. "I don't recall that much about last night. I must have been tired after the long, hectic day."

He pulled a face and she snickered impishly. "How did you sleep, Cahill?"

"Not well. I woke up several times." He stared meaningfully at her while she hid her grin behind her cup.

"Really? What kept you up?"

She knew perfectly well that she had kept him up in every way imaginable. Not that he was complaining, mind you. She could disturb him every night the rest of his life if she were so inclined. Last night was the best night without sleep he'd ever had. He wanted to tell her so but Butler entered the room to cast him a frown and a knowing stare. Quin returned it full force. Butler couldn't lecture him without sounding like a hypocrite.

"I'm still planning on moving our belongings home this morning, but not until after we canvass Phantom Springs with Lucas and Dog," Boston informed Butler.

Butler's hazel eyes widened in surprise, then he resumed his expressionless stare. The man was a master at it. "We will be packed and ready, Addie K." He glanced at Quin. "I will need to remove several items from your safe before I go."

Quin nodded agreeably, then settled down to eat with his new family—who would be gone by noon. Aw, hell! He would be greeted again by deafening silence and he'd rattle around the oversize house like a ghost looking for his lost soul. Maybe he could borrow Dog for a companion, he mused.

After all, Lucas had a wife and Quin had none.

If that didn't work, he supposed he could try to lure Bea and Butler away since they were a matched set. Let Boston see how she liked being alone all the blessed time.

The sudden rap at the door brought Quin to his feet. He rounded the corner to the foyer to see Lucas Burnett, dressed in black as usual, and Dog standing on the stoop.

"Too early?" Burnett asked.

"Not if you want a stack of melt-in-your-mouth pancakes."

Burnett grinned in anticipation. "I hear Elda is a gourmet cook. I suppose I should see for myself."

Dog followed Burnett inside and Quin looked at Dog and said, "What? No bow tie this morning?"

"Not while he's working," Burnett replied, straight-faced.

Quin reached down to pat the oversize animal. "I'll trade Dog for flapjacks and a dozen head of my best longhorns."

"No deal," said Burnett.

"Boston is leaving and I'm stuck with my own company."

Burnett shot Quin a pensive glance on his way through the door. Quin glanced down to note the wolf dog had plopped down in the opening to the dining room, as if he owned the place. He rested his oversize head on his oversize paws.

"There, you see? Dog has made himself at home already."

"The answer is still no. Get your own wife and dog," Burnett said. "I'm not sharing either one."

Quin sighed in frustration and resumed his seat at the table. "Thanks for nothing, Burnett."

"I'm here to track and scout, Cahill. That's all the help you get," he said, then grinned before he dived into the tasty pancakes.

Amazed and impressed, Adrianna watched Lucas and Quin move methodically around the site where the dead man had collapsed. They expanded the perimeters, looking for footprints and evidence of the three outlaws that had been at the scene.

Lucas squatted down on his haunches, his midnight-black eyes focused on the set of horse prints that were barely visible in the loose rock. "Someone wiped the area clean," he concluded. "Except for this overlooked partial print."

"The same way the wagon wreck site might have been wiped clean, so as not to arouse suspicion," Quin murmured contemplatively. He picked up a broken branch that was thick with leaves. "This is likely the makeshift broom they used."

When Dog appeared on the rocky ledge above, and then barked, the threesome hiked uphill to see another boot print they had overlooked.

"I wonder if this thug was the gang's lookout," Quin mused aloud. "He had the best view of the area from here."

Lucas nodded his raven head. "He was probably the sharpshooter, in case you caused more trouble than anticipated."

Adrianna shivered, unnerved by the possibility that Cahill might have been gunned down if he had been able to identify his assailant.

"We'll follow the sparse tracks to see if all three lead to town or to a nearby ranch," Lucas suggested as he sidestepped downhill. "These outlaws are holed up somewhere."

Adrianna pulled the watch from her pocket to check the time. "Blast it, I need to leave. I promised to be back before noon."

She glanced at Quin, whose closed, controlled expression revealed none of his feelings. Adrianna tried her best to mimic his expression. "Thank you for helping us,

Lucas," she said when he halted beside her. She pushed up on tiptoe to press a kiss to his bronzed cheek.

"You're welcome, but we're a long way from identifying or locating these outlaws," Lucas reminded her.

"If we can prove Cahill was a *victim,* not the shooter, we will be moving in the right direction." She zigzagged around the boulders to reach her horse. "Cahill doesn't look good in jail. The iron bars clash with his complexion."

Leaving both men chuckling, she trotted Buckshot through the trees and across the meadow to reach the house. As expected, Bea, Butler and Elda waited beside the loaded buggy. Butler had already tossed Adrianna's carpetbag beneath the seat and he was ready to roll.

"Find anything useful?" Butler asked as he boosted Bea and Elda onto the two-seated carriage.

"Afraid we didn't find much," Adrianna grumbled. "Lucas and Cahill are trying to pick up a trail leading away from the site, but most of the area was brushed clean."

"Confounded thugs were thorough," Bea muttered as she settled her calico skirts around her. "Who would have thought you could expect exceptional housecleaning skills from a band of murdering thieves?"

Adrianna thought about that for a long moment. The more she contemplated, the more she believed the men involved in the murder had also been on hand to remove evidence and tracks from the wagon wreck that killed Quin's parents. There were several similarities. Maybe this wasn't just a devious attempt to extort money from Cahill as she first thought.

She frowned, befuddled. So why had the bandits

decided to extort money and bring up incriminating information two years after the fact? Or had *one* gang member taken it upon himself to contact Cahill. Maybe his cohorts discovered his plot to make extra money for himself and disposed of him.

Adrianna scowled, frustrated with the chaos Cahill faced. She wanted answers, just as Cahill did. *Someone* around here had to know *something*. At least one of the three other men had to have seen what happened to the dead man. And what, if anything, had the dead man known about the wagon wreck? Adrianna wanted Quin to know the truth. It wouldn't bring back his parents and he might not be able to reconcile with Bowie, Chance and Leanna, but still...

Her thoughts scattered as the carriage passed the small pasture north of the 4C bunkhouse. Adrianna snapped to attention. She recognized the second horse—the strawberry roan—tied to the hitching post the night she borrowed the brown gelding with three white stockings to follow Cahill to Phantom Springs.

"Go ahead without me," she instructed her companions as she reined Buckshot north. "There's something I need to check before I meet you at home."

Butler eyed her apprehensively. "This isn't going to turn out like the Phantom Springs incident, is it?"

She flashed her best smile. "No, don't fret. I'll be home in time for supper."

"You'd better be," Butler said, then gave her a look that said, *Or else...*

The dear man was more protective of her than her own father!

When the threesome drove away, Adrianna trotted

her dapple-gray gelding to the bunkhouse where only one horse waited at the hitching post.

"Yoo-hoo!" she called out as she poked her head around the partially opened door.

The red-haired, freckle-faced cowboy—who looked to be three or four years older—smiled a greeting as he stuffed clothing into a dingy canvas knapsack. "Can I help you, Miz McKnight?"

Adrianna strode forward to extend her hand. "We haven't met formally but I've seen you around the 4C."

"I'm Otha Hadley," the bowlegged cowboy introduced.

"Are you leaving the ranch and looking for another job?" she asked curiously.

"No, ma'am. I'm getting married this weekend." His smile was so wide it affected every feature of his face. "Cahill told me if Zoe Daniels accepted my proposal I could rent the abandoned cabin on the north range and fix it up in my spare time. I'm just moving up there to spiffy it up and keep watch on 4C cattle."

"Congratulations, Otha." She discreetly surveyed the bunkhouse lined with beds that had wooden trunks for footboards. "That was generous of Cahill."

"Yes, ma'am. He's always been fair and good to me."

Adrianna sincerely hoped she hadn't misjudged the cowboy. So much was going on around here that she still wasn't sure whom she could trust. "I was wondering if you could tell me which ranch hand favors that strawberry roan gelding I noticed in your corral."

Otha set aside his knapsack and strode to the window. "That's Ezra Fields's main mount," he reported, then frowned. "Why'd you ask?"

Adrianna shrugged nonchalantly. "I saw it some-where that seemed out of place." She watched Otha intently as he shifted uneasily, then returned to his bunk to gather his clothes.

"Something's wrong. What is it?" she demanded as she followed on his heels. "If you are as loyal to Cahill as you say you are, then I need to know what's troubling you, Otha. Cahill was set up for murder. I want to know who is responsible."

Otha avoided her direct stare and neatly folded his well-patched shirt. "Well, I don't like to speak ill of folks, even ones who speak ill of others."

"Speak ill of whom? Cahill?" she questioned, con-fused.

He paused from his chore to glance at the door to make sure no one was listening. "No, Ezra is always in Cahill's ear, speaking ill of *you*. He seems suspicious of everything you do and makes everything out to be bad. 'Course, no one was happy when Rock went to work for you, but Ezra keeps talking about how you are stealing cattle and setting prairie fires to undermine 4C."

Adrianna's eyes widened in surprise. So that's why Cahill had been so wary, just as she had been wary of him because…Chester Purvis had been casting asper-sions about Cahill to *her* and Chester mentioned that supposed curse every other day.

Blast it, were those two cowboys from opposite sides of the adjoining fence in cahoots? Had they been involved in the extortion scheme that ended in murder? Had they set the fire that destroyed the new addition to her house?

"You okay, Miz McKnight?" the red-haired cowboy asked.

"I'm not sure." She glanced around the bunkhouse. "Which bunk does Ezra Fields use?"

Otha shifted uneasily. "We got a pact about not messing with another man's stuff," he said, but he pointed left.

"You didn't see this," she insisted as she made a beeline for the bunk by the door—and more specifically the trunk at the end of the bed.

She halted to lock the door, then pulled a few banknotes from the pocket of her breeches. "Consider this a wedding gift, not a bribe for silence, Otha. I need your cooperation."

He nodded somberly and refused the money, until she crammed it in his knapsack. Then she lurched around to open Ezra's trunk. The faint whiff of kerosene rose from the rolled-up garments. Anger roiled inside her as she dug to the bottom of the trunk to pluck up a pair of stained breeches.

No doubt, Ezra Fields had slopped kerosene on his clothes while starting a fire—the fire that torched her new addition. She also had the sneaking suspicion that her employee, Chester Purvis, was the one who favored the brown horse with white stockings that she had commandeered. She presumed Ches had helped Ezra ignite the fire.

A thorough inspection of Ezra's trunk didn't turn up Cahill's stolen money from Phantom Springs, but it confirmed her suspicions about Ezra's lack of loyalty. Adrianna silently fumed, certain the double-crossing cowboys were likely involved in rustling as well as arson. She wouldn't be surprised to learn they were involved in murder, as well.

Adrianna rolled up the kerosene-splattered breeches and headed for the door. "Not one word about this, Otha," she ordered, staring him down like a gunfighter at twenty paces.

"No, ma'am," he promised.

She unlocked the door, then studied the freckle-faced, bowlegged cowboy for a long intense moment. She decided she could trust him. He had too much at stake—like a good-paying job and a rented cabin to begin his married life.

Adrianna hurried outside to tuck the breeches in her saddlebag before passersby noticed. Then she hightailed it to her own bunkhouse to confirm her suspicions about Chester Purvis. He had tried to keep her at odds with Cahill and had to be involved in this devious scheme, she predicted angrily. But he wasn't going to get away with it!

Quin blew out an agitated breath when the set of tracks he and Burnett had followed for an hour disappeared into the trampled dust and dozens of other tracks on the road leading to and from Ca-Cross.

"Wild-goose chase," Burnett mumbled, voicing Quin's disgruntled thoughts aloud.

"No way of telling if the outlaws met up later or took their cuts of the money and split up until things cooled down," Quin muttered. "Worse, I don't have a description of those ruffians."

"Sorry Dog and I weren't more help." Burnett reined his Appaloosa gelding named Drizzle toward town. "Let me know if something turns up and we'll work the case together."

Quin watched his friend and Dog trot off, then he reversed direction to head home...to an empty house and deafening silence. The discouraging thought did nothing to improve his glum mood. He'd hit a dead end trying to exonerate himself. He still didn't know if his parents' deaths were a hapless accident or the result of a robbery gone bad.

And Boston had gone home... Damn it, he missed her already.

Despite the past few rotten days, his mood improved when he reached headquarters an hour later to see Boston's favorite horse tethered near his front door. Nothing would make him happier than to have her show up with an excuse to spend another night.

When he sailed through the door, she was waiting in the foyer. Impulsively, he picked her up off the floor and kissed the breath out of her.

"Mmm...I'm glad to see you, too, Cahill," she whispered as she hooked her legs around his hips, then offered him a kiss as hungry and urgent as the one he'd planted on her lips. Then she unwrapped her legs and put her feet on the floor. "But we have a problem."

"Seems like we've had a lot of those lately. Are you referring to one specifically or all of them collectively?"

He frowned warily when she retrieved a gunnysack sitting beside the coatrack near the door. She reached inside to display two pairs of breeches that smelled like kerosene.

"Where'd you find those?" he muttered, outraged. "They sure as hell aren't mine. You know I didn't—"

"I know," she cut in quickly. "One pair belongs to your man Ezra Fields. I had Otha point out his trunk so I could check his gear. By the way, that was a nice thing you did for Otha, letting him rent the cabin so he and his intended bride would have a place to call home."

"Yes, well, I didn't know if his sweetheart at the dance hall was toying with him to get him to buy her gifts or if she was sincere. I'm glad she cares about Otha." He waited a beat, then said, "What about Ezra and kerosene?"

"I remembered seeing two horses at your bunkhouse and I borrowed one to follow you to Phantom Springs," she reminded him. "I thought it strange when I realized one horse belonged at 4C and the other saddle horse came from my ranch."

Quin jerked up his head and frowned. "It isn't Rocky, is it? Damn him!"

"No, it's Chester Purvis. I found a pair of stained breeches in his trunk, too."

Quin swore foully. "So they are working together."

"They have been badmouthing each of us to keep our personal feud alive, as well as spreading speculations about that ridiculous curse," she replied. "I'm willing to bet they are involved in rustling and extortion, as well."

"Damn it to hell!" Quin roared.

"I think we should shoot them and be done with them," Boston said vindictively. "It makes me furious when I recall how much frustration they have caused by stealing our cattle, talking behind our backs and setting fires."

Quin grabbed the second pair of breeches and stuffed them in the gunnysack. "I think I'll save the shooting until later. I'll be waiting to see if those sneaky bastards join up after dark to swipe more cattle. I still haven't found the dozen calves stolen this week."

"I'm going with you," she volunteered.

"No, you are *not*," he said vehemently.

Quin knew the moment the words were out of his mouth that he'd wasted his breath. Boston flashed that fiery green glower he recognized at a glance. It offended her when he spouted orders. Every damn time. You'd think he'd have learned by now.

Her perfectly arched brow elevated to a challenging angle. "This involves me, my scorched house and my turncoat cowhand. *I'm* going. *You* are welcome to come with *me*."

"Thanks," he said caustically. "I was about to suggest the same thing myself."

She smirked, then winked. "You're learning, Cahill. You're not as bad as I first thought. In fact, I'm actually beginning to like you."

She preceded him out of the door to ride home for supper, as she had promised Butler. Quin watched the seductive sway of her curvaceous hips and sighed in defeat. He was crazy about Boston. He admired her spirit, her intellect and her keen wit. Not to mention her mesmerizing green eyes and enticing body that aroused him to the extreme. He also liked that she stood up to him, for him. She was a challenge he loved to face.

He wondered how much more she'd have to *like* him for her to move back to his big, lonely, quiet house and bring her adopted family with her.

She'd have to *love* him, he decided. Considering her mistrust of men and their ulterior motives, he doubted she'd allow herself to care that much for him or any other man.

Didn't it figure that of all the women who were eager to share his name and his fortune, he desired a woman who didn't want to marry him, even if he got down on bended knee and begged?

He'd laugh at the irony but it just wasn't that damn funny.

Chapter Thirteen

Adrianna's gaze narrowed in annoyance when she saw Ezra Fields, carrying an unlit torch, scuttle from Quin's bunkhouse after dark. He dashed around the corner like the rat he was. Beside her, Cahill muttered a creative string of obscenities when Ezra skulked into the barn. He returned a few minutes later, leading the strawberry roan that had disappeared from the pasture shortly after supper.

"What do you suppose tonight's excursion entails?" she murmured as she and Quin sat atop their horses, watching Ezra's discreet departure from 4C headquarters.

"He isn't carrying a can of kerosene," Quin whispered back. "My guess is our cattle will go missing tonight."

Adrianna reined behind the calving shed when Ezra glanced every which way to make sure no one saw him leave the premises. As expected, he lit the torch, then headed for the adjoining gate between the 4C and McKnight Ranch.

"Bastards," Quin growled when Chester Purvis, riding the brown horse with white stockings, appeared in the moonlight. He also lit a torch as he approached. "Here." Cahill handed Adrianna his spare Colt .45 but she shook her head.

"I have one of my own."

"I hope you know how to use it, Boston, and I hope you won't have to. It's not too late for you to go home."

"And let you have all the fun? Why do you think I came to Texas? It's not to sit at home in the parlor and crochet doilies."

"Well, don't get shot," he cautioned. "You won't have any fun if you're bleeding all over yourself."

"Your concern is touching," she mocked lightly. "I get all quivery inside, thinking how much you care."

He mumbled something under his breath, then took off, following the tree-lined stream that eventually became Triple Creek—the main water source for her ranch and his.

Adrianna swore softly when she saw Ches grab fence cutters from his saddlebag. Methodically, he clipped the wires as if he'd done it countless times—and chances were, he had. The two rustlers trotted off to sort out a dozen head of Cahill steers, then sent them through the opening in the fence. Then they herded a dozen longhorns that Adrianna planned to send up the trail to Dodge City in a few weeks.

She nudged Buckshot, determined to catch the thieves red-handed but Cahill grabbed her reins, bringing the gray gelding to an abrupt halt.

"Not yet. Let's see if anyone else is involved and where they're taking the cattle for safekeeping."

Adrianna chastised herself for jumping the gun. Quin was right. They needed to know if a third cowboy was waiting at another site to herd the cattle away from the two ranches or if they would pen them in a makeshift corral.

A half-hour later, the two rustlers veered toward an isolated, dead-end ravine on McKnight property. Adrianna glanced around but she didn't see another rider waiting to join Chester and Ezra.

"Well, I'll be damned," Cahill muttered sourly.

Adrianna glanced in the direction he pointed to see the men ride up to a rock ledge halfway up the hill. They picked up a note, then divided up the money waiting for them.

"What the devil is going on?" Adrianna murmured as the men pocketed the money, then rode downhill.

"Stay here, Boston," he whispered. "If gunfire breaks out and you start shooting, try not to hit me."

She waited in a grove of trees east of the ravine, despite the urge to join Cahill while he confronted those low-down, double-crossing rustlers who pretended loyalty to the 4C and McKnight Ranch. But she supposed Cahill was right. She was the element of surprise—if he needed reinforcements. But he had better not get himself shot, either, or she'd never forgive him!

With both pistols drawn, Cahill made his presence known to the thieves. When they tried to grab their pistols, Cahill growled threateningly. "Toss 'em in the dirt. *Now.*"

Ezra defied him and went for his weapon but Cahill

shot his gun hand, then hit the cartwheeling pistol in midair, making it dance sideways before it hit the ground.

"Try it again, Ez, and I'll take you in, jackknifed over your saddle. Your choice."

Adrianna decided right there and then that Cahill had gone easy on her during their previous confrontations. The man possessed amazing shooting skills and he could sound unnervingly vicious and deadly when he felt the need. In the scant moonlight and flickering torchlight, she could see Ez's and Chester's Adam's apples bobbing apprehensively.

Good, she thought, they deserved to be scared half to death after all the rotten things they had done.

When Chester tossed aside his weapon, Cahill pointed at the torches. "Drop those in the dirt." When they did as ordered, he called out to her—without taking his eyes off his captives. "There's a rope in my saddlebags, Boston. Let's tie them up and retrieve their discarded weapons."

Both men jerked up their heads when Adrianna appeared from the shadows of the trees. She didn't display her pistol or the dagger she kept tucked in her boot for desperate occasions. Those weapons were her aces in the hole.

Without a word, she reached into the leather pouches to retrieve ropes, noting the extensive length of each. She wondered if Cahill had planned it that way.

"It's a long walk in the dark but the fresh air will do you both good," Cahill remarked.

She approached the men on horseback, then demanded, "Get down, and do it carefully. Just so you know, I voted to shoot you both and be done with it, but Cahill decided to let you live...*if* you behaved." She tossed Cahill a quick glance. "I still vote to shoot 'em dead and bury 'em with their boots on. Either that or use the ropes to hang 'em high. I haven't attended a lynching yet. This will be my first."

"We'll see how it goes, Boston. For now, tie their wrists, then wrap the rope around their waists...in case I feel the need to drag them behind the horses until they tell us what we want to know."

Their Adam's apples bobbed again and she could see the whites of their eyes in the moonlight. Clearly, they didn't put the threat past Cahill. "I've heard of the tactic, but I've never seen it," she commented offhandedly as she wrapped Ezra's wrists—thrice—then encircled his hips with rope. "Is it true that you can drag a man's skin off his bones when his horse is racing at full gallop?"

"It is," Cahill confirmed grimly. "I've seen it happen accidentally during cattle drives. A cowboy can fall off and get his foot stuck in the stirrup. He can be pretty torn up by the time you stop his horse and prop him upright."

Ezra and Chester glanced uneasily at each other while Adrianna bound Chester in a similar fashion, then tied the ropes to the pommels of their saddles. When she swatted both horses on the rumps, the men gasped, then stumbled forward in an attempt to maintain their balance.

Adrianna stepped up behind Ezra to fish into the back pocket of his breeches. She retrieved the note and the money. Then she confiscated Chester's money on her way to pluck up the discarded pistols. There wasn't enough light to read the note so she tucked it, and the money, in the pocket of her jacket before she mounted Buckshot.

"Now then," Cahill said ominously, "whose idea was it to torch Boston's house?"

"We don't know," Chester muttered as he jogged to keep up with his trotting horse.

Cahill didn't give them a second warning, just eased up to swat both horses, forcing the captives into a dead run to keep up. When Ezra tripped and fell, he yelped while his horse dragged him across the rocky, uneven terrain.

"Who is giving you orders?" Cahill snarled.

"We don't know. God's truth!" Chester howled, then stumbled and bumped along, his chin bouncing on the ground.

Adrianna watched unsympathetically as the rustlers skidded across the ground. They were a long way from having their hides peeled off but to hear the cowardly bastards wail and yelp you'd swear they had been skinned alive.

"Let's try this again," Cahill barked harshly. "Who is paying you to rustle cattle, cut fences and set fires?"

"We don't know, I tell you!" Ches shrieked as he tried—and failed—to bolt to his feet.

"The same person who killed one of your partners at Phantom Springs and set me up to take the blame for murder?" Cahill snarled.

"What? Hell, no!" Ezra panted. "We don't know nothing about that. We were paid to steal cattle, set fires and keep you and Miz McKnight at odds and that's all!"

Cahill growled like an enraged grizzly, then sent the horses into a faster clip. *"Who...hired...you?"* he demanded.

"We don't know, I swear," Ezra gasped as his horse dragged him across the ground. "Somebody left notes and money in our trunks and told us to contact each other over a year ago. Now we receive our instructions and payments at the rock ledge."

"Why did you kill your partners? What do you know about Ruby and Earl's wagon wreck?" Adrianna interrogated sharply.

"Nothing!" Chester railed, then yelped in pain. "We had nothing to do with that. Just rustling and fires."

"How long have these men been cowhands?" she asked Cahill.

"About two years, give or take," he replied.

"Long enough to be involved in the wagon wreck at Ghost Canyon," she decided.

"What? No! I told you we don't know nothing about that," Ches denied frantically. "Nobody said nothing to us about a wagon accident. I *swear.*"

Quin was beginning to believe the men. Which was even more troubling. It suggested that whoever was stealing from 4C and McKnight Ranch, as well as others in the area, were not necessarily involved in the robbery plot and wagon wreck that had claimed his parents' lives.

Damn it to hell! He might never know the truth. He couldn't locate or identify the three men who rode off that night from Phantom Springs, even when Burnett and Dog helped him follow the outlaws' tracks.

Well, at least one thing went right tonight, he mused

as he halted the two horses and allowed his captives to mount up. Boston had gone along without suffering a scratch. That was a gigantic relief.

He glanced at her, watching moonbeams bathe her elegant features in light and shadows. He couldn't imagine why any man wouldn't appreciate her fiery spirit and courage, rather than seeing her as a meal ticket that could make his life comfortable.

There was so much more to Boston than her wealth and outer beauty. She had a strong sense of self and she was teeming with irrepressible intelligence. She knew who she was and what she wanted, as he did. He couldn't fault her for that.

"Something wrong, Cahill?"

He snapped to attention when she caught him staring at her. "No. Just thinking." But he didn't tell her about what.

"Me, too," she said pensively. "Should we take these two men to jail or lock them in the smokehouse for the night?"

"I've seen more of Marshal Hobbs than I care to recently," Quin mumbled. "These two men can spend the night in the shack, nursing their wounds. Tomorrow is soon enough to haul them to town and press charges."

An hour later, Quin had the captives bound and tied in the shack. When he exited to lock the door, Boston was waiting for him. The reins to her horse dangled from her fingertips.

"I suppose Butler and Company are fretting about where you are," he remarked as they walked uphill to the house.

"No, I told them I'd be gone awhile and you would be assisting me in solving the mystery about the rustling."

"Yeah?" He smiled wryly. "But Butler fusses over you. How long before he sends out a search party?"

Boston returned his grin. "I have a couple of hours to spare," she assured him.

Quin took the reins and tethered both horses near the front door. The moment he shut the door behind them he scooped Boston off the floor and headed up the steps. She didn't object when he took her to the master suite—and showed her how grateful he was for her help in capturing Ezra and Chester....

"Well? Did your evening adventure come to a satisfying conclusion, Addie K.?"

Adrianna glanced up the staircase in her home to see Butler looking as casual as she'd ever seen him. His white shirt hung outside his black breeches and he was in his stocking feet. She didn't tell him that her evening had come to a fiery, explosive encounter in Cahill's bed. That was intimate and private information she wasn't about to share with anyone. Besides, Butler was referring to her attempt to track down the rustlers and arsonists.

"Yes, as a matter of fact," she confided as she climbed the steps. "One of my cowhands and one of Cahill's has been plotting against us and we intercepted a note with orders to set a fire at one of Cahill's line shacks this week."

"Did you haul the scoundrels to jail?" Butler asked hopefully.

"No, they are spending the night in Cahill's smokehouse, awaiting transport to jail in the morning."

"Good." Butler breathed an audible sigh of relief, then sidestepped to let Adrianna pass. "Now that we have that settled and out of the way, the marshal can interrogate the perpetrators concerning their roles in the Phantom Springs murder...and Beatrice and I want to get married this weekend," he said in the same breath.

Adrianna didn't correct his assumption that she and Cahill had established a connection between the rustlers and the recent murder. She didn't want to spoil his grand announcement.

"That's wonderful!" she enthused. "I'll plan a par—"

"No," Butler cut in. "We prefer a private ceremony without fanfare to begin our new life together in Texas."

"I'm giving you and Bea full use of this house," she said generously.

His hazel eyes nearly popped out of his head. "That is too kind, Addie K. Besides, where will you and Elda live?"

She shrugged nonchalantly. "I can build another house instead of restarting the new addition. As for Elda, she seems happy working for Cahill."

He clutched her arm when she started past him. "Cahill hasn't asked for your hand?"

"No, why should he? He doesn't need mine since he has two hands of his own," she teased.

Butler didn't smile, just watched her intently. "Would you marry him if he asked?"

Adrianna didn't want to have this discussion. It was bad enough that she'd fallen head over heels in love with Cahill. The prospect of admitting her feelings aloud to him terrified her. She suspected Cahill's affection for her only lasted until they lay exhausted and content in bed.

"I don't know, Hiram," she said, then cast him a pointed glance. "Maybe in ten years. That seems to be the proper length of time for a courtship, don't you think?"

While he grumbled at her sassy retort, she strode to her room. That should keep him quiet, she mused as she undressed. Furthermore, she didn't have time to fret over the unrequited love she harbored for that silver-eyed rancher. They were in the midst of their private investigation to determine if his parents' wagon wreck was or wasn't a robbery turned disaster.

At least Cahill had included her in the search for the truth so she could spend more time with him. For now, it would be enough, she told herself before she fell asleep—with dreams of Quin's incredible passion dancing in her head.

Bright and early the next morning Adrianna rode to 4C to accompany Cahill and their prisoners to town. "I can't wait to pass along the information about these two thugs using the supposed curse as a cover to rustle and set fires," she said confidentially.

"I'm wondering if we should also let it slip that these two scoundrels *might be* involved in the murder. Whoever is responsible might become careless if someone else is blamed."

"Maybe," she said thoughtfully. "But we don't want to give Marshal Hobbs an excuse not to search out the killer and his conspirators."

Cahill shrugged his broad shoulders, then glanced back to ensure Chester and Ezra were still bound tightly and weren't plotting an escape. "I keep wondering if these two incidents are somehow connected, but I can't put it together." He blew out an exasperated breath. "It's pure torture, not knowing if my parents' accident was caused by a robbery. My chance of finding out might have died with the unidentified man at Phantom Springs."

Adrianna reached over to give his muscled forearm a sympathetic squeeze. "I know it must be maddening. Maybe you should contact your brothers and sister and let them know the possibility exists—"

"No," he interrupted quickly and decisively. "My family moved on with their lives. Until I'm certain whether it was an accident or disastrous robbery, I'm not dragging them into it. I sure as hell don't want them to think I used this as an excuse to bring them home."

He sounded so intense and determined that she decided not to debate with him. Obviously, the resentments and conflicts between siblings still existed. Cahill was too proud and stubborn to ask for help. He'd asked for assistance with the ranch duties after the funeral, only to watch his family ride off to chase their own rainbows.

As she had chased hers by coming to Texas. She cast him a pensive glance. Did he secretly hold that against *her,* too?

Adrianna stared into the distance, hearing the whistle announcing the morning train's arrival at Ca-Cross. She recalled the first time she'd stepped down from the passenger car to view the town. She'd been full of anticipation, excitement and dreams of making a place for herself as a successful lady rancher.

Thus far, all she'd done was embroil herself in a private feud with Cahill, become the victim of rustling and arson, add fodder for local gossip…and fallen in love for the first—and likely the only—time in her life.

She studied Cahill's ruggedly handsome face that sported a day's growth of stubble, remembering how his mercury-colored eyes could shimmer with passion or flash with temper. She smiled to herself and thought it was better to get her heart broken by a brawny cowboy than to be in Boston, countering the schemes of gold diggers who saw her as the key to unlocking her family fortune for them.

"What are you smiling about, Boston?" Cahill asked.

"Just wondering what adventure awaits me next," she lied convincingly. "I've been here about six weeks and my life is brimming with excitement and mystery. Those dime novels about the Wild West have become *my* life. I have no complaints."

"That's Texas for you. Never a dull moment." He winked at her. "As for me, I'd die of boredom in a place like Boston."

"I *did*," she replied, and grinned impishly. "I'm feeling much better now."

Although Quin tried to persuade Boston to chitchat with her cousin at the boutique while he incarcerated the prisoners, there was nothing doing. According to Boston, she had discovered the connection between Ezra Fields and Chester Purvis so Marshal Hobbs could deal with her, like it or not.

Which Hobbs didn't because he seemed to have an aversion to headstrong women like Boston who were quick of wit and sassy of retorts. Hobbs, like so many backward-thinking males—in the East and West—thought women should stay in their places.

Quin almost chuckled, remembering how he'd made the foolish mistake of telling Boston to go home…and stay there. Now, the thought of her living a few miles away from his ranch, while he was stuck home alone, was pure and simple torment. He'd be miserable if she moved back to her hometown.

Quin cast aside his meandering thoughts as he untied Ezra and Chester. He quick-marched them into the marshal's office. As usual, Tobias Hobbs wore his stylish three-piece suit and his bowler hat hung by the door. Hobbs raised a curious brow when he noticed the prisoners' scuffed-up condition.

"Now what?" he muttered. "You taking the law into your own hands and bringing along your sidekick?"

Quin wondered if Hobbs would ever learn to keep his mouth shut. He couldn't have riled Boston more if he tried.

"For your information, Hobbs, I did my own detective work and uncovered the plot of rustling and arson."

Quin smiled to himself, knowing she still was hassling Hobbs to take the pressure off him because he'd been a murder suspect. He also thought she enjoyed her role as agitator.

"You?" Hobbs's dark brows shot up his forehead to collide with his hairline. His startled gaze bounced between Boston and the prisoners.

"Furthermore," she added in her crisp Eastern accent,

"I have evidence to prove these two men purposely set fire to my home and I will be turning the evidence over to the court myself."

He jerked upright in his chair. "Are you suggesting—?"

"I'm suggesting," she cut in sharply, "that I am handing over evidence directly to the judge. These two men admitted they were hired to keep the story about a supposed curse alive as a diversion while they rustled on and burned my ranch and the 4C, and *I* will admit the evidence in court."

Hobbs glanced at the criminals, then turned his attention to Quin. "Apparently, you dragged the information out of them. There are laws against vigilante justice."

"After the sloppy way you handled the murder case, I'm not certain of your ability to enforce any laws," she countered caustically.

Ah, how Quin loved to watch this firebrand in action. She was indeed at home and thriving in the wide-open ranges of Texas. Hobbs was getting huffy but he deserved her harassment…which reminded Quin…

"Perhaps we have solved the murder for you, too," he insisted as he herded the captives to the cells.

Hobbs stopped being annoyed with Boston long enough to toss Quin a surprised glance. "You think they tried to extort money and set you up for murder, too?"

"We did no such thing," Chester protested loudly. "Okay, so we were hired to prey on Cahill and the woman but we didn't know who set it up. We were contacted by anonymous notes from the very beginning. And that's the truth!"

"Sound familiar? Anonymous note?" Quin prompted the marshal. "I, for one, would like to see the face behind these mysterious directives, wouldn't you?"

Grumbling, Hobbs surged to his feet to lock the captives in their cells, then he wheeled around to fetch the necessary forms from his desk.

"You can file formal charges, Cahill. I'll ask around town again to see if anyone can identify the dead man."

He glanced toward the prisoners, who had plunked onto their cots. "Did they give up a name and save me the trouble of looking?"

"No," Quin replied. "Would you admit to involvement with a dead man until you gained clemency?"

Hobbs pensively stroked his mustache with his forefinger. "No, I suppose not."

While Quin filed criminal charges, Boston breezed past Hobbs. "Unless you need my statement I'll be in Rosa's shop."

Hobbs frowned and scowled. "No, you can go… *please.*"

She flashed an ornery grin and said, "Are you glad you met me yet, Marshal?"

"Elated," he muttered caustically. When she shut the door behind her, Hobbs turned to Quin. "It is beyond me how you put up with the mouth on that feisty female."

Quin bowed his head over the form he was filling out and swallowed a grin. He loved Boston's lush mouth. Hobbs had no idea what he was missing.

Adrianna gave Rosa the boiled-down version of the capture of the men responsible for the rustling and arson. Rosa stared at her in amazement.

"You think you've put a stop to local thieving? That's marvelous! Did those scoundrels confess to silencing their partner and extorting money at Phantom Springs?"

"No," Adrianna grumbled. "But I wouldn't be dismayed if word spread the men might be involved in murder."

Rosa nodded comprehendingly. "I'm not one to spread gossip to my clients but I'll make an exception to clear Quin's name."

"Thank you. Cahill has enough problems trying to figure out if his parents made a careless mistake on the curve of the road or if they were trying to avoid a robbery and crashed at high speed at Ghost Canyon."

"I imagine that *not knowing* disturbs Quin greatly." Rosa shot her a pointed glance. "Fortunately, you are close by to console and support him."

"We moved out yesterday," Adrianna reported.

"Did you?" Rosa busied herself by selecting a bolt of fabric for one of her new creations. "A pity. I thought you and Quin made an interesting couple."

Adrianna smirked. "You mean we *deserve* each other? He's hardheaded and outspoken and I'm a hoyden at heart."

Rosa glanced over her shoulder and said, "You know what I'm asking, Addie K. What are your feelings for Quin?"

"Oh, by the way," Adrianna said, avoiding the topic and the direct stare, "Hiram and Beatrice plan to marry. I'm letting them use my house. I wonder if I might take your offer to camp out in your apartment until I can build a home for myself."

"You and Elda?" she questioned curiously.

"Elda delights in working for Cahill. He's in love with her gourmet cooking." *But not with me,* she tacked on silently.

"You can use the apartment as much as you want because I've been closing up early and riding home before dark," Rosa informed her. "Besides, we should be in our new house soon."

"Thanks, Cuz, now that we have the robberies and fires under control, perhaps I'll have more free time to visit you and Lucas. Also, I'd like to purchase some of his colts."

"I'm sure he's agreeable. We'll schedule an evening visit next week…and you can bring Quin."

"I don't need a matchmaker," she complained as Rosa toted the bolt of fabric to the workroom.

"Luckily, you get a matchmaker and dress designer all rolled into one," she said cheerily, then winked. "Have a nice day, Addie K."

Chapter Fourteen

After concluding business in town, Adrianna headed home. She had several duties to tend to before she circled back to the 4C to meet Cahill. He had taken Rocky with him to recover the cattle Ezra and Chester had stashed in the ravine to the north. They planned to check for other livestock that might have been penned up by the thieves.

She nudged Buckshot into a faster clip and her thoughts drifted back to the two traitorous cowboys undermining both ranches. Something sinister was going on here, she mused. Talk of robbery and involuntary manslaughter in Ruby and Earl's wagon wreck disturbed her. Setting Cahill up for murder annoyed her. She wanted answers but none were forthcoming.

According to Ezra and Chester—if they were to be believed, and how much was a thief's word worth?—they weren't involved in the Phantom Springs murder and the wagon wreck. What the blazes was going on and who was responsible? Were there *two* gangs of criminals lurking about, taking advantage of each other's illegal activities?

Her curiosity was aroused and Quin was in turmoil. She wanted to do all within her power to make his life easier by solving the mystery—quickly.

Her thoughts scattered when she reached home to see Butler standing on the porch, staring into the distance. She frowned warily as she dismounted. "Is there a problem?"

"No more than usual," he replied with a shrug. "I was just thinking about the two men you and Cahill put in jail. I remembered seeing the saddle horse you described. That Ezra character has been here several times this month. I guess I was too busy settling in to realize the man didn't belong here."

"Not your fault." She entered the house that still held the faint scent of smoke. "Those hooligans were operating in the area before we arrived. We were fortunate to make the connection."

"You wouldn't have if you hadn't sneaked out to follow Cahill after you were ordered to stay home under guard," he said darkly.

She flashed an undaunted grin. "I was lucky to see the two horses outside the bunkhouse and to realize there were *four* men conspiring to extort money from Cahill."

He followed her into the office, grumbling. "Still, you could have been hurt."

She shrugged off his concern as she squatted down to open the safe. "Everything turned out fine, except for the stitches in Cahill's head."

"And don't forget his stint in jail," Butler didn't fail to point out.

Adrianna wrinkled her nose at the reminder. "Dealing with that by-the-book marshal didn't help. At least he didn't put up a fuss when we brought in Ezra and Chester. But I don't think he likes me much."

Butler smirked behind her. "He might be nicer to you if he knew *exactly* how much money you're worth. Most men are."

He was right, she mused as she grabbed several stacks of banknotes. "After I pay the men's wages, I'm taking Elda back to Cahill's. That's where she wants to be. I'll be home later tonight. But I plan to stay at Rosa's apartment in town tomorrow. You and Bea can have this place to yourselves."

"You're too good to us," Butler murmured, then got all choked up. "For what it's worth, I tried to convince your father that he could never mold you into the genteel, soft-spoken woman your mother was. But he was determined to create you in her image…without success, thankfully. I like you just the way you are."

Adrianna hugged him close. "Thank you for trying to make him see who I really was, not who he wanted me to be. As for the use of the house, it's my good deed for the year," she said, grinning. "Besides, you and Bea are my family."

And what a shame Quin didn't have the support and connection with his siblings that she had with her adopted family. She would make a point to hassle him about that. Maybe his siblings had mellowed after their lengthy separation. Perhaps they wanted to reconcile—

and were waiting for someone like Quin, the eldest—to initiate a reunion.

She stepped back, then patted Butler's cheek. "If you wouldn't mind helping Elda gather her things, I'll make the rounds to pay the cowboys."

Butler nodded his brown head, squared his shoulders, then strode off. She smiled wryly. For all Butler's stoic manners, he had a sentimental heart, the sweet, endearing man.

Lurching around, Adrianna grabbed an oversize pouch from the desk to carry the payroll. Thank goodness those rustlers were in jail so she didn't have to fret about being attacked for the money. Speaking of money, she planned to offer a loan to Quin since the money for his payroll had been stolen during his attempt to buy information at Phantom Springs. He was likely too proud to accept the loan, but she knew he hadn't had time to visit the bank after incarcerating the rustlers.

She glanced northwest, hoping Rocky and Cahill would return with the confiscated cattle, hoping other thieves weren't lurking to take potshots at them. Quin didn't need holes blasted in him. He hadn't yet recovered from having his skull hammered.

"I'm ready!" Elda called from the porch, jolting Adrianna from her pensive musings.

The cook stood beside several suitcases and a sack of special utensils she'd brought all the way from Boston. When Isaac Moss, a tall, clean-cut but young cowboy brought the buggy, Elda scuttled down the steps and climbed onto the seat—with Isaac's assistance. A moment later, he had the luggage loaded and Adrianna took up the reins. She glanced northwest again but there was still no sign of Rocky and Cahill—and that made her anxious.

"That was an incredibly nice thing you did for Butler and Bea," Elda said as she settled herself on the seat. "Glad they finally decided to tie the knot." She stared pointedly at Adrianna. "All that sneaking around at night isn't good."

Adrianna ignored the comment and found herself wondering what it would be like to be married. The only man she'd consider was the one who'd never ask. Ironic, she mused with a remorseful smile. She'd heard proposals galore for seven or eight years—but never from the right man.

When they arrived at 4C, Adrianna called to Skeeter Gregory. The wiry, thirty-year-old cowboy jogged from the barn to help Elda down, then he scooped up her luggage and utensils.

"Nice to have you back, ma'am," Skeeter drawled. "Sure have been missing those mouthwatering cakes and cookies you sent to the bunkhouse for me and the other men."

Adrianna watched the plump-faced cook beam in satisfaction, then she patted Skeeter's leathery cheek. "You can expect more desserts once I'm settled in, my dear boy."

Apparently, Elda, who hadn't married and had no children, had decided to mother Cahill and his hired hands. No doubt, they showered her with constant compliments. Elda felt more useful and needed than she had at the mansion in Boston.

Adrianna understood because she felt more alive in

Texas than making a halfhearted attempt to become the woman her father expected her to be.

Once Elda was upstairs putting away her belongings, Adrianna ambled back to the buggy. She frowned warily when she noticed the same gawky Mexican boy, riding a burro, who had delivered the anonymous note the night Quin got clobbered and set up for murder.

"For Señor Cahill," the boy said with a heavy Spanish accent. Then he extended the folded note.

"Who sent you?" Adrianna demanded.

The boy shrugged beneath his tattered poncho. "It was on my burro's saddle, as before, along with a few pesos."

"You saw no one?" she questioned intently.

"No, señorita," he said before he rode away.

Adrianna unfolded the note, and noticed the hand-writing was different from the first one. Yet, the message was similar.

Bring two thousand dollars to Triple Creek to buy information about Ruby and Earl Cahill's wagon wreck.

She cursed sourly. The note gave no hint that robbery or accidental manslaughter was involved. But Adrianna was anxious for information to appease Cahill's curiosity. The anonymous notes Ezra and Chester received suggested a similar method of operation. What the devil did that mean?

Were the four men who were involved in the murder and extortion at Phantom Springs connected to the mastermind behind the arson and rustling? What about

George Spradlin, her former foreman? Was he mixed up in this? And what did anyone know—if anything— about Ruby and Earl's wagon wreck?

For sure and certain, Adrianna wouldn't allow this rendezvous to play out the way the last one had. *She* was going in Cahill's stead. He could back her up—which is how it should have played out at Phantom Springs, she told herself sensibly.

Her unexpected appearance would surprise the would-be informants, she reasoned. No one was going to set up Cahill a second time for murder—if that's what these encounters were really about. Or was it a scheme to dispose of a gang member and steal money? If Cahill followed her—and she was certain he would, mad as hell at her though he'd likely be—he could get the drop on these hooligans. His dealings with Ezra and Chester were proof enough that Cahill was a tough, deadly force to be reckoned with. He had certainly impressed Adrianna when he had outdrawn the outlaws.

Determined of purpose, she left the note in the parlor, along with a letter she'd written. She borrowed Cahill's Sunday-go-to-meeting hat and a jacket that hung by the front door. She hiked to the barn to borrow a saddle horse that looked similar to Cactus. She left her carriage by the house to ensure Cahill went looking for her.

A relieved smile pursed her lips as she glanced northwest to see Cahill and Rocky appear on a rise of ground, herding cattle to the corrals. Good, Cahill wouldn't be too far behind her. Just far enough that he couldn't discourage her from following through with her plan to disrupt the outlaws' scheme and have Cahill provide reinforcement.

With a pistol tucked in her waistband and her trusty dagger in her boot, she trotted toward the junction of the three creeks at sunset. She veered to the eastern side of the tree-lined stream so Cahill wouldn't spot her immediately. No matter what else happened, he *wasn't* going to be clubbed on the head or bushwhacked, she vowed resolutely.

The thought of him being hurt was unacceptable. She was in love with the man, after all. She would do all within her power to protect him from harm. It was her way of expressing her carefully guarded affection without blurting out her feelings and facing embarrassing rejection.

"This is your second good deed of the year," she told herself as she trotted away.

Quin herded the cattle he and Rock had found in an obscure box canyon into the corral. He'd hoped to locate another note with instructions, but no such luck. He wondered where the stolen cattle had been sold but it would take time to check around. Damn it, he wanted answers...now.

His mood improved when he noticed Boston's carriage near the house. A passionate evening spent in the privacy of the master suite held tremendous appeal. Leaving Rocky to sort 4C cattle from McKnight cattle, he trotted Cactus to the house.

"Hey, boss! Elda's back!" Skeeter called to him.

Quin nodded and smiled. Skeet had a sweet tooth that wouldn't quit. Quin's appetite, however, required a steady diet of a green-eyed, chestnut-haired firebrand named Boston.

He barreled through the front door but she wasn't there to greet him so he went looking for her. She wasn't in the kitchen or dining room and neither was Elda. His stomach dropped to his boots when he veered into the parlor to see two notes lying on the seat of his father's leather chair. With mounting dread, Quin approached, wondering if there was something symbolic about where the notes had been placed.

He plucked up the first one that offered information about his parents' wreck and he noted different handwriting. He picked up the second note in Boston's elegant script—and cursed the air black and blue. Twice.

I'm posing as you to determine if this rendezvous at Triple Creek is a hoax. I'm using my extra payroll money as bait. Maybe we'll find out if there is any truth to the possibility of foul play in your parents' deaths.
Yours truly, Boston

Yours truly? Quin swore he'd never live to see the day she signed a note "Love, Adrianna." "Dang and blast it!" he roared. "Are you trying to get yourself killed, woman?"

Damn the woman; he knew she thrived on excitement and adventure but she faced uncertain danger. She was putting herself in harm's way *for him*. That tormented him to no end.

Scowling furiously, he stalked outside to mount Cactus. Too many things could go wrong with Boston's harebrained scheme. Besides, this was his problem, not hers. "Someone needs to get control of that woman...

if that's even possible," he rumbled as he gouged the bloodred bay gelding in the flanks and raced off, praying he wouldn't arrive too late.

Adrianna dismounted in a stand of trees. She took the precaution of stashing the money pouch behind an oversize stone on the path. She intended to use the money as insurance. *No answers, no money,* she vowed as she walked toward the meeting site. Her plan was to find out everything she could and stall until Cahill arrived. As plans went, it was iffy at best. But it provided protection for Cahill.

"Toss out your pistols, Cahill," came a gruff voice from the underbrush to her left.

The sound startled her but she composed herself, gathered her courage and tossed her pistol into the clearing beside the junction of the three creeks.

"Where's your other six-gun?" the man demanded.

"I only have one," she called out.

"What the hell—?" came a deep voice from her right.

That accounted for *two* men, she thought. Where was the *third* man?

"Take off that hat!" the first bandit ordered sharply.

Adrianna removed Cahill's oversize hat and her thick braid tumbled over her shoulder.

"You?" the second outlaw crowed incredulously. "What are you doing here? We sent for Cahill."

"He wasn't home. He was herding the stolen cattle your sidekicks stashed away. Those *are* your sidekicks, right? Ezra and Chester?"

"Are those the two cowboys you stuffed in jail?" the first hombre asked.

"Yes, friends of yours?" she questioned persistently.

"No," said the second man. "Now move to the clearing. Don't try anything, lady, or you'll be damned sorry. And get those hands up where we can see 'em."

She did as she was told. Her objective was to keep the men busy talking and gather vital information. "Which one of you shot your cohort at Phantom Springs?" She walked into the clearing, then glanced sideways to note both men were wearing black hoods and long duster coats to conceal their identities.

"That don't concern you, lady," the second outlaw scowled. "Now where's the money?"

She turned slowly to face her mysterious captors. "You'll receive no money until I have information," she insisted, lowering her arms. "What do you know about Ruby and Earl Cahill's deaths? Was it a robbery attempt?"

"Maybe. Maybe not," the first bandit muttered evasively.

She rolled her eyes. "No straight answers, no money."

"Lady," the second ruffian growled, "you ain't in no position to make the rules. Now where's the damn money!"

Okay, Cahill, you can show up now, she thought anxiously. These men were short on patience.

"So you and the other two men planned to rob the Cahills on their return trip from Wolf Grove," she speculated. "They tried to outrun you in their wagon, right?"

"Shut up, lady," Number Two sneered beneath his black hood, then aimed his pistol at her chest.

"So you chased them and the Cahills lost control on

the sharp curve at Ghost Canyon?" she prompted, calling upon every ounce of bravado she could muster.

"You don't hear too good, do you, lady?" Number One said sarcastically. "Be quiet!"

"I will not be quiet." She tilted her chin defiantly. "I came here for information in exchange for money. Now, did you climb downhill to rob the Cahills of money and take their supplies after the wreck?"

"Yes, damn it," Number One muttered in exasperation.

"Then you wiped away the tracks so no one would suspect foul play," she ventured. "What did you remove from the bodies?"

"Don't you ever shut up, woman?" Number Two sneered as he took a step closer. "Maybe I'll *make* you shut up."

"We don't have the money yet," Number One reminded his angry cohort.

"Where is the third man?" she questioned, glancing this way and that. "Or did you dispose of him so you could have more money for yourselves? Was there a falling out between thieves that resulted in the death at Phantom Springs? Or did your friend try to extort money behind your back and you shot him for it?"

The question was met with silence and Adrianna swore under her breath, wondering if she would ever find the third man. Was he here now, hiding in the trees, taking her measure with a rifle?

"Lady, you are a pain in the ass," said the second outlaw.

"I hear that often," she said, undaunted. "So why did you wait two years to approach Cahill about the wreck?

Why did you set him up for murdering your buddy at Phantom Springs?"

"Enough!" the second thug snarled as he stalked toward her. "Where's the damn money!"

"Answer my questions and you can have it," she countered defiantly. "You—"

Her voice became a pained yelp when the stocky, thick-chested hooligan backhanded her, causing her to stumble and fall. Despite her stinging cheek and the stars revolving around her eyes, she scrambled to her feet to plow into the first thug. He yelped as the two of them went down in a tangle of arms and legs. Adrianna made a wild grab for his pistol but Number Two pounced on her and jerked her up by her braid.

He crammed his pistol into the underside of her neck and clamped his burly arm diagonally across her chest. The man reeked of whiskey and sweat. She stamped on his foot, hoping he'd recoil so she could launch herself away from him. No such luck. He grabbed her braid like a rope and jerked her against him again.

"Let her go," Quin snarled viciously as he appeared from the shadows of the trees. He stepped into the clearing with both pistols drawn and ready to spit lead.

Both men lurched sideways. The first man stepped behind the second—who held Boston as if she were his shield of armor.

"Give us the money and we'll let this hellcat live," the second ruffian demanded as he crammed the pistol barrel deeper into Boston's throat.

"I don't have money. I just returned to the house, then came looking for Boston."

Both men muttered beneath their concealing black

hoods. It no longer mattered if Quin received the answers to the questions that hounded him. His only concern was Boston's survival. If these men had killed his parents in a robbery attempt, he'd track them down and dispose of them later.

"Let her go. I'll bring money to you," Quin bargained, holding both men at gunpoint—while they held him at gunpoint.

"I don't trust you—awk!" The bandit's voice dried up suddenly.

Quin nearly suffered a stroke when Boston took advantage of her captor's distraction and gouged him in the soft underbelly. The outlaw cursed foully and backhanded her, sending her cartwheeling in the grass. Then he aimed his pistol at her.

Quin moved into the open to make himself a target. He fired both six-shooters simultaneously, drawing attention away from Boston. He hit the second hombre twice in the chest. The man yelped and slammed into his friend but he fired off a shot before his legs buckled and he dropped to his knees.

"No!" Boston shrieked at she stared at Quin in horror.

Quin felt the burning pain in his left side but he was too intent on holding the first man at gunpoint so he couldn't use Boston for his shield of protection.

Stalemate, he thought, breathing raggedly.

Out of the corner of his eye, he saw Boston reach into her boot to grab her concealed dagger. She sprang to her feet and charged the bandit left standing. She managed a glancing blow to his neck before he knocked her aside but she came at him again, slicing his arm.

"Where's the money?" the thief demanded as he pointed his weapon at Boston and cocked the trigger.

Somehow, Quin found the strength to shoot the pistol from the man's hand, but the outlaw swung his second revolver toward Quin, who wobbled unsteadily, then sagged to his knees.

"Get the money, lady, or I'll kill him, I swear it!"

Quin swore mightily as his strength ebbed and the world faded in and out of focus. He tried to raise his arm to fire off another shot but the bandit darted over to kick the six-shooter from his hand. The coppery scent of blood filled his nostrils. He refused to look down to see how badly he'd been injured. All that mattered was seeing Boston escape with only two bruises to the cheek.

"I've got the money with me," she insisted as she bounded to her feet. "He's been shot. He can't attack you. Just let him be."

She dashed off, then returned a minute later with a leather pouch. Defiant to the end, Boston tossed the money out of the man's reach. "Take it and go."

The gunman kept his gaze trained on Quin as he scooped up the leather poke. When he turned to leave, Boston darted toward the downed man's pistol.

"Damn it, Boston, don't draw fire," Quin panted as he tried to prop himself on his elbow.

She didn't listen to him. When had she ever? She fired off three shots as the bandit darted into the underbrush, then disappeared from sight.

A moment later, Quin heard the sound of two— maybe three—horses thundering into the darkness. He suspected the first thug had taken the second horse and had ridden hell-for-leather. Either that or a third outlaw had been watching from a safe distance. Damn it, he wished he knew for sure!

Quin dragged himself by one arm to reach the downed man. With what little strength he could muster, he shoved the thief to his back. He jerked off the hood to reveal a mop of black hair and dull brown eyes that stared dazedly at him. Bloodstains soaked the man's shirt.

"Did you purposely kill my parents during the robbery?" Quin demanded in panted breaths.

The dark-haired hombre nodded ever so slightly. "Wasn't just a robbery," he rasped. "Murder... You got no idea how deep this goes...."

When he slumped lifelessly on the ground, Quin swore ripely. He'd learned his parents had been murdered, but he still had no idea why this information had surfaced two years later or if their deaths were somehow connected to the rustling and robberies plaguing the 4C for the past few years.

"I'm so sorry," Adrianna blubbered as she stared at the bloody wound on Quin's side. "This is my fault. *I'm so sorry!*"

He sucked in a ragged breath as he slumped to the ground. "Not your fault," he whispered. "I got you into this."

Tears erupted as she ripped away the dead man's shirt to use as a makeshift bandage for Cahill. "Can you stand up? We need to get you to the doctor."

"I don't think so," he wheezed.

Heavens, thought Adrianna, the very thing she had

tried to prevent from happening had happened! "Stay here," she ordered as she sprang to her feet.

"Don't think I have much choice," he mumbled dully.

Adrianna dashed off to locate Cactus, then brought the horse to Cahill. The improvised bandage was soaked with blood so she ripped off another section of the dead man's shirt to tie around his belly. Then she grabbed Quin beneath the armpits and heaved him upward to clamp his hand around the saddle horn for support.

"You listen to me, Quin Cahill, you are going to help me get you on Cactus so we can ride to town," she raged at him through her sobs and tears. "I love you like crazy and I refuse to lose you. Now help me, blast it!"

Adrianna wasn't sure how they managed to hoist him onto the saddle before he collapsed against Cactus. After she mounted up, she led Quin to town for help—and prayed nonstop that he would survive.

And damn the man! she railed silently. She had tried repeatedly to draw attention away from *him* but he had left himself open to attack to draw gunfire away from *her*. He had taken a bullet for her and that tormented her beyond words.

"Blast it, you just can't do some people a favor, and you're one of them, Cahill," she muttered. "Now look at you."

He didn't comment, just lay over Cactus like a feed sack.

Adrianna bawled her head off all the way to town. Anger, guilt and regret hounded her every step. Her attempt to spare Cahill from danger had backfired.

Plus, the dead outlaw had only lived long enough to impart a tidbit of information. The other bandit had escaped with the money—and no more than minor stab wounds on his neck and arm.

Adrianna had no idea whether the third thief had stood guard, then rode off. There was no conclusive sign of him. The third bandit could be dead already, for all she knew.

Even worse, Cahill could be a dead man riding. She might have killed the only man she had ever loved—by trying to *protect* him! The tormenting thought circled her mind like a vulture. She would give her fortune if it could save Cahill.

Muffling a sniff, she glanced back to see Cahill's motionless form and pale face in the moonlight. Her heart twisted in her chest and another sob burst from her lips.

It wasn't enough that Cahill had to deal with that stupid curse and rumors constantly circulating around town. *She* had become the worst curse of his life…or what he had left of it….

Chapter Fifteen

Quin groaned miserably. He felt like death warmed on a dim flame and he wondered if he was still alive. He couldn't tell for sure. He'd hoped dead would feel better than this, but who could say for certain?

Before he could take inventory to see if he still had most of his body parts, a fuzzy haze overtook him and he dozed off.

A few hours later—or maybe it was a century, he wasn't certain—he regained consciousness. He opened his eyes to realize he was sprawled in bed at Doc Lewis's infirmary. He turned his head sideways to see Boston draped uncomfortably in the chair beside him.

Quin tried to ease onto his side so he could reach out to limn the refined features of her enchanting face, but it hurt to move. He groaned involuntarily, causing Boston to come awake instantly. Her green eyes were noticeably puffy from crying. There were red welts on her cheek and a concerned frown etched her brow.

"How are you feeling?" she whispered as she combed her hand through his tousled hair.

"Like hell," he croaked. "How about you?"

"The same. It's killing me to know I'm responsible for your injury. I was trying to help and I made matters worse."

"I already told you it's not your fault."

She glanced away, shifted uncomfortably, then murmured, "Do you remember what I said after we managed to drag you onto Cactus's back?"

"Sorry, no. I guess I blacked out. What'd you say?"

She bit her lip, then smiled ruefully. "I don't know if it will make you feel better or worse. Maybe I should let it be."

"Spit it out, Boston. It isn't like you to mince words."

She took an enormous breath, as if she were diving off a cliff into fathomless depths. "I'm in love with you."

Quin smiled faintly. "Are you saying that because you know I'm dying?"

She shook her head adamantly, sending the chestnut-colored braid rippling over her shoulder. "I realized I loved you before I managed to get you shot. You aren't dying. The bullet missed vital organs but it nicked muscles and ligaments. Doc Lewis patched you up and said you'd be stiff and sore for a couple of weeks." She squeezed his hand. "Just because I love you doesn't mean you're obligated—"

He pressed his forefinger to her lips, wishing he had the strength to pull her into his arms and hold her close. "I love you, too, Boston," he whispered earnestly. "There aren't the right words to describe how much you mean to me."

"Well, why didn't you say so?" she huffed, but grinned—and he felt a hundred times better when he basked in the warmth of her glorious smile.

"I kept silent because I didn't think you wanted me and I didn't want to crowd your independent space," he replied.

She pressed her lush mouth to his. "I want you like crazy and you can crowd my space anytime you please, Cahill." Her long thick lashes fluttered down to shield her gaze as she trailed her fingertip over his jaw and cheek. "Are you going to ask me to marry you?"

"No. Every man you know proposes to you," he reminded her. "I don't want to be anything like them because I'm not after your money." He grinned rakishly—and wondered if he'd been able to pull it off since he wasn't an accomplished ladies' man. "I'm fascinated with your fiery spirit, your intelligence and your gorgeous body. All of the person you are. But you'll have to ask *me* if you want to move to 4C and stay forever because that's how long I promise to love you, Boston. You are my heart."

"I want to be with you always, Cahill," she choked out as tears dribbled down her cheeks. *"Marry me."*

"Name the time and place," he insisted as he rerouted her tears with the pad of his thumb.

"On two conditions," she negotiated.

"Here it comes," he grumbled playfully. "What do I have to do to keep you with me forevermore?"

"I want to add my herd of longhorns to yours and find out what it's like to make the trail drive to Dodge City. Doc says you'll be up and around by then."

Quin blew out his breath. "Damn it, Boston. Spring

trail drives are notorious for violent storms, bandits, stampedes, dangerous river crossings and renegade Indians on the way to Kansas."

She got that determined tilt to her chin that he'd come to recognize at a glance. "You are not going without me and that's that, Cahill. I crave new experiences and adventure."

"I was hoping our marriage would be adventure enough," he mumbled.

She grinned and said, "Has it occurred to you that I don't want to be away from you? Besides, I want to make certain you don't overdo it after getting shot on my account."

Quin sighed audibly, knowing this was likely the first of many times he wouldn't be able to tell Boston no. "Fine. We'll go together. And what's the second stipulation?"

Her smile disappeared and she stared intently at him. "I want you to contact your brothers and sister. Let them know you're injured and your parents' wagon wreck wasn't an accident."

"No," he muttered. "Having my siblings gather around while I'm injured and vulnerable offends my pride. I'm the eldest, damn it. I'm supposed to be in charge—"

His voice dried up when Boston skimmed her moist lips over his mouth, then said, "I understand how you feel. I suffered the same kind of conflict with my father. I loved him, but he angered me because he forced unreasonable demands on me. He disappointed me because he couldn't accept me for who I was."

Quin couldn't imagine her father finding fault and trying to stifle her spirit. It was who *she* was.

She smiled ruefully as she traced the curve of his lips. "You are caught between aggravation, disappointment and love, too. But your brothers and sister are part of who you are and, deep down, you care about them. You're angry because they left you to hold the ranch together by yourself. They disappoint you because they don't share your dreams and your interests. But each of us has to be who we are, Cahill."

"I know you're right, but they left me alone to pick up the pieces, manage the ranch and deal with the gossip," he mumbled. "It wasn't easy."

"I know, but your parents' deaths altered their lives, too," she reminded him. "They have a right to decide if they want to be involved in this investigation. There is one man running around loose who knows what happened two years ago. We need to find out what happened to the fourth gang member. Whoever killed your parents should pay for what they did to your family. Your brothers and sister can help serve justice. Bowie is a sheriff, after all. What better place to start than calling him in to continue the investigation while you're recovering and driving the cattle herds to Kansas?"

She kissed him so tenderly that every objection he'd formulated fizzled out. Maybe it *was* time to contact his family. According to the man who died at Triple Creek, there was far more to learn about his parents' deaths.

"Please, Quin," she whispered softly. "Let your family help solve this awful crime while you recover your strength and tend your ranching duties…. Did I tell you I love you…?"

"Not often enough, sweetheart." He stared into those mystifying green eyes and saw his future. "I'll marry *you* on one condition," he stipulated.

"Name it," she said without hesitation.

"Love me until the end of time, Boston."

Her radiant smile lit up the room—and his lonely soul. "Done. I'll have the parson here first thing in the morning for our wedding ceremony. Rosa and Lucas can bear witness."

Quin used her thick braid like a rope to draw her head back to his. "Tomorrow can't come soon enough. Then you won't have an excuse to leave me alone again."

"I'm not going anywhere." She smiled adoringly at him. "Stampeding longhorns couldn't drive me away."

After tomorrow she would *belong* to him, *with* him, he mused as they sealed their promise with a kiss. Quin had enough sense not to spout those specific words to a woman with Boston's feisty, independent temperament. He loved her the way he'd never loved anyone or anything in his whole life. Quin vowed to spend every day telling her so. Or better yet, he'd show her that she was everything he needed to be happy for now…and until long past the end of eternity.

* * * * *

HISTORICAL

Where Love is Timeless™

HARLEQUIN® HISTORICAL

COMING NEXT MONTH
AVAILABLE NOVEMBER 22, 2011

THE MARSHAL AND MISS MERRITT
Cahill Cowboys
Debra Cowan
(Western)

COMING HOME FOR CHRISTMAS
Carla Kelly
(19th century)

UNMASKING THE DUKE'S MISTRESS
Gentlemen of Disrepute
Margaret McPhee
(Regency)

THE LADY FORFEITS
The Copeland Sisters
Carole Mortimer
(Regency)

You can find more information on upcoming
Harlequin® titles, free excerpts and more
at www.HarlequinInsideRomance.com.

REQUEST YOUR FREE BOOKS!

 HARLEQUIN® HISTORICAL:
Where love is timeless

2 FREE NOVELS PLUS 2 FREE GIFTS!

YES! Please send me 2 FREE Harlequin® Historical novels and my 2 FREE gifts (gifts are worth about $10). After receiving them, if I don't wish to receive any more books, I can return the shipping statement marked "cancel." If I don't cancel, I will receive 6 brand-new novels every month and be billed just $5.19 per book in the U.S. or $5.74 per book in Canada. That's a savings of at least 17% off the cover price! It's quite a bargain! Shipping and handling is just 50¢ per book in the U.S. and 75¢ per book in Canada.* I understand that accepting the 2 free books and gifts places me under no obligation to buy anything. I can always return a shipment and cancel at any time. Even if I never buy another book, the two free books and gifts are mine to keep forever.

246/349 HDN FEQQ

Name _____ (PLEASE PRINT) _____

Address _____ Apt. #

City _____ State/Prov. _____ Zip/Postal Code

Signature (if under 18, a parent or guardian must sign)

Mail to the **Reader Service:**
IN U.S.A.: P.O. Box 1867, Buffalo, NY 14240-1867
IN CANADA: P.O. Box 609, Fort Erie, Ontario L2A 5X3

Not valid for current subscribers to Harlequin Historical books.

Want to try two free books from another line?
Call 1-800-873-8635 or visit www.ReaderService.com.

* Terms and prices subject to change without notice. Prices do not include applicable taxes. Sales tax applicable in N.Y. Canadian residents will be charged applicable taxes. Offer not valid in Quebec. This offer is limited to one order per household. All orders subject to credit approval. Credit or debit balances in a customer's account(s) may be offset by any other outstanding balance owed by or to the customer. Please allow 4 to 6 weeks for delivery. Offer available while quantities last.

Your Privacy—The Reader Service is committed to protecting your privacy. Our Privacy Policy is available online at www.ReaderService.com or upon request from the Reader Service.

We make a portion of our mailing list available to reputable third parties that offer products we believe may interest you. If you prefer that we not exchange your name with third parties, or if you wish to clarify or modify your communication preferences, please visit us at www.ReaderService.com/consumerschoice or write to us at Reader Service Preference Service, P.O. Box 9062, Buffalo, NY 14269. Include your complete name and address.

HHI1B

Lucy Flemming and Ross Mitchell shared a magical,
sexy Christmas weekend together six years ago.
This Christmas, history may repeat itself when they find
themselves stranded in a major snowstorm...
and alone at last.

Read on for a sneak peek from
IT HAPPENED ONE CHRISTMAS
by Leslie Kelly.

Available December 2011, only from Harlequin® Blaze™.

EYEING THE GRAY, THICK SKY through the expansive wall of
windows, Lucy began to pack up her photography gear.
The Christmas party was winding down, only a dozen or so
people remaining on this floor, which had been transformed
from cubicles and meeting rooms to a holiday funland. She
smiled at those nearest to her, then, seeing the glances at her
silly elf hat, she reached up to tug it off her head.

Before she could do it, however, she heard a voice. A
deep, male voice—smooth and sexy, and so not Santa's.

"I appreciate you filling in on such short notice. I've
heard you do a terrific job."

Lucy didn't turn around, letting her brain process what
she was hearing. Her whole body had stiffened, the hairs on
the back of her neck standing up, her skin tightening into
tiny goose bumps. Because that voice sounded so familiar.
Impossibly familiar.

It can't be.

"It sounds like the kids had a great time."

Unable to stop herself, Lucy began to turn around,
wondering if her ears—and all her other senses—were
deceiving her. After all, six years was a long time, the mind

could play tricks. What were the odds that she'd bump into *him*, here? And today of all days. December 23.

Six years exactly. Was that really possible?

One look—and the accompanying frantic thudding of her heart—and she knew her ears and brain were working just fine. Because it was *him*.

"Oh, my God," he whispered, shocked, frozen, staring as thoroughly as she was. "Lucy?"

She nodded slowly, not taking her eyes off him, wondering why the years had made him even more attractive than ever. It didn't seem fair. Not when she'd spent the past six years thinking he must have started losing that thick, golden-brown hair, or added a spare tire to that trim, muscular form.

No.

The man was gorgeous. Truly, without-a-doubt, mouthwateringly handsome, every bit as hot as he'd been the first time she'd laid eyes on him. She'd been twenty-two, he one year older.

They'd shared an amazing holiday season.

And had never seen one another again.

Until now.

Find out what happens in
IT HAPPENED ONE CHRISTMAS
by Leslie Kelly.
Available December 2011, only from Harlequin® Blaze™